The Duel
and Other Stories

DOVER · THRIFT · EDITIONS

The Duel
and Other Stories

ANTON CHEKHOV

DOVER PUBLICATIONS, INC.
Mineola, New York

DOVER THRIFT EDITIONS

GENERAL EDITOR: PAUL NEGRI

EDITOR OF THIS VOLUME: THOMAS CRAWFORD

Bibliographical Note

The Duel and Other Stories, first published by Dover Publications, Inc. in 2003, is a new selection of stories reprinted from the Constance Garnett translations published by The Macmillan Company, New York, in the following years: "The Darling" (1916); "The Duel" (1916); "The Kiss" (1917); "'Anna on the Neck'" (1917); "The Man in a Case" (1918); and "A Malefactor" (1918). An introductory Note has been specially prepared for this edition.

Library of Congress Cataloging-in-Publication Data

Chekhov, Anton Pavlovich, 1860–1904.
    [Short stories. English. Selections]
    The duel and other stories / Anton Chekhov.
        p. cm.
    Translations by Constance Garnett.
    Contents: A malefactor — The kiss — The duel — "Anna on the neck" — The man in a case — The darling.
    ISBN 0-486-42676-9 (pbk.)
      1. Chekhov, Anton Pavlovich, 1860–1904—Translations into English. I. Garnett, Constance Black, 1862–1946. II. Title.

PG3456.A13 G38 2003
891.73'3—dc21

                                 2002034980

Manufactured in the United States of America
Dover Publications, Inc., 31 East 2nd Street, Mineola, N.Y. 11501

Note

"After any of your stories, however insignificant, everything appears crude, as if written not by a pen, but by a cudgel."
— Maxim Gorky

Chekhov earned this tribute from his Russian compatriot and fellow writer through the balance, objectivity, compassion and exquisite sensitivity of his work. Author of over 800 stories, Anton Chekhov (1860–1904) honed his skills to the point that he became a master of the genre, one of the most beloved Russian storytellers, and one of the greatest of all time. Although many of his earlier stories are of a comic nature, his mature work leans toward darker themes: hopelessness, futility, the inability of human beings to communicate or connect in any meaningful way, and the common human condition of despair. As the protagonist thinks to himself in "The Kiss": "And the whole world, the whole of life, seemed to Ryabovich an unintelligible, aimless jest . . . his life struck him as extraordinarily meager, poverty-stricken, and drab . . . "

Despite the often melancholy nature of Chekhov's stories, they are nevertheless full of human interest as he puts peasants, government officials, doctors, scientists and the aristocracy under the microscope and examines their lives with his characteristic objectivity and non-judgmental attitude. Of Chekhov's lack of moralizing, Shelby Foote notes, "For the most part, though, he kept his opinions and judgments to himself—especially in his fiction, where, as he said, he aimed not at solutions to problems but rather at their correct presentation." Moreover, Chekhov illuminates the lives of his characters with striking economy of means, telling his stories in a precise, simple way that illustrates his own dictum: "Conciseness is the sister of talent."

This collection offers six stories comprising a representative cross-section of the Russian master's short story production, beginning with "A Malefactor" (1885) a semi-comic sketch with a serious underlying theme, and ending with "The Darling," (1899). "The Duel" (1891), almost novella-length, is a masterly consideration of social and philosophical issues, portraying the conflict of sharply differing concepts of life. It is also a superb study of a human being at the end of his emotional rope. Included as well are "The Kiss" (1887), "'Anna on the Neck'" (1895), and "The Man in a Case" (1898)—all among Chekhov's most admired stories.

Perhaps the most telling explanation for the tenor and tone of Chekhov's work comes from the writer himself:

> "All I wanted was to say honestly to people: 'Have a look at yourselves and see how bad and dreary your lives are!' The important thing is that people should realize that, for when they do, they will most certainly create another and better life for themselves. I will not live to see it, but I know that it will be quite different, quite unlike our present life."

In his passionate desire to convey the harsh realities of life in late nineteenth-century Russia, including the decay of the aristocracy, and the poverty, both real and spiritual, of the common man, Chekhov created stories that are profoundly human, reflecting the difficulties of living a meaningful life in the face of oppression, boredom, poverty, listlessness, apathy and despair. Reprinted here in the highly regarded Constance Garnett translations, these stories combine the dispassionate attitude of a scientist and doctor (Chekhov was a physician) with the sensitivity and psychological understanding of an artist.

Contents

A MALEFACTOR

AN EXCEEDINGLY lean little peasant, in a striped hempen shirt and patched drawers, stands facing the investigating magistrate. His face overgrown with hair and pitted with smallpox, and his eyes scarcely visible under thick, overhanging eyebrows have an expression of sullen moroseness. On his head there is a perfect mop of tangled, unkempt hair, which gives him an even more spider-like air of moroseness. He is barefooted.

"Denis Grigoryev!" the magistrate begins. "Come nearer, and answer my questions. On the seventh of this July the railway watchman, Ivan Semyonovitch Akinfov, going along the line in the morning, found you at the hundred-and-forty-first mile engaged in unscrewing a nut by which the rails are made fast to the sleepers. Here it is, the nut! . . . With the aforesaid nut he detained you. Was that so?"

"Wha-at?"

"Was this all as Akinfov states?"

"To be sure, it was."

"Very good; well, what were you unscrewing the nut for?"

"Wha-at?"

"Drop that 'wha-at' and answer the question; what were you unscrewing the nut for?"

"If I hadn't wanted it I shouldn't have unscrewed it," croaks Denis, looking at the ceiling.

"What did you want that nut for?"

"The nut? We make weights out of those nuts for our lines."

"Who is 'we'?"

"We, people. . . . The Klimovo peasants, that is."

"Listen, my man; don't play the idiot to me, but speak sensibly. It's no use telling lies here about weights!"

"I've never been a liar from a child, and now I'm telling lies . . ." mutters Denis, blinking. "But can you do without a weight, your honour?

1

If you put live bait or maggots on a hook, would it go to the bottom without a weight? . . . I am telling lies," grins Denis. . . . "What the devil is the use of the worm if it swims on the surface! The perch and the pike and the eel-pout always go to the bottom, and a bait on the surface is only taken by a shillisper, not very often then, and there are no shillispers in our river. . . . That fish likes plenty of room."

"Why are you telling me about shillispers?"

"Wha-at? Why, you asked me yourself! The gentry catch fish that way too in our parts. The silliest little boy would not try to catch a fish without a weight. Of course anyone who did not understand might go to fish without a weight. There is no rule for a fool."

"So you say you unscrewed this nut to make a weight for your fishing line out of it?"

"What else for? It wasn't to play knuckle-bones with!"

"But you might have taken lead, a bullet . . . a nail of some sort. . . ."

"You don't pick up lead in the road, you have to buy it, and a nail's no good. You can't find anything better than a nut. . . . It's heavy, and there's a hole in it."

"He keeps pretending to be a fool! as though he'd been born yesterday or dropped from heaven! Don't you understand, you blockhead, what unscrewing these nuts leads to? If the watchman had not noticed it the train might have run off the rails, people would have been killed—you would have killed people."

"God forbid, your honour! What should I kill them for? Are we heathens or wicked people? Thank God, good gentlemen, we have lived all our lives without ever dreaming of such a thing. . . . Save, and have mercy on us, Queen of Heaven! . . . What are you saying?"

"And what do you suppose railway accidents do come from? Unscrew two or three nuts and you have an accident."

Denis grins, and screws up his eye at the magistrate incredulously.

"Why! how many years have we all in the village been unscrewing nuts, and the Lord has been merciful; and you talk of accidents, killing people. If I had carried away a rail or put a log across the line, say, then maybe it might have upset the train, but . . . pouf! a nut!"

"But you must understand that the nut holds the rail fast to the sleepers!"

"We understand that. . . . We don't unscrew them all . . . we leave some. . . . We don't do it thoughtlessly . . . we understand. . . ."

Denis yawns and makes the sign of the cross over his mouth.

"Last year the train went off the rails here," says the magistrate. "Now I see why!"

"What do you say, your honour?"

"I am telling you that now I see why the train went off the rails last year. . . . I understand!"

"That's what you are educated people for, to understand, you kind gentlemen. The Lord knows to whom to give understanding. . . . Here you have reasoned how and what, but the watchman, a peasant like ourselves, with no understanding at all, catches one by the collar and hauls one along. . . . You should reason first and then haul me off. It's a saying that a peasant has a peasant's wit. . . . Write down, too, your honour, that he hit me twice—in the jaw and in the chest."

"When your hut was searched they found another nut. . . . At what spot did you unscrew that, and when?"

"You mean the nut which lay under the red box?"

"I don't know where it was lying, only it was found. When did you unscrew it?"

"I didn't unscrew it; Ignashka, the son of one-eyed Semyon, gave it me. I mean the one which was under the box, but the one which was in the sledge in the yard Mitrofan and I unscrewed together."

"What Mitrofan?"

"Mitrofan Petrov. . . . Haven't you heard of him? He makes nets in our village and sells them to the gentry. He needs a lot of those nuts. Reckon a matter of ten for each net."

"Listen. Article 1081 of the Penal Code lays down that every wilful damage of the railway line committed when it can expose the traffic on that line to danger, and the guilty party knows that an accident must be caused by it . . . (Do you understand? Knows! And you could not help knowing what this unscrewing would lead to . . .) is liable to penal servitude."

"Of course, you know best. . . . We are ignorant people. . . . What do we understand?"

"You understand all about it! You are lying, shamming!"

"What should I lie for? Ask in the village if you don't believe me. Only a bleak is caught without a weight, and there is no fish worse than a gudgeon, yet even that won't bite without a weight."

"You'd better tell me about the shillisper next," said the magistrate, smiling.

"There are no shillispers in our parts. . . . We cast our line without a weight on the top of the water with a butterfly; a mullet may be caught that way, though that is not often."

"Come, hold your tongue."

A silence follows. Denis shifts from one foot to the other, looks at the table with the green cloth on it, and blinks his eyes violently as though what was before him was not the cloth but the sun. The magistrate writes rapidly.

"Can I go?" asks Denis after a long silence.

"No. I must take you under guard and send you to prison."

Denis leaves off blinking and, raising his thick eyebrows, looks inquiringly at the magistrate.

"How do you mean, to prison? Your honour! I have no time to spare, I must go to the fair; I must get three roubles from Yegor for some tallow! . . ."

"Hold your tongue; don't interrupt."

"To prison. . . . If there was something to go for, I'd go; but just to go for nothing! What for? I haven't stolen anything, I believe, and I've not been fighting. . . . If you are in doubt about the arrears, your honour, don't believe the elder. . . . You ask the agent . . . he's a regular heathen, the elder, you know."

"Hold your tongue."

"I am holding my tongue, as it is," mutters Denis; "but that the elder has lied over the account, I'll take my oath for it. . . . There are three of us brothers: Kuzma Grigoryev, then Yegor Grigoryev, and me, Denis Grigoryev."

"You are hindering me. . . . Hey, Semyon," cries the magistrate, "take him away!"

"There are three of us brothers," mutters Denis, as two stalwart soldiers take him and lead him out of the room. "A brother is not responsible for a brother. Kuzma does not pay, so you, Denis, must answer for it. . . . Judges indeed! Our master the general is dead—the Kingdom of Heaven be his—or he would have shown you judges. . . . You ought to judge sensibly, not at random. . . . Flog if you like, but flog someone who deserves it, flog with conscience."

THE KISS

AT EIGHT o'clock on the evening of the twentieth of May all the six batteries of the N——— Reserve Artillery Brigade halted for the night in the village of Myestetchki on their way to camp. When the general commotion was at its height, while some officers were busily occupied around the guns, while others, gathered together in the square near the church enclosure, were listening to the quartermasters, a man in civilian dress, riding a strange horse, came into sight round the church. The little dun-coloured horse with a good neck and a short tail came, moving not straight forward, but as it were sideways, with a sort of dance step, as though it were being lashed about the legs. When he reached the officers the man on the horse took off his hat and said:

"His Excellency Lieutenant-General von Rabbek invites the gentlemen to drink tea with him this minute. . . ."

The horse turned, danced, and retired sideways; the messenger raised his hat once more, and in an instant disappeared with his strange horse behind the church.

"What the devil does it mean?" grumbled some of the officers, dispersing to their quarters. "One is sleepy, and here this Von Rabbek with his tea! We know what tea means."

The officers of all the six batteries remembered vividly an incident of the previous year, when during manœuvres they, together with the officers of a Cossack regiment, were in the same way invited to tea by a count who had an estate in the neighbourhood and was a retired army officer: the hospitable and genial count made much of them, fed them, and gave them drink, refused to let them go to their quarters in the village and made them stay the night. All that, of course, was very nice—nothing better could be desired, but the worst of it was, the old army officer was so carried away by the pleasure of the young men's company that till sunrise he was telling the officers anecdotes of his glorious past, taking them over the house, showing them expensive pictures, old engravings, rare guns, reading them autograph letters from great people, while the weary and exhausted officers looked and listened, longing for their beds and yawning in their sleeves; when at last their host let them go, it was too late for sleep.

Might not this Von Rabbek be just such another? Whether he were or not, there was no help for it. The officers changed their uniforms, brushed themselves, and went all together in search of the gentleman's house. In the square by the church they were told they could get to His Excellency's by the lower path—going down behind the church to the river, going along the bank to the garden, and there an avenue would taken them to the house; or by the upper way—straight from the church by the road which, half a mile from the village, led right up to His Excellency's granaries. The officers decided to go by the upper way.

"What Von Rabbek is it?" they wondered on the way. "Surely not the one who was in command of the N—— cavalry division at Plevna?"

"No, that was not Von Rabbek, but simply Rabbe and no 'von.'"

"What lovely weather!"

At the first of the granaries the road divided in two: one branch went straight on and vanished in the evening darkness, the other led to the owner's house on the right. The officers turned to the right and began to speak more softly. . . . On both sides of the road stretched stone granaries with red roofs, heavy and sullen-looking, very much like barracks of a district town. Ahead of them gleamed the windows of the manor-house.

"A good omen, gentlemen," said one of the officers. "Our setter is the foremost of all; no doubt he scents game ahead of us! . . ."

Lieutenant Lobytko, who was walking in front, a tall and stalwart fellow, though entirely without moustache (he was over five-and-twenty, yet for some reason there was no sign of hair on his round, well-fed face), renowned in the brigade for his peculiar faculty for divining the presence of women at a distance, turned round and said:

"Yes, there must be women here; I feel that by instinct."

On the threshold the officers were met by Von Rabbek himself, a comely-looking man of sixty in civilian dress. Shaking hands with his guests, he said that he was very glad and happy to see them, but begged them earnestly for God's sake to excuse him for not asking them to stay the night; two sisters with their children, some brothers, and some neighbours, had come on a visit to him, so that he had not one spare room left.

The General shook hands with every one, made his apologies, and smiled, but it was evident by his face that he was by no means so delighted as their last year's count, and that he had invited the officers simply because, in his opinion, it was a social obligation to do so. And the officers themselves, as they walked up the softly carpeted stairs, as they listened to him, felt that they had been invited to this house simply because it would have been awkward not to invite them; and at the sight of the footmen, who hastened to light the lamps in the entrance below and in the anteroom above, they began to feel as though they had brought uneasiness and discomfort into the house with them. In a house in which two sisters and their children, brothers, and neighbours were gathered together, probably on account of some family festivity, or event, how could the presence of nineteen unknown officers possibly be welcome?

At the entrance to the drawing-room the officers were met by a tall, graceful old lady with black eyebrows and a long face, very much like the Empress Eugénie. Smiling graciously and majestically, she said she was glad and happy to see her guests, and apologized that her husband and she were on this occasion unable to invite *messieurs les officiers* to stay the night. From her beautiful majestic smile, which instantly vanished from her face every time she turned away from her guests, it was evident that she had seen numbers of officers in her day, that she was in no humour for them now, and if she invited them to her house and apologized for not doing more, it was only because her breeding and position in society required it of her.

When the officers went into the big dining-room, there were about a dozen people, men and ladies, young and old, sitting at tea at the end of a long table. A group of men was dimly visible behind their chairs, wrapped in a haze of cigar smoke; and in the midst of them stood a lanky young man with red whiskers, talking loudly, with a lisp, in English. Through a door beyond the group could be seen a light room with pale blue furniture.

"Gentlemen, there are so many of you that it is impossible to introduce you all!" said the General in a loud voice, trying to sound very cheerful. "Make each other's acquaintance, gentlemen, without any ceremony!"

The officers—some with very serious and even stern faces, others with forced smiles, and all feeling extremely awkward—somehow made their bows and sat down to tea.

The most ill at ease of them all was Ryabovitch—a little officer in spectacles, with sloping shoulders, and whiskers like a lynx's. While some of his comrades assumed a serious expression, while others wore forced smiles, his face, his lynx-like whiskers, and spectacles seemed to say: "I am the shyest, most modest, and most undistinguished officer in the whole brigade!" At first, on going into the room and sitting down to the table, he could not fix his attention on any one face or object. The faces, the dresses, the cut-glass decanters of brandy, the steam from the glasses, the moulded cornices—all blended in one general impression that inspired in Ryabovitch alarm and a desire to hide his head. Like a lecturer making his first appearance before the public, he saw everything that was before his eyes, but apparently only had a dim understanding of it (among physiologists this condition, when the subject sees but does not understand, is called psychical blindness). After a little while, growing accustomed to his surroundings, Ryabovitch saw clearly and began to observe. As a shy man, unused to society, what struck him first was that in which he had always been deficient—namely, the extraordinary boldness of his new acquaintances. Von Rabbek, his wife, two elderly ladies, a young lady in a lilac dress, and the young man with the red whiskers, who was, it appeared, a younger son of Von Rabbek, very cleverly, as though they had rehearsed it beforehand, took seats between the officers, and at once got up a heated discussion in which the visitors could not help taking part. The lilac young lady hotly asserted that the artillery had a much better time than the cavalry and the infantry, while Von Rabbek and the elderly ladies maintained the opposite. A brisk interchange of talk followed. Ryabovitch watched the lilac young lady who argued so hotly about what was unfamiliar and utterly uninteresting to her, and watched artificial smiles come and go on her face.

Von Rabbek and his family skilfully drew the officers into the discussion, and meanwhile kept a sharp lookout over their glasses and mouths, to see whether all of them were drinking, whether all had enough sugar, why some one was not eating cakes or not drinking brandy. And the longer Ryabovitch watched and listened, the more he was attracted by this insincere but splendidly disciplined family.

After tea the officers went into the drawing-room. Lieutenant Lobytko's instinct had not deceived him. There were a great number of girls and young married ladies. The "setter" lieutenant was soon standing by a very young, fair girl in a black dress, and, bending down to her jauntily, as though leaning on an unseen sword, smiled and shrugged his shoulders coquettishly. He probably talked very interesting nonsense, for the fair girl looked at his well-fed face condescendingly and asked indifferently, "Really?" And from that uninterested "Really?" the setter, had he been intelligent, might have concluded that she would never call him to heel.

The piano struck up; the melancholy strains of a valse floated out of the wide open windows, and every one, for some reason, remembered that it was spring, a May evening. Every one was conscious of the fragrance of roses, of lilac, and of the young leaves of the poplar. Ryabovitch, in whom the brandy he had drunk made itself felt, under the influence of the music stole a glance towards the window, smiled, and began watching the movements of the women, and it seemed to him that the smell of roses, of poplars, and lilac came not from the garden, but from the ladies' faces and dresses.

Von Rabbek's son invited a scraggy-looking young lady to dance, and waltzed round the room twice with her. Lobytko, gliding over the parquet floor, flew up to the lilac young lady and whirled her away. Dancing began. . . . Ryabovitch stood near the door among those who were not dancing and looked on. He had never once danced in his whole life, and he had never once in his life put his arm round the waist of a respectable woman. He was highly delighted that a man should in the sight of all take a girl he did not know round the waist and offer her his shoulder to put her hand on, but he could not imagine himself in the position of such a man. There were times when he envied the boldness and swagger of his companions and was inwardly wretched; the consciousness that he was timid, that he was round-shouldered and uninteresting, that he had a long waist and lynx-like whiskers, had deeply mortified him, but with years he had grown used to this feeling, and now, looking at his comrades dancing or loudly talking, he no longer envied them, but only felt touched and mournful.

When the quadrille began, young Von Rabbek came up to those who were not dancing and invited two officers to have a game at billiards. The officers accepted and went with him out of the drawing-room. Ryabovitch, having nothing to do and wishing to take part in the general movement, slouched after them. From the big drawing-room they went into the little drawing-room, then into a narrow corridor with a glass roof, and thence into a room in which on their entrance three sleepy-looking footmen jumped up quickly from the sofa. At last, after passing through a long succession of rooms, young Von Rabbek and the officers came into a small room where there was a billiard-table. They began to play.

Ryabovitch, who had never played any game but cards, stood near the billiard-table and looked indifferently at the players, while they in unbuttoned coats, with cues in their hands, stepped about, made puns, and kept shouting out unintelligible words.

The players took no notice of him, and only now and then one of them, shoving him with his elbow or accidentally touching him with the end of his cue, would turn round and say "Pardon!" Before the first game was over he was weary of it, and began to feel he was not wanted and in the way. . . . He felt disposed to return to the drawing-room, and he went out.

On his way back he met with a little adventure. When he had gone half-way he noticed he had taken a wrong turning. He distinctly remembered that he ought to meet three sleepy footmen on his way, but he had passed five or six rooms, and those sleepy figures seemed to have vanished into the earth. Noticing his mistake, he walked back a little way and turned to the right; he found himself in a little dark room which he had not seen on his way to the billiard-room. After standing there a little while, he resolutely opened the first door that met his eyes and walked into an absolutely dark room. Straight in front could be seen the crack in the doorway through which there was a gleam of vivid light; from the other side of the door came the muffled sound of a melancholy mazurka. Here, too, as in the drawing-room, the windows were wide open and there was a smell of poplars, lilac and roses. . . .

Ryabovitch stood still in hesitation. . . . At that moment, to his surprise, he heard hurried footsteps and the rustling of a dress, a breathless feminine voice whispered "At last!" And two soft, fragrant, unmistakably feminine arms were clasped about his neck; a warm cheek was pressed to his cheek, and simultaneously there was the sound of a kiss. But at once the bestower of the kiss uttered a faint shriek and skipped back from him, as it seemed to Ryabovitch, with aversion. He, too, almost shrieked and rushed towards the gleam of light at the door. . . .

When he went back into the drawing-room his heart was beating and his hands were trembling so noticeably that he made haste to hide them behind his back. At first he was tormented by shame and dread that the whole drawing-room knew that he had just been kissed and embraced by a woman. He shrank into himself and looked uneasily about him, but as he became convinced that people were dancing and talking as calmly as ever, he gave himself up entirely to the new sensation which he had never experienced before in his life. Something strange was happening to him. . . . His neck, round which soft, fragrant arms had so lately been clasped, seemed to him to be anointed with oil; on his left cheek near his moustache where the unknown had kissed him there was a faint chilly tingling sensation as from peppermint drops, and the more he rubbed the place the more distinct was the chilly sensation; all over, from head to foot, he was full of a strange new feeling which grew stronger and stronger. . . . He wanted to dance, to talk, to run into the garden, to laugh aloud. . . . He quite forgot that he was round-shouldered and uninteresting, that he had lynx-like whiskers and an "undistinguished appearance" (that was how his appearance had been described by some ladies whose conversation he had accidentally overheard). When Von Rabbek's wife happened to pass by him, he gave her such a broad and friendly smile that she stood still and looked at him inquiringly.

"I like your house immensely!" he said, setting his spectacles straight.

The General's wife smiled and said that the house had belonged to her father; then she asked whether his parents were living, whether he had long been in the army, why he was so thin, and so on. . . . After receiving answers to her questions, she went on, and after his conversation with her his smiles were more friendly than ever, and he thought he was surrounded by splendid people. . . .

At supper Ryabovitch ate mechanically everything offered him, drank, and without listening to anything, tried to understand what had just happened to him. . . . The adventure was of a mysterious and romantic character, but it was not difficult to explain it. No doubt some girl or young married lady had arranged a tryst with some one in the dark room; had waited a long time, and being nervous and excited had taken Ryabovitch for her hero; this was the more probable as Ryabovitch had stood still hesitating in the dark room, so that he, too, had seemed like a person expecting something. . . . This was how Ryabovitch explained to himself the kiss he had received.

"And who is she?" he wondered, looking round at the women's faces. "She must be young, for elderly ladies don't give rendezvous. That she was a lady, one could tell by the rustle of her dress, her perfume, her voice. . . ."

His eyes rested on the lilac young lady, and he thought her very attractive; she had beautiful shoulders and arms, a clever face, and a delightful voice. Ryabovitch, looking at her, hoped that she and no one else was his unknown. . . . But she laughed somehow artificially and wrinkled up her long nose, which seemed to him to make her look old. Then he turned his eyes upon the fair girl in a black dress. She was younger, simpler, and more genuine, had a charming brow, and drank very daintily out of her wineglass. Ryabovitch now hoped that it was she. But soon he began to think her face flat, and fixed his eyes upon the one next her.

"It's difficult to guess," he thought, musing. "If one takes the shoulders and arms of the lilac one only, adds the brow of the fair one and the eyes of the one on the left of Lobytko, then . . ."

He made a combination of these things in his mind and so formed the image of the girl who had kissed him, the image that he wanted her to have, but could not find at the table. . . .

After supper, replete and exhilarated, the officers began to take leave and say thank you. Von Rabbek and his wife began again apologizing that they could not ask them to stay the night.

"Very, very glad to have met you, gentlemen," said Von Rabbek, and this time sincerely (probably because people are far more sincere and good-humoured at speeding their parting guests than on meeting them). "Delighted. I hope you will come on your way back! Don't stand on ceremony! Where are you going? Do you want to go by the upper way? No, go across the garden; it's nearer here by the lower way."

The officers went out into the garden. After the bright light and the noise the garden seemed very dark and quiet. They walked in silence all the way to the gate. They were a little drunk, pleased, and in good spirits, but the darkness and silence made them thoughtful for a minute. Probably the same idea occurred to each one of them as to Ryabovitch: would there ever come a time for them when, like Von Rabbek, they would have a large house, a family, a garden—when they, too, would be able to welcome people, even though insincerely, feed them, make them drunk and contented?

Going out of the garden gate, they all began talking at once and laughing loudly about nothing. They were walking now along the little path that led down to the river, and then ran along the water's edge, winding round the bushes on the bank, the pools, and the willows that overhung the water. The bank and the path were scarcely visible, and the other bank was entirely plunged in darkness. Stars were reflected here and there on the dark water; they quivered and were broken up on the surface—and from that alone it could be seen that the river was flowing rapidly. It was still. Drowsy curlews cried plaintively on the further bank, and in one of the bushes on the nearest side a nightingale was trilling loudly, taking no notice of the crowd of officers. The officers stood round the bush, touched it, but the nightingale went on singing.

"What a fellow!" they exclaimed approvingly. "We stand beside him and he takes not a bit of notice! What a rascal!"

At the end of the way the path went uphill, and, skirting the church enclosure, turned into the road. Here the officers, tired with walking uphill, sat down and lighted their cigarettes. On the other side of the river a murky red fire came into sight, and having nothing better to do, they spent a long time in discussing whether it was a camp fire or a light in a window, or something else. . . . Ryabovitch, too, looked at the light, and he fancied that the light looked and winked at him, as though it knew about the kiss.

On reaching his quarters, Ryabovitch undressed as quickly as possible and got into bed. Lobytko and Lieutenant Merzlyakov—a peaceable, silent fellow, who was considered in his own circle a highly educated officer, and was always, whenever it was possible, reading the "Vyestnik Evropi," which he carried about with him everywhere—were quartered in the same hut with Ryabovitch. Lobytko undressed, walked up and down the room for a long while with the air of a man who has not been satisfied, and sent his orderly for beer. Merzlyakov got into bed, put a candle by his pillow and plunged into reading the "Vyestnik Evropi."

"Who was she?" Ryabovitch wondered, looking at the smoky ceiling.

His neck still felt as though he had been anointed with oil, and there was still the chilly sensation near his mouth as though from peppermint drops. The shoulders and arms of the young lady in lilac, the brow and the truthful eyes of the fair girl in black, waists, dresses, and brooches, floated through his imagination. He tried to fix his attention on these images, but they danced about, broke up and flickered. When these images vanished altogether from the broad dark background which every man sees when he closes his eyes, he began to hear hurried footsteps, the rustle of skirts, the sound of a kiss and—an intense groundless joy took possession of him. . . . Abandoning himself to this joy, he heard the orderly return and announce that there was no beer. Lobytko was terribly indignant, and began pacing up and down again.

"Well, isn't he an idiot?" he kept saying, stopping first before Ryabovitch and then before Merzlyakov. "What a fool and a dummy a man must be not to get hold of any beer! Eh? Isn't he a scoundrel?"

"Of course you can't get beer here," said Merzlyakov, not removing his eyes from the "Vyestnik Evropi."

"Oh! Is that your opinion?" Lobytko persisted. "Lord have mercy upon us, if you dropped me on the moon I'd find you beer and women directly! I'll go and find some at once. . . . You may call me an impostor if I don't!"

He spent a long time in dressing and pulling on his high boots, then finished smoking his cigarette in silence and went out.

"Rabbek, Grabbek, Labbek," he muttered, stopping in the outer room. "I don't care to go alone, damn it all! Ryabovitch, wouldn't you like to go for a walk? Eh?"

Receiving no answer, he returned, slowly undressed and got into bed. Merzlyakov sighed, put the "Vyestnik Evropi" away, and put out the light.

"H'm! . . ." muttered Lobytko, lighting a cigarette in the dark.

Ryabovitch pulled the bed-clothes over his head, curled himself up in bed, and tried to gather together the floating images in his mind and to combine them into one whole. But nothing came of it. He soon fell asleep, and his last thought was that some one had caressed him and made him happy—that something extraordinary, foolish, but joyful and delightful, had come into his life. The thought did not leave him even in his sleep.

When he woke up the sensations of oil on his neck and the chill of peppermint about his lips had gone, but joy flooded his heart just as the day before. He looked enthusiastically at the window-frames, gilded by the light of the rising sun, and listened to the movement of the passers-by in the street. People were talking loudly close to the window.

Lebedetsky, the commander of Ryabovitch's battery, who had only just overtaken the brigade, was talking to his sergeant at the top of his voice, being always accustomed to shout.

"What else?" shouted the commander.

"When they were shoeing yesterday, your high nobility, they drove a nail into Pigeon's hoof. The vet. put on clay and vinegar; they are leading him apart now. And also, your honour, Artemyev got drunk yesterday, and the lieutenant ordered him to be put in the limber of a spare gun-carriage."

The sergeant reported that Karpov had forgotten the new cords for the trumpets and the rings for the tents, and that their honours, the officers, had spent the previous evening visiting General Von Rabbek. In the middle of this conversation the red-bearded face of Lebedetsky appeared in the window. He screwed up his short-sighted eyes, looking at the sleepy faces of the officers, and said good-morning to them.

"Is everything all right?" he asked.

"One of the horses has a sore neck from the new collar," answered Lobytko, yawning.

The commander sighed, thought a moment, and said in a loud voice:

"I am thinking of going to see Alexandra Yevgrafovna. I must call on her. Well, good-bye. I shall catch you up in the evening."

A quarter of an hour later the brigade set off on its way. When it was moving along the road by the granaries, Ryabovitch looked at the house on the right. The blinds were down in all the windows. Evidently the household was still asleep. The one who had kissed Ryabovitch the day before was asleep, too. He tried to imagine her asleep. The wide-open windows of the bedroom, the green branches peeping in, the morning freshness, the scent of the poplars, lilac, and roses, the bed, a chair, and on it the skirts that had rustled the day before, the little slippers, the little watch on the table—all this he pictured to himself clearly and distinctly, but the features of the face, the sweet sleepy smile, just what was characteristic and important, slipped through his imagination like quicksilver through the fingers. When he had ridden on half a mile, he looked back: the yellow church, the house, and the river, were all bathed in light; the river with its bright green banks, with the blue sky reflected in it and glints of silver in the sunshine here and there, was very beautiful. Ryabovitch gazed for the last time at Myestetchki, and he felt as sad as though he were parting with something very near and dear to him.

And before him on the road lay nothing but long familiar, uninteresting pictures. . . . To right and to left, fields of young rye and buckwheat with rooks hopping about in them. If one looked ahead, one saw dust and the backs of men's heads; if one looked back, one saw the

same dust and faces. . . . Foremost of all marched four men with
sabres—this was the vanguard. Next, behind, the crowd of singers, and
behind them the trumpeters on horseback. The vanguard and the cho-
rus of singers, like torch-bearers in a funeral procession, often forgot to
keep the regulation distance and pushed a long way ahead. . . .
Ryabovitch was with the first cannon of the fifth battery. He could see
all the four batteries moving in front of him. For any one not a military
man this long tedious procession of a moving brigade seems an intri-
cate and unintelligible muddle; one cannot understand why there are
so many people round one cannon, and why it is drawn by so many
horses in such a strange network of harness, as though it really were so
terrible and heavy. To Ryabovitch it was all perfectly comprehensible
and therefore uninteresting. He had known for ever so long why at the
head of each battery there rode a stalwart bombardier, and why he was
called a bombardier; immediately behind this bombardier could be
seen the horsemen of the first and then of the middle units. Ryabovitch
knew that the horses on which they rode, those on the left, were called
one name, while those on the right were called another—it was
extremely uninteresting. Behind the horsemen came two shaft-horses.
On one of them sat a rider with the dust of yesterday on his back and a
clumsy and funny-looking piece of wood on his leg. Ryabovitch knew
the object of this piece of wood, and did not think it funny. All the riders waved their whips mechanically and shouted from time to time.
The cannon itself was ugly. On the fore part lay sacks of oats covered
with canvas, and the cannon itself was hung all over with kettles,
soldiers' knapsacks, bags, and looked like some small harmless animal
surrounded for some unknown reason by men and horses. To the lee-
ward of it marched six men, the gunners, swinging their arms. After the
cannon there came again more bombardiers, riders, shaft-horses, and
behind them another cannon, as ugly and unimpressive as the first.
After the second followed a third, a fourth; near the fourth an officer,
and so on. There were six batteries in all in the brigade, and four can-
nons in each battery. The procession covered half a mile; it ended in a
string of wagons near which an extremely attractive creature—the ass,
Magar, brought by a battery commander from Turkey—paced pensively with his long-eared head drooping.

Ryabovitch looked indifferently before and behind, at the backs of
heads and at faces; at any other time he would have been half asleep,
but now he was entirely absorbed in his new agreeable thoughts. At first
when the brigade was setting off on the march he tried to persuade
himself that the incident of the kiss could only be interesting as a mysterious little adventure, that it was in reality trivial, and to think of it
seriously, to say the least of it, was stupid; but now he bade farewell to

logic and gave himself up to dreams. . . . At one moment he imagined himself in Von Rabbek's drawing-room beside a girl who was like the young lady in lilac and the fair girl in black; then he would close his eyes and see himself with another, entirely unknown girl, whose features were very vague. In his imagination he talked, caressed her, leaned on her shoulder, pictured war, separation, then meeting again, supper with his wife, children. . . .

"Brakes on!" the word of command rang out every time they went downhill.

He, too, shouted "Brakes on!" and was afraid this shout would disturb his reverie and bring him back to reality. . . .

As they passed by some landowner's estate Ryabovitch looked over the fence into the garden. A long avenue, straight as a ruler, strewn with yellow sand and bordered with young birch-trees, met his eyes. . . . With the eagerness of a man given up to dreaming, he pictured to himself little feminine feet tripping along yellow sand, and quite unexpectedly had a clear vision in his imagination of the girl who had kissed him and whom he had succeeded in picturing to himself the evening before at supper. This image remained in his brain and did not desert him again.

At midday there was a shout in the rear near the string of wagons:

"Easy! Eyes to the left! Officers!"

The general of the brigade drove by in a carriage with a pair of white horses. He stopped near the second battery, and shouted something which no one understood. Several officers, among them Ryabovitch, galloped up to them.

"Well?" asked the general, blinking his red eyes. "Are there any sick?"

Receiving an answer, the general, a little skinny man, chewed, thought for a moment and said, addressing one of the officers:

"One of your drivers of the third cannon has taken off his leg-guard and hung it on the fore part of the cannon, the rascal. Reprimand him."

He raised his eyes to Ryabovitch and went on:

"It seems to me your front strap is too long."

Making a few other tedious remarks, the general looked at Lobytko and grinned.

"You look very melancholy today, Lieutenant Lobytko," he said. "Are you pining for Madame Lopuhov? Eh? Gentlemen, he is pining for Madame Lopuhov."

The lady in question was a very stout and tall person who had long passed her fortieth year. The general, who had a predilection for solid ladies, whatever their ages, suspected a similar taste in his officers. The officers smiled respectfully. The general, delighted at having said something very amusing and biting, laughed loudly, touched his coachman's back, and saluted. The carriage rolled on. . . .

"All I am dreaming about now which seems to me so impossible and unearthly is really quite an ordinary thing," thought Ryabovitch, looking at the clouds of dust racing after the general's carriage. "It's all very ordinary, and every one goes through it. . . . That general, for instance, has once been in love; now he is married and has children. Captain Vahter, too, is married and beloved, though the nape of his neck is very red and ugly and he has no waist. . . . Salmanov is coarse and very Tatar, but he has had a love affair that has ended in marriage. . . . I am the same as every one else, and I, too, shall have the same experience as every one else, sooner or later. . . ."

And the thought that he was an ordinary person, and that his life was ordinary, delighted him and gave him courage. He pictured *her* and his happiness as he pleased, and put no rein on his imagination. . . .

When the brigade reached their halting-place in the evening, and the officers were resting in their tents, Ryabovitch, Merzlyakov, and Lobytko were sitting round a box having supper. Merzlyakov ate without haste, and, as he munched deliberately, read the "Vyestnik Evropi," which he held on his knees. Lobytko talked incessantly and kept filling up his glass with beer, and Ryabovitch, whose head was confused from dreaming all day long, drank and said nothing. After three glasses he got a little drunk, felt weak, and had an irresistible desire to impart his new sensations to his comrades.

"A strange thing happened to me at those Von Rabbeks'," he began, trying to put an indifferent and ironical tone into his voice. "You know I went into the billiard-room. . . ."

He began describing very minutely the incident of the kiss, and a moment later relapsed into silence. . . . In the course of that moment he had told everything, and it surprised him dreadfully to find how short a time it took him to tell it. He had imagined that he could have been telling the story of the kiss till next morning. Listening to him, Lobytko, who was a great liar and consequently believed no one, looked at him sceptically and laughed. Merzlyakov twitched his eyebrows and, without removing his eyes from the "Vyestnik Evropi," said:

"That's an odd thing! How strange! . . . throws herself on a man's neck, without addressing him by name. .. . She must be some sort of hysterical neurotic."

"Yes, she must," Ryabovitch agreed.

"A similar thing once happened to me," said Lobytko, assuming a scared expression. "I was going last year to Kovno. . . . I took a second-class ticket. The train was crammed, and it was impossible to sleep. I gave the guard half a rouble; he took my luggage and led me to another compartment. . . . I lay down and covered myself with a rug. . . . It was dark, you understand. Suddenly I felt some one touch me on the shoulder and

breathe in my face. I made a movement with my hand and felt somebody's elbow. . . . I opened my eyes and only imagine—a woman. Black
eyes, lips red as a prime salmon, nostrils breathing passionately—a
bosom like a buffer. . . ."

"Excuse me," Merzlyakov interrupted calmly, "I understand about
the bosom, but how could you see the lips if it was dark?"

Lobytko began trying to put himself right and laughing at Merzlyakov's
unimaginativeness. It made Ryabovitch wince. He walked away from the
box, got into bed, and vowed never to confide again.

Camp life began. . . . The days flowed by, one very much like
another. All those days Ryabovitch felt, thought, and behaved as
though he were in love. Every morning when his orderly handed him
water to wash with, and he sluiced his head with cold water, he thought
there was something warm and delightful in his life.

In the evenings when his comrades began talking of love and women,
he would listen, and draw up closer; and he wore the expression of a soldier when he hears the description of a battle in which he has taken part.
And on the evenings when the officers, out on the spree with the setter—
Lobytko—at their head, made Don Juan excursions to the "suburb," and
Ryabovitch took part in such excursions, he always was sad, felt profoundly
guilty, and inwardly begged *her* forgiveness. . . . In hours of leisure or on
sleepless nights, when he felt moved to recall his childhood, his father and
mother—everything near and dear, in fact, he invariably thought of
Myestetchki, the strange horse, Von Rabbek, his wife who was like the
Empress Eugénie, the dark room, the crack of light at the door. . . .

On the thirty-first of August he went back from the camp, not with
the whole brigade, but with only two batteries of it. He was dreaming
and excited all the way, as though he were going back to his native
place. He had an intense longing to see again the strange horse, the
church, the insincere family of the Von Rabbeks, the dark room. The
"inner voice," which so often deceives lovers, whispered to him for
some reason that he would be sure to see her . . . and he was tortured
by the questions, How he should meet her? What he would talk to her
about? Whether she had forgotten the kiss? If the worst came to the
worst, he thought, even if he did not meet her, it would be a pleasure
to him merely to go through the dark room and recall the past. . . .

Towards evening there appeared on the horizon the familiar church
and white granaries. Ryabovitch's heart beat. . . . He did not hear the
officer who was riding beside him and saying something to him, he
forgot everything, and looked eagerly at the river shining in the distance, at the roof of the house, at the dovecote round which the
pigeons were circling in the light of the setting sun.

When they reached the church and were listening to the billeting orders, he expected every second that a man on horseback would come round the church enclosure and invite the officers to tea, but . . . the billeting orders were read, the officers were in haste to go on to the village, and the man on horseback did not appear.

"Von Rabbek will hear at once from the peasants that we have come and will send for us," thought Ryabovitch, as he went into the hut, unable to understand why a comrade was lighting a candle and why the orderlies were hurriedly setting samovars. . . .

A painful uneasiness took possession of him. He lay down, then got up and looked out of the window to see whether the messenger were coming. But there was no sign of him.

He lay down again, but half an hour later he got up, and, unable to restrain his uneasiness, went into the street and strode towards the church. It was dark and deserted in the square near the church. . . . Three soldiers were standing silent in a row where the road began to go downhill. Seeing Ryabovitch, they roused themselves and saluted. He returned the salute and began to go down the familiar path.

On the further side of the river the whole sky was flooded with crimson: the moon was rising; two peasant women, talking loudly, were picking cabbage in the kitchen garden; behind the kitchen garden there were some dark huts. . . . And everything on the near side of the river was just as it had been in May: the path, the bushes, the willows overhanging the water . . . but there was no sound of the brave nightingale, and no scent of poplar and fresh grass.

Reaching the garden, Ryabovitch looked in at the gate. The garden was dark and still. . . . He could see nothing but the white stems of the nearest birch-trees and a little bit of the avenue; all the rest melted together into a dark blur. Ryabovitch looked and listened eagerly, but after waiting for a quarter of an hour without hearing a sound or catching a glimpse of a light, he trudged back. . . .

He went down to the river. The General's bath-house and the bath-sheets on the rail of the little bridge showed white before him. . . . He went on to the bridge, stood a little, and, quite unnecessarily, touched the sheets. They felt rough and cold. He looked down at the water. . . . The river ran rapidly and with a faintly audible gurgle round the piles of the bath-house. The red moon was reflected near the left bank; little ripples ran over the reflection, stretching it out, breaking it into bits, and seemed trying to carry it away. . . .

"How stupid, how stupid!" thought Ryabovitch, looking at the running water. "How unintelligent it all is!"

Now that he expected nothing, the incident of the kiss, his impatience, his vague hopes and disappointment, presented themselves in a clear light. It no longer seemed to him strange that he had not seen the

General's messenger, and that he would never see the girl who had accidentally kissed him instead of some one else; on the contrary, it would have been strange if he had seen her. . . .

The water was running, he knew not where or why, just as it did in May. In May it had flowed into the great river, from the great river into the sea; then it had risen in vapour, turned into rain, and perhaps the very same water was running now before Ryabovitch's eyes again. . . . What for? Why?

And the whole world, the whole of life, seemed to Ryabovitch an unintelligible, aimless jest. . . . And turning his eyes from the water and looking at the sky, he remembered again how fate in the person of an unknown woman had by chance caressed him, he remembered his summer dreams and fancies, and his life struck him as extraordinarily meagre, poverty-stricken, and colourless. . . .

When he went back to his hut he did not find one of his comrades. The orderly informed him that they had all gone to "General von Rabbek's, who had sent a messenger on horseback to invite them. . . ."

For an instant there was a flash of joy in Ryabovitch's heart, but he quenched it at once, got into bed, and in his wrath with his fate, as though to spite it, did not go to the General's.

THE DUEL

I

IT WAS eight o'clock in the morning—the time when the officers, the local officials, and the visitors usually took their morning dip in the sea after the hot, stifling night, and then went into the pavilion to drink tea or coffee. Ivan Andreitch Laevsky, a thin, fair young man of twenty-eight, wearing the cap of a clerk in the Ministry of Finance and with slippers on his feet, coming down to bathe, found a number of acquaintances on the beach, and among them his friend Samoylenko, the army doctor.

With his big cropped head, short neck, his red face, his big nose, his shaggy black eyebrows and grey whiskers, his stout puffy figure and his hoarse military bass, this Samoylenko made on every newcomer the unpleasant impression of a gruff bully; but two or three days after making his acquaintance, one began to think his face extraordinarily good-natured, kind, and even handsome. In spite of his clumsiness and rough manner, he was a peaceable man, of infinite kindliness and goodness of heart, always ready to be of use. He was on familiar terms with every one in the town, lent every one money, doctored every one, made matches, patched up quarrels, arranged picnics at which he cooked *shashlik* and an awfully good soup of grey mullets. He was always looking after other people's affairs and trying to interest some one on their behalf, and was always delighted about something. The general opinion about him was that he was without faults of character. He had only two weaknesses: he was ashamed of his own good nature, and tried to disguise it by a surly expression and an assumed gruffness; and he liked his assistants and his soldiers to call him "Your Excellency," although he was only a civil councillor.

21

"Answer one question for me, Alexandr Daviditch," Laevsky began, when both he and Samoylenko were in the water up to their shoulders. "Suppose you had loved a woman and had been living with her for two or three years, and then left off caring for her, as one does, and began to feel that you had nothing in common with her. How would you behave in that case?"

"It's very simple. 'You go where you please, madam'—and that would be the end of it."

"It's easy to say that! But if she has nowhere to go? A woman with no friends or relations, without a farthing, who can't work . . ."

"Well? Five hundred roubles down or an allowance of twenty-five roubles a month—and nothing more. It's very simple."

"Even supposing you have five hundred roubles and can pay twenty-five roubles a month, the woman I am speaking of is an educated woman and proud. Could you really bring yourself to offer her money? And how would you do it?"

Samoylenko was going to answer, but at that moment a big wave covered them both, then broke on the beach and rolled back noisily over the shingle. The friends got out and began dressing.

"Of course, it is difficult to live with a woman if you don't love her," said Samoylenko, shaking the sand out of his boots. "But one must look at the thing humanely, Vanya. If it were my case, I should never show a sign that I did not love her, and I should go on living with her till I died."

He was at once ashamed of his own words; he pulled himself up and said:

"But for aught I care, there might be no females at all. Let them all go to the devil!"

The friends dressed and went into the pavilion. There Samoylenko was quite at home, and even had a special cup and saucer. Every morning they brought him on a tray a cup of coffee, a tall cut glass of iced water, and a tiny glass of brandy. He would first drink the brandy, then the hot coffee, then the iced water, and this must have been very nice, for after drinking it his eyes looked moist with pleasure, he would stroke his whiskers with both hands, and say, looking at the sea:

"A wonderfully magnificent view!"

After a long night spent in cheerless, unprofitable thoughts which prevented him from sleeping, and seemed to intensify the darkness and sultriness of the night, Laevsky felt listless and shattered. He felt no better for the bathe and the coffee.

"Let us go on with our talk, Alexandr Daviditch," he said. "I won't make a secret of it; I'll speak to you openly as to a friend. Things are in a bad way with Nadyezhda Fyodorovna and me . . . a very bad way!

Forgive me for forcing my private affairs upon you, but I must speak out."

Samoylenko, who had a misgiving of what he was going to speak about, dropped his eyes and drummed with his fingers on the table.

"I've lived with her for two years and have ceased to love her," Laevsky went on; "or, rather, I realised that I never had felt any love for her. . . . These two years have been a mistake."

It was Laevsky's habit as he talked to gaze attentively at the pink palms of his hands, to bite his nails, or to pinch his cuffs. And he did so now.

"I know very well you can't help me," he said. "But I tell you, because unsuccessful and superfluous people like me find their salvation in talking. I have to generalise about everything I do. I'm bound to look for an explanation and justification of my absurd existence in somebody else's theories, in literary types—in the idea that we, upper-class Russians, are degenerating, for instance, and so on. Last night, for example, I comforted myself by thinking all the time: 'Ah, how true Tolstoy is, how mercilessly true!' And that did me good. Yes, really, brother, he is a great writer, say what you like!"

Samoylenko, who had never read Tolstoy and was intending to do so every day of his life, was a little embarrassed, and said:

"Yes, all other authors write from imagination, but he writes straight from nature."

"My God!" sighed Laevsky; "how distorted we all are by civilisation! I fell in love with a married woman and she with me. . . . To begin with, we had kisses, and calm evenings, and vows, and Spencer, and ideals, and interests in common. . . . What a deception! We really ran away from her husband, but we lied to ourselves and made out that we ran away from the emptiness of the life of the educated class. We pictured our future like this: to begin with, in the Caucasus, while we were getting to know the people and the place, I would put on the Government uniform and enter the service; then at our leisure we would pick out a plot of ground, would toil in the sweat of our brow, would have a vineyard and a field, and so on. If you were in my place, or that zoologist of yours, Von Koren, you might live with Nadyezhda Fyodorovna for thirty years, perhaps, and might leave your heirs a rich vineyard and three thousand acres of maize; but I felt like a bankrupt from the first day. In the town you have insufferable heat, boredom, and no society; if you go out into the country, you fancy poisonous spiders, scorpions, or snakes lurking under every stone and behind every bush, and beyond the fields—mountains and the desert. Alien people, an alien country, a wretched form of civilisation—all that is not so easy, brother, as walking on the Nevsky Prospect in one's fur coat, arm-in-arm with Nadyezhda Fyodorovna, dreaming of the sunny South. What is needed here is a life and death struggle, and I'm not a fighting man. A wretched neurasthenic, an idle gentleman. . . . From the first day I knew that my dreams of a life of labour and of a vineyard were worthless. As for love, I ought to tell you that living with a woman who has read Spencer and has followed you to the ends of the earth is no more interesting than living with any Anfissa or Akulina. There's the same smell of ironing, of powder, and of medicines, the same curl-papers every morning, the same self-deception."

"You can't get on in the house without an iron," said Samoylenko, blushing at Laevsky's speaking to him so openly of a lady he knew. "You are out of humour to-day, Vanya, I notice. Nadyezhda Fyodorovna is a splendid woman, highly educated, and you are a man of the highest intellect. Of course, you are not married," Samoylenko went on, glancing round at the adjacent tables, "but that's not your fault; and besides . . . one ought to be above conventional prejudices and rise to the level of modern ideas. I believe in free love myself, yes. . . . But to my thinking, once you have settled together, you ought to go on living together all your life."

"Without love?"

"I will tell you directly," said Samoylenko. "Eight years ago there was an old fellow, an agent, here—a man of very great intelligence. Well, he used to say that the great thing in married life was patience. Do you hear, Vanya? Not love, but patience. Love cannot last long. You have lived two years in love, and now evidently your married life has reached the period when, in order to preserve equilibrium, so to speak, you ought to exercise all your patience. . . ."

"You believe in your old agent; to me his words are meaningless. Your old man could be a hypocrite; he could exercise himself in the virtue of patience, and, as he did so, look upon a person he did not love as an object indispensable for his moral exercises; but I have not yet fallen so low. If I want to exercise myself in patience, I will buy dumbbells or a frisky horse, but I'll leave human beings alone."

Samoylenko asked for some white wine with ice. When they had drunk a glass each, Laevsky suddenly asked:

"Tell me, please, what is the meaning of softening of the brain?"

"How can I explain it to you? . . . It's a disease in which the brain becomes softer . . . as it were, dissolves."

"Is it curable?"

"Yes, if the disease is not neglected. Cold douches, blisters. . . . Something internal, too."

"Oh! . . . Well, you see my position; I can't live with her: it is more than I can do. While I'm with you I can be philosophical about it and smile, but at home I lose heart completely; I am so utterly miserable, that if I were told, for instance, that I should have to live another month with her, I should blow out my brains. At the same time, parting with her is out of the question. She has no friends or relations; she cannot work, and neither she nor I have any money. . . . What could become of her? To whom could she go? There is nothing one can think of. . . . Come, tell me, what am I to do?"

"H'm! . . ." growled Samoylenko, not knowing what to answer. "Does she love you?"

"Yes, she loves me in so far as at her age and with her temperament she wants a man. It would be as difficult for her to do without me as to do without her powder or her curl-papers. I am for her an indispensable, integral part of her boudoir."

Samoylenko was embarrassed.

"You are out of humour to-day, Vanya," he said. "You must have had a bad night."

"Yes, I slept badly. . . . Altogether, I feel horribly out of sorts, brother. My head feels empty; there's a sinking at my heart, a weakness. . . . I must run away."

"Run where?"

"There, to the North. To the pines and the mushrooms, to people and ideas. . . . I'd give half my life to bathe now in some little stream in the province of Moscow or Tula; to feel chilly, you know, and then to stroll for three hours even with the feeblest student, and to talk and talk endlessly. . . . And the scent of the hay! Do you remember it? And in the evening, when one walks in the garden, sounds of the piano float from the house; one hears the train passing. . . ."

Laevsky laughed with pleasure; tears came into his eyes, and to cover them, without getting up, he stretched across the next table for the matches.

"I have not been in Russia for eighteen years," said Samoylenko. "I've forgotten what it is like. To my mind, there is not a country more splendid than the Caucasus."

"Vereshtchagin has a picture in which some men condemned to death are languishing at the bottom of a very deep well. Your magnificent Caucasus strikes me as just like that well. If I were offered the choice of a chimney-sweep in Petersburg or a prince in the Caucasus, I should choose the job of chimney-sweep."

Laevsky grew pensive. Looking at his stooping figure, at his eyes fixed dreamily at one spot, at his pale, perspiring face and sunken temples, at his bitten nails, at the slipper which had dropped off his heel, displaying a badly darned sock, Samoylenko was moved to pity, and probably because Laevsky reminded him of a helpless child, he asked:

"Is your mother living?"

"Yes, but we are on bad terms. She could not forgive me for this affair."

Samoylenko was fond of his friend. He looked upon Laevsky as a good-natured fellow, a student, a man with no nonsense about him, with whom one could drink, and laugh, and talk without reserve. What he understood in him he disliked extremely. Laevsky drank a great deal and at unsuitable times; he played cards, despised his work, lived beyond his means, frequently made use of unseemly expressions in conversation, walked about the streets in his slippers, and quarrelled with Nadyezhda Fyodorovna before other people—and Samoylenko did not like this. But the fact that Laevsky had once been a student in the Faculty of Arts, subscribed to two fat reviews, often talked so cleverly that only a few people understood him, was living with a well-educated woman—all this Samoylenko did not understand, and he liked this and respected Laevsky, thinking him superior to himself.

"There is another point," said Laevsky, shaking his head. "Only it is between ourselves. I'm concealing it from Nadyezhda Fyodorovna for the time. . . . Don't let it out before her. . . . I got a letter the day before yesterday, telling me that her husband has died from softening of the brain."

"The Kingdom of Heaven be his!" sighed Samoylenko. "Why are you concealing it from her?"

"To show her that letter would be equivalent to 'Come to church to be married.' And we should first have to make our relations clear. When she understands that we can't go on living together, I will show her the letter. Then there will be no danger in it."

"Do you know what, Vanya," said Samoylenko, and a sad and imploring expression came into his face, as though he were going to ask him about something very touching and were afraid of being refused. "Marry her, my dear boy!"

"Why?"

"Do your duty to that splendid woman! Her husband is dead, and so Providence itself shows you what to do!"

"But do understand, you queer fellow, that it is impossible. To marry without love is as base and unworthy of a man as to perform mass without believing in it."

"But it's your duty to."

"Why is it my duty?" Laevsky asked irritably.

"Because you took her away from her husband and made yourself responsible for her."

"But now I tell you in plain Russian, I don't love her!"

"Well, if you've no love, show her proper respect, consider her wishes. . . ."

"'Show her respect, consider her wishes,'" Laevsky mimicked him. "As though she were some Mother Superior! . . . You are a poor psychologist and physiologist if you think that living with a woman one can get off with nothing but respect and consideration. What a woman thinks most of is her bedroom."

"Vanya, Vanya!" said Samoylenko, overcome with confusion.

"You are an elderly child, a theorist, while I am an old man in spite of my years, and practical, and we shall never understand one another. We had better drop this conversation. Mustapha!" Laevsky shouted to the waiter. "What's our bill?"

"No, no . . ." the doctor cried in dismay, clutching Laevsky's arm. "It is for me to pay. I ordered it. Make it out to me," he cried to Mustapha.

The friends got up and walked in silence along the sea-front. When they reached the boulevard, they stopped and shook hands at parting.

"You are awfully spoilt, my friend!" Samoylenko sighed. "Fate has sent you a young, beautiful, cultured woman, and you refuse the gift, while if God were to give me a crooked old woman, how pleased I should be if only she were kind and affectionate! I would live with her in my vineyard and . . ."

Samoylenko caught himself up and said:

"And she might get the samovar ready for me there, the old hag."

After parting with Laevsky he walked along the boulevard. When, bulky and majestic, with a stern expression on his face, he walked along the boulevard in his snow-white tunic and superbly polished boots, squaring his chest, decorated with the Vladimir cross on a ribbon, he was very much pleased with himself, and it seemed as though the whole world were looking at him with pleasure. Without turning his head, he looked to each side and thought that the boulevard was extremely well laid out; that the young cypress-trees, the eucalyptuses, and the ugly, anæmic palm-trees were very handsome and would in time give abundant shade; that the Circassians were an honest and hospitable people.

"It's strange that Laevsky does not like the Caucasus," he thought, "very strange."

Five soldiers, carrying rifles, met him and saluted him. On the right side of the boulevard the wife of a local official was walking along the pavement with her son, a schoolboy.

"Good-morning, Marya Konstantinovna," Samoylenko shouted to her with a pleasant smile. "Have you been to bathe? Ha, ha, ha! . . . My respects to Nikodim Alexandritch!"

And he went on, still smiling pleasantly, but seeing an assistant of the military hospital coming towards him, he suddenly frowned, stopped him, and asked:

"Is there any one in the hospital?"

"No one, Your Excellency."

"Eh?"

"No one, Your Excellency."

"Very well, run along. . . ."

Swaying majestically, he made for the lemonade stall, where sat a full-bosomed old Jewess, who gave herself out to be a Georgian, and said to her as loudly as though he were giving the word of command to a regiment:

"Be so good as to give me some soda-water!"

II

Laevsky's not loving Nadyezhda Fyodorovna showed itself chiefly in the fact that everything she said or did seemed to him a lie, or equivalent to a lie, and everything he read against women and love seemed to him to apply perfectly to himself, to Nadyezhda Fyodorovna and her husband. When he returned home, she was sitting at the window, dressed and with her hair done, and with a preoccupied face was drinking coffee and turning over the leaves of a fat magazine; and he thought the drinking of coffee was not such a remarkable event that she need put on a preoccupied expression over it, and that she had been wasting her time doing her hair in a fashionable style, as there was no one here to attract and no need to be attractive. And in the magazine he saw nothing but falsity. He thought she had dressed and done her hair so as to look handsomer, and was reading in order to seem clever.

"Will it be all right for me to go to bathe to-day?" she said.

"Why? There won't be an earthquake whether you go or not, I suppose. . . ."

"No, I only ask in case the doctor should be vexed."

"Well, ask the doctor, then; I'm not a doctor."

On this occasion what displeased Laevsky most in Nadyezhda Fyodorovna was her white open neck and the little curls at the back of her head. And he remembered that when Anna Karenin got tired of her husband, what she disliked most of all was his ears, and thought: "How true it is, how true!"

Feeling weak and as though his head were perfectly empty, he went into his study, lay down on his sofa, and covered his face with a handkerchief that he might not be bothered by the flies. Despondent and oppressive thoughts always about the same thing trailed slowly across his brain like a long string of waggons on a gloomy autumn evening, and he sank into a state of drowsy oppression. It seemed to him that he

had wronged Nadyezhda Fyodorovna and her husband, and that it was
through his fault that her husband had died. It seemed to him that he
had sinned against his own life, which he had ruined, against the world
of lofty ideas, of learning, and of work, and he conceived that wonderful world as real and possible, not on this sea-front with hungry Turks
and lazy mountaineers sauntering upon it, but there in the North,
where there were operas, theatres, newspapers, and all kinds of intellectual activity. One could only there—not here—be honest, intelligent, lofty, and pure. He accused himself of having no ideal, no guid-
ing principle in life, though he had a dim understanding now what it
meant. Two years before, when he fell in love with Nadyezhda
Fyodorovna, it seemed to him that he had only to go with her as his
wife to the Caucasus, and he would be saved from vulgarity and emptiness; in the same way now, he was convinced that he had only to part
from Nadyezhda Fyodorovna and to go to Petersburg, and he would get
everything he wanted.

"Run away," he muttered to himself, sitting up and biting his nails.
"Run away!"

He pictured in his imagination how he would go aboard the steamer
and then would have some lunch, would drink some cold beer, would
talk on deck with ladies, then would get into the train at Sevastopol and
set off. Hurrah for freedom! One station after another would flash by,
the air would keep growing colder and keener, then the birches and the
fir-trees, then Kursk, Moscow. . . .

In the restaurants cabbage soup, mutton with kasha, sturgeon, beer,
no more Asiaticism, but Russia, real Russia. The passengers in the train
would talk about trade, new singers, the Franco-Russian *entente*; on all
sides there would be the feeling of keen, cultured, intellectual, eager
life. . . . Hasten on, on! At last Nevsky Prospect, and Great Morskaya
Street, and then Kovensky Place, where he used to live at one time
when he was a student, the dear grey sky, the drizzling rain, the
drenched cabmen. . . .

"Ivan Andreitch!" some one called from the next room. "Are you at
home?"

"I'm here," Laevsky responded. "What do you want?"

"Papers."

Laevsky got up languidly, feeling giddy, walked into the other room,
yawning and shuffling with his slippers. There, at the open window that
looked into the street, stood one of his young fellow-clerks, laying out
some government documents on the window-sill.

"One minute, my dear fellow," Laevsky said softly, and he went to
look for the ink; returning to the window, he signed the papers without
looking at them, and said: "It's hot!"

"Yes. Are you coming to-day?"

"I don't think so. . . . I'm not quite well. Tell Sheshkovsky that I will come and see him after dinner."

The clerk went away. Laevsky lay down on his sofa again and began thinking:

"And so I must weigh all the circumstances and reflect on them. Before I go away from here I ought to pay up my debts. I owe about two thousand roubles. I have no money. . . . Of course, that's not important; I shall pay part now, somehow, and I shall send the rest, later, from Petersburg. The chief point is Nadyezhda Fyodorovna. . . . First of all we must define our relations. . . . Yes."

A little later he was considering whether it would not be better to go to Samoylenko for advice.

"I might go," he thought, "but what use would there be in it? I shall only say something inappropriate about boudoirs, about women, about what is honest or dishonest. What's the use of talking about what is honest or dishonest, if I must make haste to save my life, if I am suffocating in this cursed slavery and am killing myself? . . . One must realise at last that to go on leading the life I do is something so base and so cruel that everything else seems petty and trivial beside it. To run away," he muttered, sitting down, "to run away."

The deserted seashore, the insatiable heat, and the monotony of the smoky lilac mountains, ever the same and silent, everlastingly solitary, overwhelmed him with depression, and, as it were, made him drowsy and sapped his energy. He was perhaps very clever, talented, remarkably honest; perhaps if the sea and the mountains had not closed him in on all sides, he might have become an excellent Zemstvo leader, a statesman, an orator, a political writer, a saint. Who knows? If so, was it not stupid to argue whether it were honest or dishonest when a gifted and useful man—an artist or musician, for instance—to escape from prison, breaks a wall and deceives his jailers? Anything is honest when a man is in such a position.

At two o'clock Laevsky and Nadyezhda Fyodorovna sat down to dinner. When the cook gave them rice and tomato soup, Laevsky said:

"The same thing every day. Why not have cabbage soup?"

"There are no cabbages."

"It's strange. Samoylenko has cabbage soup and Marya Konstantinovna has cabbage soup, and only I am obliged to eat this mawkish mess. We can't go on like this, darling."

As is common with the vast majority of husbands and wives, not a single dinner had in earlier days passed without scenes and fault-finding between Nadyezhda Fyodorovna and Laevsky; but ever since Laevsky had made up his mind that he did not love her, he had tried to give way to Nadyezhda Fyodorovna in everything, spoke to her gently and politely, smiled, and called her " darling."

"This soup tastes like liquorice," he said, smiling; he made an effort to control himself and seem amiable, but could not refrain from saying: "Nobody looks after the housekeeping. . . . If you are too ill or busy with reading, let me look after the cooking."

In earlier days she would have said to him, "Do by all means," or, "I see you want to turn me into a cook"; but now she only looked at him timidly and flushed crimson.

"Well, how do you feel to-day?" he asked kindly.

"I am all right to-day. There is nothing but a little weakness."

"You must take care of yourself, darling. I am awfully anxious about you."

Nadyezhda Fyodorovna was ill in some way. Samoylenko said she had intermittent fever, and gave her quinine; the other doctor, Ustimovitch, a tall, lean, unsociable man, who used to sit at home in the daytime, and in the evenings walk slowly up and down on the sea-front coughing, with his hands folded behind him and a cane stretched along his back, was of the opinion that she had a female complaint, and prescribed warm compresses. In old days, when Laevsky loved her, Nadyezhda Fyodorovna's illness had excited his pity and terror; now he saw falsity even in her illness. Her yellow, sleepy face, her lustreless eyes, her apathetic expression, and the yawning that always followed her attacks of fever, and the fact that during them she lay under a shawl and looked more like a boy than a woman, and that it was close and stuffy in her room—all this, in his opinion, destroyed the illusion and was an argument against love and marriage.

The next dish given him was spinach with hard-boiled eggs, while Nadyezhda Fyodorovna, as an invalid, had jelly and milk. When with a preoccupied face she touched the jelly with a spoon and then began languidly eating it, sipping milk, and he heard her swallowing, he was possessed by such an overwhelming aversion that it made his head tingle. He recognised that such a feeling would be an insult even to a dog, but he was angry, not with himself but with Nadyezhda Fyodorovna, for arousing such a feeling, and he understood why lovers sometimes murder their mistresses. He would not murder her, of course, but if he had been on a jury now, he would have acquitted the murderer.

"Merci, darling," he said after dinner, and kissed Nadyezhda Fyodorovna on the forehead.

Going back into his study, he spent five minutes in walking to and fro, looking at his boots; then he sat down on his sofa and muttered:

"Run away, run away! We must define the position and run away!"

He lay down on the sofa and recalled again that Nadyezhda Fyodorovna's husband had died, perhaps, by his fault.

"To blame a man for loving a woman, or ceasing to love a woman, is stupid," he persuaded himself, lying down and raising his legs in order to put on his high boots. "Love and hatred are not under our control. As for her husband, maybe I was in an indirect way one of the causes of his death; but again, is it my fault that I fell in love with his wife and she with me?"

Then he got up, and finding his cap, set off to the lodgings of his colleague, Sheshkovsky, where the Government clerks met every day to play *vint* and drink beer.

"My indecision reminds me of Hamlet," thought Laevsky on the way. "How truly Shakespeare describes it! Ah, how truly!"

III

For the sake of sociability and from sympathy for the hard plight of newcomers without families, who, as there was not an hotel in the town, had nowhere to dine, Dr. Samoylenko kept a sort of table d'hôte. At this time there were only two men who habitually dined with him: a young zoologist called Von Koren, who had come for the summer to the Black Sea to study the embryology of the medusa, and a deacon called Pobyedov, who had only just left the seminary and been sent to the town to take the duty of the old deacon who had gone away for a cure. Each of them paid twelve roubles a month for their dinner and supper, and Samoylenko made them promise to turn up at two o'clock punctually.

Von Koren was usually the first to appear. He sat down in the drawing-room in silence, and taking an album from the table, began attentively scrutinising the faded photographs of unknown men in full trousers and top-hats, and ladies in crinolines and caps. Samoylenko only remembered a few of them by name, and of those whom he had forgotten he said with a sigh: "A very fine fellow, remarkably intelligent!" When he had finished with the album, Von Koren took a pistol from the whatnot, and screwing up his left eye, took deliberate aim at the portrait of Prince Vorontsov, or stood still at the looking-glass and gazed a long time at his swarthy face, his big forehead, and his black hair, which curled like a negro's, and his shirt of dull-coloured cotton with big flowers on it like a Persian rug, and the broad leather belt he wore instead of a waistcoat. The contemplation of his own image seemed to afford him almost more satisfaction than looking at photographs or playing with the pistols. He was very well satisfied with his face, and his becomingly clipped beard, and the broad shoulders, which were unmistakable evidence of his excellent health and physical strength. He was satisfied, too, with his stylish get-up, from the cravat, which matched the colour of his shirt, down to his brown boots.

While he was looking at the album and standing before the glass, at that moment, in the kitchen and in the passage near, Samoylenko, without his coat and waistcoat, with his neck bare, excited and bathed in perspiration, was bustling about the tables, mixing the salad, or making some sauce, or preparing meat, cucumbers, and onion for the cold soup, while he glared fiercely at the orderly who was helping him, and brandished first a knife and then a spoon at him.

"Give me the vinegar!" he said. "That's not the vinegar—it's the salad oil!" he shouted, stamping. "Where are you off to, you brute?"

"To get the butter, Your Excellency," answered the flustered orderly in a cracked voice.

"Make haste; it's in the cupboard! And tell Daria to put some fennel in the jar with the cucumbers! Fennel! Cover the cream up, gaping laggard, or the flies will get into it!"

And the whole house seemed resounding with his shouts. When it was ten or fifteen minutes to two the deacon would come in; he was a lanky young man of twenty-two, with long hair, with no beard and a hardly perceptible moustache. Going into the drawing-room, he crossed himself before the ikon, smiled, and held out his hand to Von Koren.

"Good-morning," the zoologist said coldly. "Where have you been?"

"I've been catching sea-gudgeon in the harbour."

"Oh, of course. . . . Evidently, deacon, you will never be busy with work."

"Why not? Work is not like a bear; it doesn't run off into the woods," said the deacon, smiling and thrusting his hands into the very deep pockets of his white cassock.

"There's no one to whip you!" sighed the zoologist.

Another fifteen or twenty minutes passed and they were not called to dinner, and they could still hear the orderly running into the kitchen and back again, noisily treading with his boots, and Samoylenko shouting:

"Put it on the table! Where are your wits? Wash it first."

The famished deacon and Von Koren began tapping on the floor with their heels, expressing in this way their impatience like the audience at a theatre. At last the door opened and the harassed orderly announced that dinner was ready! In the dining-room they were met by Samoylenko, crimson in the face, wrathful, perspiring from the heat of the kitchen; he looked at them furiously, and with an expression of horror, took the lid off the soup tureen and helped each of them to a plateful; and only when he was convinced that they were eating it with relish and liked it, he gave a sigh of relief and settled himself in his deep arm-chair. His face looked blissful and his eyes grew moist. . . . He deliberately poured himself out a glass of vodka and said:

"To the health of the younger generation."

After his conversation with Laevsky, from early morning till dinner Samoylenko had been conscious of a load at his heart, although he was in the best of humours; he felt sorry for Laevsky and wanted to help him. After drinking a glass of vodka before the soup, he heaved a sigh and said:

"I saw Vanya Laevsky to-day. He is having a hard time of it, poor fellow! The material side of life is not encouraging for him, and the worst of it is all this psychology is too much for him. I'm sorry for the lad."

"Well, that is a person I am not sorry for," said Von Koren. "If that charming individual were drowning, I would push him under with a stick and say, 'Drown, brother, drown away.' . . ."

"That's untrue. You wouldn't do it."

"Why do you think that?" The zoologist shrugged his shoulders. "I'm just as capable of a good action as you are."

"Is drowning a man a good action?" asked the deacon, and he laughed.

"Laevsky? Yes."

I think there is something amiss with the soup . . ." said Samoylenko, anxious to change the conversation.

"Laevsky is absolutely pernicious and is as dangerous to society as the cholera microbe," Von Koren went on. "To drown him would be a service."

"It does not do you credit to talk like that about your neighbour. Tell us: what do you hate him for?"

"Don't talk nonsense, doctor. To hate and despise a microbe is stupid, but to look upon everybody one meets without distinction as one's neighbour, whatever happens—thanks very much, that is equivalent to giving up criticism, renouncing a straightforward attitude to people, washing one's hands of responsibility, in fact! I consider your Laevsky a blackguard; I do not conceal it, and I am perfectly conscientious in treating him as such. Well, you look upon him as your neighbour—and you may kiss him if you like: you look upon him as your neighbour, and that means that your attitude to him is the same as to me and to the deacon; that is no attitude at all. You are equally indifferent to all."

"To call a man a blackguard!" muttered Samoylenko, frowning with distaste—"that is so wrong that I can't find words for it!"

"People are judged by their actions," Von Koren continued. "Now you decide, deacon. . . . I am going to talk to you, deacon. Mr. Laevsky's career lies open before you, like a long Chinese puzzle, and you can read it from beginning to end. What has he been doing these two years that he has been living here? We will reckon his doings on our fingers. First, he has taught the inhabitants of the town to play *vint*: two years ago that game was unknown here; now they all play it from morning till late at night, even the women and the boys. Secondly, he has taught the residents to drink beer, which was not known here either; the inhabitants are indebted to him for the knowledge of various sorts of spirits, so that now they can distinguish Kospelov's vodka from Smirnov's No. 21, blindfold. Thirdly, in former days, people here made love to other men's wives in secret, from the same motives as thieves steal in secret and not openly; adultery was considered something they were ashamed to make a public display of. Laevsky has come as a pioneer in that line; he lives with another man's wife openly. . . . Fourthly . . ."

Von Koren hurriedly ate up his soup and gave his plate to the orderly.

"I understood Laevsky from the first month of our acquaintance," he went on, addressing the deacon. "We arrived here at the same time. Men like him are very fond of friendship, intimacy, solidarity, and all the rest of it, because they always want company for *vint*, drinking, and eating; besides, they are talkative and must have listeners. We made friends—that is, he turned up every day, hindered me working, and indulged in confidences in regard to his mistress. From the first he struck me by his exceptional falsity, which simply made me sick. As a friend I pitched into him, asking him why he drank too much, why he lived beyond his means and got into debt, why he did nothing and read nothing, why he had so little culture and so little knowledge; and in answer to all my questions he used to smile bitterly, sigh, and say: 'I am a failure, a superfluous man'; or: 'What do you expect, my dear fellow, from us, the débris of the serf-owning class?' or: 'We are degenerate. . . .' Or he would begin a long rigmarole about Onyegin, Petchorin, Byron's Cain, and Bazarov, of whom he would say: 'They are our fathers in flesh and in spirit.' So we are to understand that it was not his fault that Government envelopes lay unopened in his office for weeks together, and that he drank and taught others to drink, but Onyegin, Petchorin, and Turgenev, who had invented the failure and the superfluous man, were responsible for it. The cause of his extreme dissoluteness and unseemliness lies, do you see, not in himself, but somewhere outside in space. And so—an ingenious idea!—it is not only he who is dissolute, false, and disgusting, but we . . . 'we men of the eighties,' 'we the spiritless, nervous offspring of the serf-owning class'; 'civilisation has crippled us' . . . in fact, we are to understand that such a great man as Laevsky is great even in his fall: that his dissoluteness, his lack of culture and of moral purity, is a phenomenon of natural history, sanctified by inevitability; that the causes of it are world-wide, elemental; and that we ought to hang up a lamp before Laevsky, since he is the fated victim of the age, of influences, of heredity, and so on. All the officials and their ladies were in ecstasies when they listened to him, and I could not make out for a long time what sort of man I had to deal with, a cynic or a clever rogue. Such types as he, on the surface intellectual with a smattering of education and a great deal of talk about their own nobility, are very clever in posing as exceptionally complex natures."

"Hold your tongue!" Samoylenko flared up. "I will not allow a splendid fellow to be spoken ill of in my presence!"

"Don't interrupt, Alexandr Daviditch," said Von Koren coldly; "I am just finishing. Laevsky is by no means a complex organism. Here is his moral skeleton: in the morning, slippers, a bathe, and coffee; then till dinner-time, slippers, a constitutional, and conversation; at two o'clock slippers, dinner, and wine; at five o'clock a bathe, tea and wine, then *vint* and lying; at ten o'clock supper and wine; and after midnight sleep and *la femme*. His existence is confined within this narrow programme like an egg within its shell. Whether he walks or sits, is angry, writes, rejoices, it may all be reduced to wine, cards, slippers, and women. Woman plays a fatal, overwhelming part in his life. He tells us himself that at thirteen he was in love; that when he was a student in his first year he was living with a lady who had a good influence over him, and to whom he was indebted for his musical education. In his second year he bought a prostitute from a brothel and raised her to his level—that is, took her as his kept mistress, and she lived with him for six months and then ran away back to the brothel-keeper, and her flight caused him much spiritual suffering. Alas! his sufferings were so great that he had to leave the university and spend two years at home doing nothing. But this was all for the best. At home he made friends with a widow who advised him to leave the Faculty of Jurisprudence and go into the Faculty of Arts. And so he did. When he had taken his degree, he fell passionately in love with his present . . . what's her name? . . . married lady, and was obliged to flee with her here to the Caucasus for the sake of his ideals, he would have us believe, seeing that . . . to-morrow, if not to-day, he will be tired of her and flee back again to Petersburg, and that, too, will be for the sake of his ideals."

"How do you know?" growled Samoylenko, looking angrily at the zoologist. "You had better eat your dinner."

The next course consisted of boiled mullet with Polish sauce. Samoylenko helped each of his companions to a whole mullet and poured out the sauce with his own hand. Two minutes passed in silence.

"Woman plays an essential part in the life of every man," said the deacon. "You can't help that."

"Yes, but to what degree? For each of us woman means mother, sister, wife, friend. To Laevsky she is everything, and at the same time nothing but a mistress. She—that is, cohabitation with her—is the happiness and object of his life; he is gay, sad, bored, disenchanted—on account of woman; his life grows disagreeable—woman is to blame; the dawn of a new life begins to glow, ideals turn up—and again look for the woman. . . . He only derives enjoyment from books and pictures in which there is woman. Our age is, to his thinking, poor and inferior to the forties and the sixties only because we do not know how to abandon ourselves obliviously to the passion and ecstasy of love. These voluptuaries must have in their brains a special growth of the nature of sarcoma, which stifles the brain and directs their whole psychology. Watch Laevsky when he is sitting anywhere in company. You notice: when one raises any general question in his presence, for instance, about the cell or instinct, he sits apart, and neither speaks nor listens; he looks languid and disillusioned; nothing has any interest for him, everything is vulgar and trivial. But as soon as you speak of male and female—for instance, of the fact that the female spider, after fertilisation, devours the male—his eyes glow with curiosity, his face brightens, and the man revives, in fact. All his thoughts, however noble, lofty, or neutral they may be, they all have one point of resemblance. You walk along the street with him and meet a donkey, for instance. . . . 'Tell me, please,' he asks, 'what would happen if you mated a donkey with a camel?' And his dreams! Has he told you of his dreams? It is magnificent! First, he dreams that he is married to the moon, then that he is summoned before the police and ordered to live with a guitar . . ."

The deacon burst into resounding laughter; Samoylenko frowned and wrinkled up his face angrily so as not to laugh, but could not restrain himself, and laughed.

"And it's all nonsense!" he said, wiping his tears. "Yes, by Jove, it's nonsense!"

IV

The deacon was very easily amused, and laughed at every trifle till he got a stitch in his side, till he was helpless. It seemed as though he only liked to be in people's company because there was a ridiculous side to them, and because they might be given ridiculous nicknames. He had nicknamed Samoylenko "the tarantula," his orderly "the drake," and was in ecstasies when on one occasion Von Koren spoke of Laevsky and Nadyezhda Fyodorovna as "Japanese monkeys." He watched people's faces greedily, listened without blinking, and it could be seen that his eyes filled with laughter and his face was tense with expectation of the moment when he could let himself go and burst into laughter.

"He is a corrupt and depraved type," the zoologist continued, while the deacon kept his eyes riveted on his face, expecting he would say something funny. "It is not often one can meet with such a nonentity. In body he is inert, feeble, prematurely old, while in intellect he differs in no respect from a fat shopkeeper's wife who does nothing but eat, drink, and sleep on a feather-bed, and who keeps her coachman as a lover."

The deacon began guffawing again.

"Don't laugh, deacon," said Von Koren. "It grows stupid, at last. I should not have paid attention to his insignificance," he went on, after waiting till the deacon had left off laughing; "I should have passed him by if he were not so noxious and dangerous. His noxiousness lies first of all in the fact that he has great success with women, and so threatens to leave descendants—that is, to present the world with a dozen Laevskys as feeble and as depraved as himself. Secondly, he is in the highest degree contaminating. I have spoken to you already of *vint* and beer. In another year or two he will dominate the whole Caucasian coast. You know how the mass, especially its middle stratum, believe in intellectuality, in a university education, in gentlemanly manners, and in literary language. Whatever filthy thing he did, they would all believe that it was as it should be, since he is an intellectual man, of liberal ideas and university education. What is more, he is a failure, a superfluous man, a neurasthenic, a victim of the age, and that means he can do anything. He is a charming fellow, a regular good sort, he is so genuinely indulgent to human weaknesses; he is compliant, accommodating, easy and not proud; one can drink with him and gossip and talk evil of people. . . . The masses, always inclined to anthropomorphism in religion and morals, like best of all the little gods who have the same weaknesses as themselves. Only think what a wide field he has for contamination! Besides, he is not a bad actor and is a clever hypocrite, and knows very well how to twist things round. Only take his little shifts and dodges, his attitude to civilisation, for instance. He has scarcely sniffed at civilisation, yet: 'Ah, how we have been crippled by civilisation! Ah, how I envy those savages, those children of nature, who know nothing of civilisation!' We are to understand, you see, that at one time, in ancient days, he has been devoted to civilisation with his whole soul, has served it, has sounded it to its depths, but it has exhausted him, disillusioned him, deceived him; he is a Faust, do you see?—a second Tolstoy. . . . As for Schopenhauer and Spencer, he treats them like small boys and slaps them on the shoulder in a fatherly way: 'Well, what do you say, old Spencer?' He has not read Spencer, of course, but how charming he is when with light, careless irony he says of his lady friend: 'She has read Spencer!' And they all listen to him, and no one cares to understand that this charlatan has not the right to kiss the sole of Spencer's foot, let alone speaking about him in that tone! Sapping the foundations of civilisation, of authority, of other people's altars, spattering them with filth, winking jocosely at them only to justify and conceal one's own rottenness and moral poverty is only possible for a very vain, base, and nasty creature."

"I don't know what it is you expect of him, Kolya," said Samoylenko, looking at the zoologist, not with anger now, but with a guilty air. "He is a man the same as every one else. Of course, he has his weaknesses, but he is abreast of modern ideas, is in the service, is of use to his country. Ten years ago there was an old fellow serving as agent here, a man of the greatest intelligence . . . and he used to say . . ."

"Nonsense, nonsense!" the zoologist interrupted. "You say he is in the service; but how does he serve? Do you mean to tell me that things have been done better because he is here, and the officials are more punctual, honest, and civil? On the contrary, he has only sanctioned their slackness by his prestige as an intellectual university man. He is only punctual on the 20th of the month, when he gets his salary; on the other days he lounges about at home in slippers and tries to look as if he were doing the Government a great service by living in the Caucasus. No, Alexandr Daviditch, don't stick up for him. You are insincere from beginning to end. If you really loved him and considered him your neighbour, you would above all not be indifferent to his weaknesses, you would not be indulgent to them, but for his own sake would try to make him innocuous."

"That is?"

"Innocuous. Since he is incorrigible, he can only be made innocuous in one way. . . ." Von Koren passed his finger round his throat. "Or he might be drowned . . . ," he added. "In the interests of humanity and in their own interests, such people ought to be destroyed. They certainly ought."

"What are you saying?" muttered Samoylenko, getting up and looking with amazement at the zoologist's calm, cold face. " Deacon, what is he saying? Why—are you in your senses?"

"I don't insist on the death penalty," said Von Koren. "If it is proved that it is pernicious, devise something else. If we can't destroy Laevsky, why then, isolate him, make him harmless, send him to hard labour."

"What are you saying!" said Samoylenko in horror. "With pepper, with pepper," he cried in a voice of despair, seeing that the deacon was eating stuffed aubergines without pepper. "You with your great intellect, what are you saying! Send our friend, a proud intellectual man, to penal servitude!"

"Well, if he is proud and tries to resist, put him in fetters!"

Samoylenko could not utter a word, and only twiddled his fingers; the deacon looked at his flabbergasted and really absurd face, and laughed.

"Let us leave off talking of that," said the zoologist. "Only remember one thing, Alexandr Daviditch: primitive man was preserved from such as Laevsky by the struggle for existence and by natural selection; now our civilisation has considerably weakened the struggle and the selection, and we ought to look after the destruction of the rotten and worthless for ourselves; otherwise, when the Laevskys multiply, civilisation will perish and mankind will degenerate utterly. It will be our fault."

"If it depends on drowning and hanging," said Samoylenko, "damnation take your civilisation, damnation take your humanity! Damnation take it! I tell you what: you are a very learned and intelligent man and the pride of your country, but the Germans have ruined you. Yes, the Germans! The Germans!"

Since Samoylenko had left Dorpat, where he had studied medicine, he had rarely seen a German and had not read a single German book, but, in his opinion, every harmful idea in politics or science was due to the Germans. Where he had got this notion he could not have said himself, but he held it firmly.

"Yes, the Germans!" he repeated once more. "Come and have some tea."

All three stood up, and putting on their hats, went out into the little garden, and sat there under the shade of the light green maples, the pear-trees, and a chestnut-tree. The zoologist and the deacon sat on a bench by the table, while Samoylenko sank into a deep wicker chair with a sloping back. The orderly handed them tea, jam, and a bottle of syrup.

It was very hot, thirty degrees Réaumur in the shade. The sultry air was stagnant and motionless, and a long spider-web, stretching from the chestnut-tree to the ground, hung limply and did not stir.

The deacon took up the guitar, which was constantly lying on the ground near the table, tuned it, and began singing softly in a thin voice:

"'Gathered round the tavern were the seminary lads,'"

but instantly subsided, overcome by the heat, mopped his brow and glanced upwards at the blazing blue sky. Samoylenko grew drowsy; the sultry heat, the stillness and the delicious after-dinner languor, which quickly pervaded all his limbs, made him feel heavy and sleepy; his arms dropped at his sides, his eyes grew small, his head sank on his breast. He looked with almost tearful tenderness at Von Koren and the deacon, and muttered:

"The younger generation. . . A scientific star and a luminary of the Church. . . . I shouldn't wonder if the long-skirted alleluia will be shooting up into a bishop; I dare say I may come to kissing his hand . . . Well . . . please God. . . ."

Soon a snore was heard. Von Koren and the deacon finished their tea and went out into the street.

"Are you going to the harbour again to catch sea-gudgeon?" asked the zoologist.

"No, it's too hot."

"Come and see me. You can pack up a parcel and copy something for me. By the way, we must have a talk about what you are to do. You must work, deacon. You can't go on like this."

"Your words are just and logical," said the deacon. "But my laziness finds an excuse in the circumstances of my present life. You know yourself that an uncertain position has a great tendency to make people apathetic. God only knows whether I have been sent here for a time or permanently. I am living here in uncertainty, while my wife is vegetating at her father's and is missing me. And I must confess my brain is melting with the heat."

"That's all nonsense," said the zoologist. "You can get used to the heat, and you can get used to being without the deaconess. You mustn't be slack; you must pull yourself together."

V

Nadyezhda Fyodorovna went to bathe in the morning, and her cook, Olga, followed her with a jug, a copper basin, towels, and a sponge. In the bay stood two unknown steamers with dirty white funnels, obviously foreign cargo vessels. Some men dressed in white and wearing white shoes were walking along the harbour, shouting loudly in French, and were answered from the steamers. The bells were ringing briskly in the little church of the town.

"To-day is Sunday!" Nadyezhda Fyodorovna remembered with pleasure.

She felt perfectly well, and was in a gay holiday humour. In a new loose-fitting dress of coarse thick tussore silk, and a big wide-brimmed straw hat which was bent down over her ears, so that her face looked out as though from a basket, she fancied she looked very charming. She thought that in the whole town there was only one young, pretty, intellectual woman, and that was herself, and that she was the only one who knew how to dress herself cheaply, elegantly, and with taste. That dress, for example, cost only twenty-two roubles, and yet how charming it was! In the whole town she was the only one who could be attractive, while there were numbers of men, so they must all, whether they would or not, be envious of Laevsky.

She was glad that of late Laevsky had been cold to her, reserved and polite, and at times even harsh and rude; in the past she had met all his outbursts, all his contemptuous, cold or strange incomprehensible glances, with tears, reproaches, and threats to leave him or to starve herself to death; now she only blushed, looked guiltily at him, and was glad he was not affectionate to her. If he had abused her, threatened her, it would have been better and pleasanter, since she felt hopelessly guilty towards him. She felt she was to blame, in the first place, for not sympathising with the dreams of a life of hard work, for the sake of which he had given up Petersburg and had come here to the Caucasus, and she was convinced that he had been angry with her of late for precisely that. When she was travelling to the Caucasus, it seemed that she would find here on the first day a cosy nook by the sea, a snug little garden with shade, with birds, with little brooks, where she could grow flowers and vegetables, rear ducks and hens, entertain her neighbours, doctor poor peasants and distribute little books amongst them. It had turned out that the Caucasus was nothing but bare mountains, forests, and huge valleys, where it took a long time and a great deal of effort to find anything and settle down; that there were no neighbours of any sort; that it was very hot and one might be robbed. Laevsky had been in no hurry to obtain a piece of land; she was glad of it, and they seemed to be in a tacit compact never to allude to a life of hard work. He was silent about it, she thought, because he was angry with her for being silent about it.

In the second place, she had without his knowledge during those two years bought various trifles to the value of three hundred roubles at Atchmianov's shop. She had bought the things by degrees, at one time materials, at another time silk or a parasol, and the debt had grown imperceptibly.

"I will tell him about it to-day . . . ," she used to decide, but at once reflected that in Laevsky's present mood it would hardly be convenient to talk to him of debts.

Thirdly, she had on two occasions in Laevsky's absence received a visit from Kirilin, the police captain: once in the morning when Laevsky had gone to bathe, and another time at midnight when he was playing cards. Remembering this, Nadyezhda Fyodorovna flushed crimson, and looked round at the cook as though she might overhear her thoughts. The long, insufferably hot, wearisome days, beautiful languorous evenings and stifling nights, and the whole manner of living, when from morning to night one is at a loss to fill up the useless hours, and the persistent thought that she was the prettiest young woman in the town, and that her youth was passing and being wasted, and Laevsky himself, though honest and idealistic, always the same, always lounging about in his slippers, biting his nails, and wearying her with his caprices, led by degrees to her becoming possessed by desire, and as though she were mad, she thought of nothing else day and night. Breathing, looking, walking, she felt nothing but desire. The sound of the sea told her she must love; the darkness of evening—the same; the mountains—the same. . . . And when Kirilin began paying her attentions, she had neither the power nor the wish to resist, and surrendered to him. . . .

Now the foreign steamers and the men in white reminded her for some reason of a huge hall; together with the shouts of French she heard the strains of a waltz, and her bosom heaved with unaccountable delight. She longed to dance and talk French.

She reflected joyfully that there was nothing terrible about her infidelity. Her soul had no part in her infidelity; she still loved Laevsky, and that was proved by the fact that she was jealous of him, was sorry for him, and missed him when he was away. Kirilin had turned out to be very mediocre, rather coarse though handsome; everything was broken off with him already and there would never be anything more. What had happened was over; it had nothing to do with any one, and if Laevsky found it out he would not believe in it.

There was only one bathing-house for ladies on the sea-front; men bathed under the open sky. Going into the bathing-house, Nadyezhda Fyodorovna found there an elderly lady, Marya Konstantinovna Bityugov, and her daughter Katya, a schoolgirl of fifteen; both of them were sitting on a bench undressing. Marya Konstantinovna was a good-natured, enthusiastic, and genteel person, who talked in a drawling and pathetic voice. She had been a governess until she was thirty-two, and then had married Bityugov, a Government official—a bald little man with his hair combed on to his temples and with a very meek disposition. She was still in love with him, was jealous, blushed at the word "love," and told every one she was very happy.

"My dear," she cried enthusiastically, on seeing Nadyezhda Fyodorovna, assuming an expression which all her acquaintances called "almond-oily." "My dear, how delightful that you have come! We'll bathe together—that's enchanting!"

Olga quickly flung off her dress and chemise, and began undressing her mistress.

"It's not quite so hot to-day as yesterday?" said Nadyezhda Fyodorovna, shrinking at the coarse touch of the naked cook. "Yesterday I almost died of the heat."

"Oh, yes, my dear; I could hardly breathe myself. Would you believe it? I bathed yesterday three times! Just imagine, my dear, three times! Nikodim Alexandritch was quite uneasy."

"Is it possible to be so ugly?" thought Nadyezhda Fyodorovna, looking at Olga and the official's wife; she glanced at Katya and thought: "The little girl's not badly made."

"Your Nikodim Alexandritch is very charming!" she said. "I'm simply in love with him."

"Ha, ha, ha!" cried Marya Konstantinovna, with a forced laugh; "that's quite enchanting."

Free from her clothes, Nadyezhda Fyodorovna felt a desire to fly. And it seemed to her that if she were to wave her hands she would fly upwards. When she was undressed, she noticed that Olga looked scornfully at her white body. Olga, a young soldier's wife, was living with her lawful husband, and so considered herself superior to her mistress. Marya Konstantinovna and Katya were afraid of her, and did not respect her. This was disagreeable, and to raise herself in their opinion, Nadyezhda Fyodorovna said:

"At home, in Petersburg, summer villa life is at its height now. My husband and I have so many friends! We ought to go and see them."

"I believe your husband is an engineer?" said Marya Konstantinovna timidly.

"I am speaking of Laevsky. He has a great many acquaintances. But unfortunately his mother is a proud aristocrat, not very intelligent. . . ."

Nadyezhda Fyodorovna threw herself into the water without finishing; Marya Konstantinovna and Katya made their way in after her.

"There are so many conventional ideas in the world," Nadyezhda Fyodorovna went on, "and life is not so easy as it seems."

Marya Konstantinovna, who had been a governess in aristocratic families and who was an authority on social matters, said:

"Oh yes! Would you believe me, my dear, at the Garatynskys' I was expected to dress for lunch as well as for dinner, so that, like an actress, I received a special allowance for my wardrobe in addition to my salary."

She stood between Nadyezhda Fyodorovna and Katya as though to screen her daughter from the water that washed the former.

Through the open doors looking out to the sea they could see some one swimming a hundred paces from their bathing-place.

"Mother, it's our Kostya," said Katya.

"Ach, ach!" Marya Konstantinovna cackled in her dismay. "Ach, Kostya!" she shouted, "Come back! Kostya, come back!"

Kostya, a boy of fourteen, to show off his prowess before his mother and sister, dived and swam farther, but began to be exhausted and hurried back, and from his strained and serious face it could be seen that he could not trust his own strength.

"The trouble one has with these boys, my dear!" said Marya Konstantinovna, growing calmer. "Before you can turn round, he will break his neck. Ah, my dear, how sweet it is, and yet at the same time how difficult, to be a mother! One's afraid of everything."

Nadyezhda Fyodorovna put on her straw hat and dashed out into the open sea. She swam some thirty feet and then turned on her back. She could see the sea to the horizon, the steamers, the people on the sea-front, the town; and all this, together with the sultry heat and the soft, transparent waves, excited her and whispered that she must live, live. . . . A sailing-boat darted by her rapidly and vigorously, cleaving the waves and the air; the man sitting at the helm looked at her, and she liked being looked at. . . .

After bathing, the ladies dressed and went away together.

"I have fever every alternate day, and yet I don't get thin," said Nadyezhda Fyodorovna, licking her lips, which were salt from the bathe, and responding with a smile to the bows of her acquaintances. "I've always been plump, and now I believe I'm plumper than ever."

"That, my dear, is constitutional. If, like me, one has no constitutional tendency to stoutness, no diet is of any use. . . . But you've wetted your hat, my dear."

"It doesn't matter; it will dry."

Nadyezhda Fyodorovna saw again the men in white who were walking on the sea-front and talking French; and again she felt a sudden thrill of joy, and had a vague memory of some big hall in which she had once danced, or of which, perhaps, she had once dreamed. And something at the bottom of her soul dimly and obscurely whispered to her that she was a petty, common, miserable, worthless woman. . . .

Marya Konstantinovna stopped at her gate and asked her to come in and sit down for a little while.

"Come in, my dear," she said in an imploring voice, and at the same time she looked at Nadyezhda Fyodorovna with anxiety and hope; perhaps she would refuse and not come in!

"With pleasure," said Nadyezhda Fyodorovna, accepting. "You know how I love being with you!"

And she went into the house. Marya Konstantinovna sat her down and gave her coffee, regaled her with milk rolls, then showed her photographs of her former pupils, the Garatynskys, who were by now married. She showed her, too, the examination reports of Kostya and Katya. The reports were very good, but to make them seem even better, she complained, with a sigh, how difficult the lessons at school were now. . . . She made much of her visitor, and was sorry for her, though at the same time she was harassed by the thought that Nadyezhda Fyodorovna might have a corrupting influence on the morals of Kostya and Katya, and was glad that her Nikodim Alexandritch was not at home. Seeing that in her opinion all men are fond of "women like that," Nadyezhda Fyodorovna might have a bad effect on Nikodim Alexandritch too.

As she talked to her visitor, Marya Konstantinovna kept remembering that they were to have a picnic that evening, and that Von Koren had particularly begged her to say nothing about it to the "Japanese monkeys"—that is, Laevsky and Nadyezhda Fyodorovna; but she dropped a word about it unawares, crimsoned, and said in confusion:

"I hope you will come too!"

VI

It was agreed to drive about five miles out of town on the road to the south, to stop near a *duhan* at the junction of two streams—the Black River and the Yellow River—and to cook fish soup. They started out soon after five. Foremost of the party in a char-à-banc drove Samoylenko and Laevsky; they were followed by Marya Konstantinovna, Nadyezhda Fyodorovna, Katya and Kostya, in a coach with three horses, carrying with them the crockery and a basket with provisions. In the next carriage came the police captain, Kirilin, and the young Atchmianov, the son of the shopkeeper to whom Nadyezhda Fyodorovna owed three hundred roubles; opposite them, huddled up on the little seat with his feet tucked under him, sat Nikodim Alexandritch, a neat little man with hair combed on to his temples. Last of all came Von Koren and the deacon; at the deacon's feet stood a basket of fish.

"R-r-right!" Samoylenko shouted at the top of his voice when he met a cart or a mountaineer riding on a donkey.

"In two years' time, when I shall have the means and the people ready, I shall set off on an expedition," Von Koren was telling the deacon. "I shall go by the sea-coast from Vladivostok to the Behring Straits, and then from the Straits to the mouth of the Yenisei. We shall make the map, study the fauna and the flora, and make detailed geological, anthropological, and ethnographical researches. It depends upon you to go with me or not."

"It's impossible," said the deacon.

"Why?"

"I'm a man with ties and a family."

"Your wife will let you go; we will provide for her. Better still if you were to persuade her for the public benefit to go into a nunnery; that would make it possible for you to become a monk, too, and join the expedition as a priest. I can arrange it for you."

The deacon was silent.

"Do you know your theology well?" asked the zoologist.

"No, rather badly."

"H'm! . . . I can't give you any advice on that score, because I don't know much about theology myself. You give me a list of books you need, and I will send them to you from Petersburg in the winter. It will be necessary for you to read the notes of religious travellers, too; among them are some good ethnologists and Oriental scholars. When you are familiar with their methods, it will be easier for you to set to work. And you needn't waste your time till you get the books; come to me, and we will study the compass and go through a course of meteorology. All that's indispensable."

"To be sure . . ." muttered the deacon, and he laughed. "I was trying to get a place in Central Russia, and my uncle, the head priest, promised to help me. If I go with you I shall have troubled them for nothing."

"I don't understand your hesitation. If you go on being an ordinary deacon, who is only obliged to hold a service on holidays, and on the other days can rest from work, you will be exactly the same as you are now in ten years' time, and will have gained nothing but a beard and moustache; while on returning from this expedition in ten years' time you will be a different man, you will be enriched by the consciousness that something has been done by you."

From the ladies' carriage came shrieks of terror and delight. The carriages were driving along a road hollowed in a literally overhanging precipitous cliff, and it seemed to every one that they were galloping along a shelf on a steep wall, and that in a moment the carriages would drop into the abyss. On the right stretched the sea; on the left was a rough brown wall with black blotches and red veins and with climbing roots; while on the summit stood shaggy fir-trees bent over, as though looking down in terror and curiosity. A minute later there were shrieks and laughter again: they had to drive under a huge overhanging rock.

"I don't know why the devil I'm coming with you," said Laevsky. "How stupid and vulgar it is! I want to go to the North, to run away, to escape; but here I am, for some reason, going to this stupid picnic."

"But look, what a view!" said Samoylenko as the horses turned to the left, and the valley of the Yellow River came into sight and the stream itself gleamed in the sunlight, yellow, turbid, frantic.

"I see nothing fine in that, Sasha," answered Laevsky. "To be in continual ecstasies over nature shows poverty of imagination. In comparison with what my imagination can give me, all these streams and rocks are trash, and nothing else."

The carriages now were by the banks of the stream. The high mountain banks gradually grew closer, the valley shrank together and ended in a gorge; the rocky mountain round which they were driving had been piled together by nature out of huge rocks, pressing upon each other with such terrible weight, that Samoylenko could not help gasping every time he looked at them. The dark and beautiful mountain was cleft in places by narrow fissures and gorges from which came a breath of dewy moisture and mystery; through the gorges could be seen other mountains, brown, pink, lilac, smoky, or bathed in vivid sunlight. From time to time as they passed a gorge they caught the sound of water falling from the heights and splashing on the stones.

"Ach, the damned mountains!" sighed Laevsky. "How sick I am of them!"

At the place where the Black River falls into the Yellow, and the water black as ink stains the yellow and struggles with it, stood the Tatar Kerbalay's *duhan*, with the Russian flag on the roof and with an inscription written in chalk: "The Pleasant Duhan." Near it was a little garden, enclosed in a hurdle fence, with tables and chairs set out in it, and in the midst of a thicket of wretched thorn-bushes stood a single solitary cypress, dark and beautiful.

Kerbalay, a nimble little Tatar in a blue shirt and a white apron, was standing in the road, and, holding his stomach, he bowed low to welcome the carriages, and smiled, showing his glistening white teeth.

"Good-evening, Kerbalay," shouted Samoylenko. "We are driving on a little further, and you take along the samovar and chairs! Look sharp!"

Kerbalay nodded his shaven head and muttered something, and only those sitting in the last carriage could hear: "We've got trout, your Excellency."

"Bring them, bring them!" said Von Koren.

Five hundred paces from the *duhan* the carriages stopped. Samoylenko selected a small meadow round which there were scattered stones convenient for sitting on, and a fallen tree blown down by the storm with roots overgrown by moss and dry yellow needles. Here there was a fragile wooden bridge over the stream, and just opposite on the other bank there was a little barn for drying maize, standing on four low piles, and looking like the hut on hen's legs in the fairy tale; a little ladder sloped from its door.

The first impression in all was a feeling that they would never get out of that place again. On all sides wherever they looked, the mountains rose up and towered above them, and the shadows of evening were stealing rapidly, rapidly from the *duhan* and dark cypress, making the narrow winding valley of the Black River narrower and the mountains higher. They could hear the river murmuring and the unceasing chirrup of the grasshoppers.

"Enchanting!" said Marya Konstantinovna, heaving deep sighs of ecstasy. "Children, look how fine! What peace!"

"Yes, it really is fine," assented Laevsky, who liked the view, and for some reason felt sad as he looked at the sky and then at the blue smoke rising from the chimney of the *duhan*. "Yes, it is fine," he repeated.

"Ivan Andreitch, describe this view," Marya Konstantinovna said tearfully.

"Why?" asked Laevsky. "The impression is better than any description. The wealth of sights and sounds which every one receives from nature by direct impression is ranted about by authors in a hideous and unrecognisable way."

"Really?" Von Koren asked coldly, choosing the biggest stone by the side of the water, and trying to clamber up and sit upon it. "Really?" he repeated, looking directly at Laevsky. "What of 'Romeo and Juliet'? Or, for instance, Pushkin's 'Night in the Ukraine'? Nature ought to come and bow down at their feet."

"Perhaps," said Laevsky, who was too lazy to think and oppose him. "Though what is 'Romeo and Juliet' after all?" he added after a short pause. "The beauty of poetry and holiness of love are simply the roses under which they try to hide its rottenness. Romeo is just the same sort of animal as all the rest of us."

"Whatever one talks to you about, you always bring it round to . . ." Von Koren glanced round at Katya and broke off.

"What do I bring it round to?" asked Laevsky.

"One tells you, for instance, how beautiful a bunch of grapes is, and you answer: 'Yes, but how ugly it is when it is chewed and digested in one's stomach!' Why say that? It's not new, and . . . altogether it is a queer habit."

Laevsky knew that Von Koren did not like him, and so was afraid of him, and felt in his presence as though every one were constrained and some one were standing behind his back. He made no answer and walked away, feeling sorry he had come.

"Gentlemen, quick march for brushwood for the fire!" commanded Samoylenko.

They all wandered off in different directions, and no one was left but Kirilin, Atchmianov, and Nikodim Alexandritch. Kerbalay brought chairs, spread a rug on the ground, and set a few bottles of wine.

The police captain, Kirilin, a tall, good-looking man, who in all weathers wore his great-coat over his tunic, with his haughty deportment, stately carriage, and thick, rather hoarse voice, looked like a young provincial chief of police; his expression was mournful and sleepy, as though he had just been waked against his will.

"What have you brought this for, you brute?" he asked Kerbalay, deliberately articulating each word. "I ordered you to give us *kvarel*, and what have you brought, you ugly Tatar? Eh? What?"

"We have plenty of wine of our own, Yegor Alekseitch," Nikodim Alexandritch observed, timidly and politely.

"What? But I want us to have my wine, too; I'm taking part in the picnic and I imagine I have full right to contribute my share. I im-magine so! Bring ten bottles of *kvarel*."

"Why so many?" asked Nikodim Alexandritch, in wonder, knowing Kirilin had no money.

"Twenty bottles! Thirty!" shouted Kirilin.

"Never mind, let him," Atchmianov whispered to Nikodim Alexandritch; "I'll pay."

Nadyezhda Fyodorovna was in a light-hearted, mischievous mood; she wanted to skip and jump, to laugh, to shout, to tease, to flirt. In her cheap cotton dress with blue pansies on it, in her red shoes and the same straw hat, she seemed to herself, little, simple, light, ethereal as a butterfly. She ran over the rickety bridge and looked for a minute into the water, in order to feel giddy; then, shrieking and laughing, ran to the other side to the drying-shed, and she fancied that all the men were admiring her, even Kerbalay. When in the rapidly falling darkness the trees began to melt into the mountains and the horses into the carriages, and a light gleamed in the windows of the *duhan*, she climbed up the mountain by the little path which zigzagged between stones and thorn-bushes and sat on a stone. Down below, the camp-fire was burning. Near the fire, with his sleeves tucked up, the deacon was moving to and fro, and his long black shadow kept describing a circle round it; he put on wood, and with a spoon tied to a long stick he stirred the cauldron. Samoylenko, with a copper-red face, was fussing round the fire just as though he were in his own kitchen, shouting furiously:

"Where's the salt, gentlemen? I bet you've forgotten it. Why are you all sitting about like lords while I do the work?"

Laevsky and Nikodim Alexandritch were sitting side by side on the fallen tree looking pensively at the fire. Marya Konstantinovna, Katya, and Kostya were taking the cups, saucers, and plates out of the baskets. Von Koren, with his arms folded and one foot on a stone, was standing on a bank at the very edge of the water, thinking about something. Patches of red light from the fire moved together with the shadows over the ground near the dark human figures, and quivered on the mountain, on the trees, on the bridge, on the drying-shed; on the other side the steep, scooped-out bank was all lighted up and glimmering in the stream, and the rushing turbid water broke its reflection into little bits.

The deacon went for the fish which Kerbalay was cleaning and washing on the bank, but he stood still half-way and looked about him.

"My God, how nice it is!" he thought. "People, rocks, the fire, the twilight, a monstrous tree—nothing more, and yet how fine it is!"

On the further bank some unknown persons made their appearance near the drying-shed. The flickering light and the smoke from the camp-fire puffing in that direction made it impossible to get a full view of them all at once, but glimpses were caught now of a shaggy hat and a grey beard, now of a blue shirt, now of a figure, ragged from shoulder to knee, with a dagger across the body; then a swarthy young face with black eyebrows, as thick and bold as though they had been drawn in charcoal. Five of them sat in a circle on the ground, and the other five went into the drying-shed. One was standing at the door with his back to the fire, and with his hands behind his back was telling something, which must have been very interesting, for when Samoylenko threw on twigs and the fire flared up, and scattered sparks and threw a glaring light on the shed, two calm countenances with an expression on them of deep attention could be seen, looking out of the door, while those who were sitting in a circle turned round and began listening to the speaker. Soon after, those sitting in a circle began softly singing something slow and melodious, that sounded like Lenten Church music. . . . Listening to them, the deacon imagined how it would be with him in ten years' time, when he would come back from the expedition: he would be a young priest and monk, an author with a name and a splendid past; he would be consecrated an archimandrite, then a bishop; and he would serve mass in the cathedral; in a golden mitre he would come out into the body of the church with the ikon on his breast, and blessing the mass of the people with the triple and the double candelabra, would proclaim: "Look down from Heaven, O God, behold and visit this vineyard which Thy Hand has planted," and the children with their angel voices would sing in response: "Holy God. . . ."

"Deacon, where is that fish?" he heard Samoylenko's voice.

As he went back to the fire, the deacon imagined the Church procession going along a dusty road on a hot July day; in front the peasants carrying the banners and the women and children the ikons, then the boy choristers and the sacristan with his face tied up and a straw in his hair, then in due order himself, the deacon, and behind him the priest wearing his *calotte* and carrying a cross, and behind them, tramping in the dust, a crowd of peasants—men, women, and children; in the crowd his wife and the priest's wife with kerchiefs on their heads. The choristers sing, the babies cry, the corncrakes call, the lark carols. . . .

Then they make a stand and sprinkle the herd with holy water. . . .
They go on again, and then kneeling pray for rain. Then lunch and
talk. . . .

"And that's nice too . . ." thought the deacon.

VII

Kirilin and Atchmianov climbed up the mountain by the path.
Atchmianov dropped behind and stopped, while Kirilin went up to
Nadyezhda Fyodorovna.

"Good-evening," he said, touching his cap.

"Good-evening."

"Yes!" said Kirilin, looking at the sky and pondering.

"Why 'yes'?" asked Nadyezhda Fyodorovna after a brief pause, noticing that Atchmianov was watching them both.

"And so it seems," said the officer, slowly, "that our love has withered
before it has blossomed, so to speak. How do you wish me to understand it? Is it a sort of coquetry on your part, or do you look upon me
as a nincompoop who can be treated as you choose."

"It was a mistake! Leave me alone!" Nadyezhda Fyodorovna said
sharply, on that beautiful, marvellous evening, looking at him with terror and asking herself with bewilderment, could there really have been
a moment when that man attracted her and had been near to her?

"So that's it!" said Kirilin; he thought in silence for a few minutes
and said: "Well, I'll wait till you are in a better humour, and meanwhile
I venture to assure you I am a gentleman, and I don't allow any one to
doubt it. Adieu!"

He touched his cap again and walked off, making his way between
the bushes. After a short interval Atchmianov approached hesitatingly.

"What a fine evening!" he said with a slight Armenian accent.

He was nice-looking, fashionably dressed, and behaved unaffectedly
like a well-bred youth, but Nadyezhda Fyodorovna did not like him
because she owed his father three hundred roubles; it was displeasing
to her, too, that a shopkeeper had been asked to the picnic, and she was
vexed at his coming up to her that evening when her heart felt so pure.

"The picnic is a success altogether," he said, after a pause.

"Yes," she agreed, and as though suddenly remembering her debt,
she said carelessly: "Oh, tell them in your shop that Ivan Andreitch will
come round in a day or two and will pay three hundred roubles. . . . I
don't remember exactly what it is."

"I would give another three hundred if you would not mention that
debt every day. Why be prosaic?"

Nadyezhda Fyodorovna laughed; the amusing idea occurred to her that if she had been willing and sufficiently immoral she might in one minute be free from her debt. If she, for instance, were to turn the head of this handsome young fool! How amusing, absurd, wild it would be really! And she suddenly felt a longing to make him love her, to plunder him, throw him over, and then to see what would come of it.

"Allow me to give you one piece of advice," Atchmianov said timidly. "I beg you to beware of Kirilin. He says horrible things about you everywhere."

"It doesn't interest me to know what every fool says of me," Nadyezhda Fyodorovna said coldly, and the amusing thought of playing with handsome young Atchmianov suddenly lost its charm.

"We must go down," she said; "they're calling us."

The fish soup was ready by now. They were ladling it out by platefuls, and eating it with the religious solemnity with which this is only done at a picnic; and every one thought the fish soup very good, and thought that at home they had never eaten anything so nice. As is always the case at picnics, in the mass of dinner napkins, parcels, useless greasy papers fluttering in the wind, no one knew where was his glass or where his bread. They poured the wine on the carpet and on their own knees, spilt the salt, while it was dark all round them and the fire burnt more dimly, and every one was too lazy to get up and put wood on. They all drank wine, and even gave Kostya and Katya half a glass each. Nadyezhda Fyodorovna drank one glass and then another, got a little drunk and forgot about Kirilin.

"A splendid picnic, an enchanting evening," said Laevsky, growing lively with the wine. "But I should prefer a fine winter to all this. 'His beaver collar is silver with hoar-frost.'"

"Every one to his taste," observed Von Koren.

Laevsky felt uncomfortable; the heat of the camp-fire was beating upon his back, and the hatred of Von Koren upon his breast and face: this hatred on the part of a decent, clever man, a feeling in which there probably lay hid a well-grounded reason, humiliated him and enervated him, and unable to stand up against it, he said in a propitiatory tone:

"I am passionately fond of nature, and I regret that I'm not a naturalist. I envy you."

"Well, I don't envy you, and don't regret it," said Nadyezhda Fyodorovna. "I don't understand how any one can seriously interest himself in beetles and ladybirds while the people are suffering."

Laevsky shared her opinion. He was absolutely ignorant of natural science, and so could never reconcile himself to the authoritative tone and the learned and profound air of the people who devoted themselves to the whiskers of ants and the claws of beetles, and he always felt vexed that these people, relying on these whiskers, claws, and something they called protoplasm (he always imagined it in the form of an oyster), should undertake to decide questions involving the origin and life of man. But in Nadyezhda Fyodorovna's words he heard a note of falsity, and simply to contradict her he said: "The point is not the ladybirds, but the deductions made from them."

VIII

It was late, eleven o'clock, when they began to get into the carriages to go home. They took their seats, and the only ones missing were Nadyezhda Fyodorovna and Atchmianov, who were running after one another, laughing, the other side of the stream.

"Make haste, my friends," shouted Samoylenko.

"You oughtn't to give ladies wine," said Von Koren in a low voice.

Laevsky, exhausted by the picnic, by the hatred of Von Koren, and by his own thoughts, went to meet Nadyezhda Fyodorovna, and when, gay and happy, feeling light as a feather, breathless and laughing, she took him by both hands and laid her head on his breast, he stepped back and said dryly:

"You are behaving like a . . . cocotte."

It sounded horribly coarse, so that he felt sorry for her at once. On his angry, exhausted face she read hatred, pity and vexation with himself, and her heart sank at once. She realised instantly that she had gone too far, had been too free and easy in her behaviour, and overcome with misery, feeling herself heavy, stout, coarse, and drunk, she got into the first empty carriage together with Atchmianov. Laevsky got in with Kirilin, the zoologist with Samoylenko, the deacon with the ladies, and the party set off.

"You see what the Japanese monkeys are like," Von Koren began, rolling himself up in his cloak and shutting his eyes. "You heard she doesn't care to take an interest in beetles and ladybirds because the people are suffering. That's how all the Japanese monkeys look upon people like us. They're a slavish, cunning race, terrified by the whip and the fist for ten generations; they tremble and burn incense only before violence; but let the monkey into a free state where there's no one to take it by the collar, and it relaxes at once and shows itself in its true colours. Look how bold they are in picture galleries, in museums, in theatres, or when they talk of science: they puff themselves out and get excited, they are abusive and critical . . . they are bound to criticise — it's the sign of the slave. You listen: men of the liberal professions are more often sworn at than pickpockets — that's because three-quarters of society are made up of slaves, of just such monkeys. It never happens that a slave holds out his hand to you and sincerely says 'Thank you' to you for your work."

"I don't know what you want," said Samoylenko, yawning; "the poor thing, in the simplicity of her heart, wanted to talk to you of scientific subjects, and you draw a conclusion from that. You're cross with him for something or other, and with her, too, to keep him company. She's a splendid woman."

"Ah, nonsense! An ordinary kept woman, depraved and vulgar. Listen, Alexandr Daviditch; when you meet a simple peasant woman, who isn't living with her husband, who does nothing but giggle, you tell her to go and work. Why are you timid in this case and afraid to tell the truth? Simply because Nadyezhda Fyodorovna is kept, not by a sailor, but by an official."

"What am I to do with her?" said Samoylenko, getting angry. "Beat her or what?"

"Not flatter vice. We curse vice only behind its back, and that's like making a long nose at it round a corner. I am a zoologist or a sociologist, which is the same thing; you are a doctor; society believes in us; we ought to point out the terrible harm which threatens it and the next generation from the existence of ladies like Nadyezhda Ivanovna."

"Fyodorovna," Samoylenko corrected. "But what ought society to do?"

"Society? That's its affair. To my thinking the surest and most direct method is—compulsion. *Manu militari* she ought to be returned to her husband; and if her husband won't take her in, then she ought to be sent to penal servitude or some house of correction."

"Ouf!" sighed Samoylenko. He paused and asked quietly: "You said the other day that people like Laevsky ought to be destroyed. . . . Tell me, if you . . . if the State or society commissioned you to destroy him, could you . . . bring yourself to it?"

"My hand would not tremble."

IX

When they got home, Laevsky and Nadyezhda Fyodorovna went into their dark, stuffy, dull rooms. Both were silent. Laevsky lighted a candle, while Nadyezhda Fyodorovna sat down, and without taking off her cloak and hat, lifted her melancholy, guilty eyes to him.

He knew that she expected an explanation from him, but an explanation would be wearisome, useless and exhausting, and his heart was heavy because he had lost control over himself and been rude to her. He chanced to feel in his pocket the letter which he had been intending every day to read to her, and thought if he were to show her that letter now, it would turn her thoughts in another direction.

"It is time to define our relations," he thought. "I will give it her; what is to be will be."

He took out the letter and gave it her.

"Read it. It concerns you."

Saying this, he went into his own room and lay down on the sofa in the dark without a pillow. Nadyezhda Fyodorovna read the letter, and it seemed to her as though the ceiling were falling and the walls were closing in on her. It seemed suddenly dark and shut in and terrible. She crossed herself quickly three times and said:

"Give him peace, O Lord . . . give him peace. . . ."

And she began crying.

"Vanya," she called. "Ivan Andreitch!"

There was no answer. Thinking that Laevsky had come in and was standing behind her chair, she sobbed like a child, and said:

"Why did you not tell me before that he was dead? I wouldn't have gone to the picnic; I shouldn't have laughed so horribly. . . . The men said horrid things to me. What a sin, what a sin! Save me, Vanya, save me. . . . I have been mad. . . . I am lost. . . ."

Laevsky heard her sobs. He felt stifled and his heart was beating violently. In his misery he got up, stood in the middle of the room, groped his way in the dark to an easy-chair by the table, and sat down.

"This is a prison . . ." he thought. "I must get away. . . . I can't bear it."

It was too late to go and play cards; there were no restaurants in the town. He lay down again and covered his ears that he might not hear her sobbing, and he suddenly remembered that he could go to Samoylenko. To avoid going near Nadyezhda Fyodorovna, he got out of the window into the garden, climbed over the garden fence and went along the street. It was dark. A steamer, judging by its lights, a big passenger one, had just come in. . . . He heard the clank of the anchor chain. A red light was moving rapidly from the shore in the direction of the steamer: it was the Customs boat going out to it.

"The passengers are asleep in their cabins . . ." thought Laevsky, and he envied the peace of mind of other people.

The windows in Samoylenko's house were open. Laevsky looked in at one of them, then in at another; it was dark and still in the rooms.

"Alexandr Daviditch, are you asleep?" he called. "Alexandr Daviditch!"

He heard a cough and an uneasy shout:

"Who's there? What the devil?"

"It is I, Alexandr Daviditch; excuse me."

A little later the door opened; there was a glow of soft light from the lamp, and Samoylenko's huge figure appeared all in white, with a white nightcap on his head.

"What now?" he asked, scratching himself and breathing hard from sleepiness. "Wait a minute; I'll open the door directly."

"Don't trouble; I'll get in at the window. . . ."

Laevsky climbed in at the window, and when he reached Samoylenko, seized him by the hand.

"Alexandr Daviditch," he said in a shaking voice, "save me! I beseech you, I implore you. Understand me! My position is agonising. If it goes on for another two days I shall strangle myself like . . . like a dog."

"Wait a bit. . . . What are you talking about exactly?"

"Light a candle."

"Oh . . . oh! . . ." sighed Samoylenko, lighting a candle. "My God! My God! . . . Why, it's past one, brother."

"Excuse me, but I can't stay at home," said Laevsky, feeling great comfort from the light and the presence of Samoylenko. "You are my best, my only friend, Alexandr Daviditch. . . . You are my only hope. For God's sake, come to my rescue, whether you want to or not. I must get away from here, come what may! . . . Lend me the money!"

"Oh, my God, my God! . . . sighed Samoylenko, scratching himself. "I was dropping asleep and I hear the whistle of the steamer, and now you . . . Do you want much?"

"Three hundred roubles at least. I must leave her a hundred, and I need two hundred for the journey. . . . I owe you about four hundred already, but I will send it you all . . . all. . . ."

Samoylenko took hold of both his whiskers in one hand, and standing with his legs wide apart, pondered.

"Yes . . ." he muttered, musing. "Three hundred. . . . Yes. . . . But I haven't got so much. I shall have to borrow it from some one."

"Borrow it, for God's sake!" said Laevsky, seeing from Samoylenko's face that he wanted to lend him the money and certainly would lend it. "Borrow it, and I'll be sure to pay you back. I will send it from Petersburg as soon as I get there. You can set your mind at rest about that. I'll tell you what, Sasha," he said, growing more animated; "let us have some wine."

"Yes . . . we can have some wine, too."

They both went into the dining-room.

"And how about Nadyezhda Fyodorovna?" asked Samoylenko, setting three bottles and a plate of peaches on the table. "Surely she's not remaining?"

"I will arrange it all, I will arrange it all," said Laevsky, feeling an unexpected rush of joy. "I will send her the money afterwards and she will join me. . . . Then we will define our relations. To your health, friend."

"Wait a bit," said Samoylenko. "Drink this first. . . . This is from my vineyard. This bottle is from Navaridze's vineyard and this one is from Ahatulov's. . . . Try all three kinds and tell me candidly. . . . There seems a little acidity about mine. Eh? Don't you taste it?"

"Yes. You have comforted me, Alexandr Daviditch. Thank you. . . . I feel better."

"Is there any acidity?"

"Goodness only knows, I don't know. But you are a splendid, wonderful man!"

Looking at his pale, excited, good-natured face, Samoylenko remembered Von Koren's view that men like that ought to be destroyed, and Laevsky seemed to him a weak, defenceless child, whom any one could injure and destroy.

"And when you go, make it up with your mother," he said. "It's not right."

"Yes, yes; I certainly shall."

They were silent for a while. When they had emptied the first bottle, Samoylenko said:

"You ought to make it up with Von Koren too. You are both such splendid, clever fellows, and you glare at each other like wolves."

"Yes, he's a fine, very intelligent fellow," Laevsky assented, ready now to praise and forgive every one. "He's a remarkable man, but it's impossible for me to get on with him. No! Our natures are too different. I'm an indolent, weak, submissive nature. Perhaps in a good minute I might hold out my hand to him, but he would turn away from me . . . with contempt."

Laevsky took a sip of wine, walked from corner to corner and went on, standing in the middle of the room:

"I understand Von Koren very well. His is a resolute, strong, despotic nature. You have heard him continually talking of 'the expedition,' and it's not mere talk. He wants the wilderness, the moonlit night: all around in little tents, under the open sky, lie sleeping his sick and hungry Cossacks, guides, porters, doctor, priest, all exhausted with their weary marches, while only he is awake, sitting like Stanley on a camp-stool, feeling himself the monarch of the desert and the master of these men. He goes on and on and on, his men groan and die, one after another, and he goes on and on, and in the end perishes himself, but still is monarch and ruler of the desert, since the cross upon his tomb can be seen by the caravans for thirty or forty miles over the desert. I am sorry the man is not in the army. He would have made a splendid military genius. He would not have hesitated to drown his cavalry in the river and make a bridge out of dead bodies. And such hardihood is more needed in war than any kind of fortification or strategy. Oh, I understand him perfectly! Tell me: why is he wasting his substance here? What does he want here?"

"He is studying the marine fauna."

"No, no, brother, no!" Laevsky sighed. "A scientific man who was on the steamer told me the Black Sea was poor in animal life, and that in its depths, thanks to the abundance of sulphuric hydrogen, organic life was impossible. All the serious zoologists work at the biological station at Naples or Villefranche. But Von Koren is independent and obstinate: he works on the Black Sea because nobody else is working there; he is at loggerheads with the university, does not care to know his comrades and other scientific men because he is first of all a despot and only secondly a zoologist. And you'll see he'll do something. He is already dreaming that when he comes back from his expedition he will purify our universities from intrigue and mediocrity, and will make the scientific men mind their ps and qs. Despotism is just as strong in science as in the army. And he is spending his second summer in this stinking little town because he would rather be first in a village than second in a town. Here he is a king and an eagle; he keeps all the inhabitants under his thumb and oppresses them with his authority. He has appropriated every one, he meddles in other people's affairs; everything is of use to him, and every one is afraid of him. I am slipping out of his clutches, he feels that and hates me. Hasn't he told you that I ought to be destroyed or sent to hard labour?"

"Yes," laughed Samoylenko.

Laevsky laughed too, and drank some wine.

"His ideals are despotic too," he said, laughing, and biting a peach. "Ordinary mortals think of their neighbour—me, you, man in fact—if they work for the common weal. To Von Koren men are puppets and nonentities, too trivial to be the object of his life. He works, will go for his expedition and break his neck there, not for the sake of love for his neighbour, but for the sake of such abstractions as humanity, future generations, an ideal race of men. He exerts himself for the improvement of the human race, and we are in his eyes only slaves, food for the cannon, beasts of burden; some he would destroy or stow away in Siberia, others he would break by discipline, would, like Araktcheev, force them to get up and go to bed to the sound of the drum; would appoint eunuchs to preserve our chastity and morality, would order them to fire at any one who steps out of the circle of our narrow conservative morality; and all this in the name of the improvement of the human race. . . . And what is the human race? Illusion, mirage . . . despots have always been illusionists. I understand him very well, brother. I appreciate him and don't deny his importance; this world rests on men like him, and if the world were left only to such men as us, for all our good-nature and good intentions, we should make as great a mess of it as the flies have of that picture. Yes."

Laevsky sat down beside Samoylenko, and said with genuine feeling: "I'm a foolish, worthless, depraved man. The air I breathe, this wine, love, life in fact—for all that, I have given nothing in exchange so far but lying, idleness, and cowardice. Till now I have deceived myself and other people; I have been miserable about it, and my misery was cheap and common. I bow my back humbly before Von Koren's hatred because at times I hate and despise myself."

Laevsky began again pacing from one end of the room to the other in excitement, and said:

"I'm glad I see my faults clearly and am conscious of them. That will help me to reform and become a different man. My dear fellow, if only you knew how passionately, with what anguish, I long for such a change. And I swear to you I'll be a man! I will! I don't know whether it is the wine that is speaking in me, or whether it really is so, but it seems to me that it is long since I have spent such pure and lucid moments as I have just now with you."

It's time to sleep, brother," said Samoylenko.

"Yes, yes. . . . Excuse me; I'll go directly."

Laevsky moved hurriedly about the furniture and windows, looking for his cap.

"Thank you," he muttered, sighing. "Thank you. . . . Kind and friendly words are better than charity. You have given me new life."

He found his cap, stopped, and looked guiltily at Samoylenko.

"Alexandr Daviditch," he said in an imploring voice.

"What is it?"

"Let me stay the night with you, my dear fellow!"

"Certainly. . . . Why not?"

Laevsky lay down on the sofa, and went on talking to the doctor for a long time.

X

Three days after the picnic, Marya Konstantinovna unexpectedly called on Nadyezhda Fyodorovna, and without greeting her or taking off her hat, seized her by both hands, pressed them to her breast and said in great excitement:

"My dear, I am deeply touched and moved: our dear kind-hearted doctor told my Nikodim Alexandritch yesterday that your husband was dead. Tell me, my dear . . . tell me, is it true?

"Yes, it's true; he is dead," answered Nadyezhda Fyodorovna.

"That is awful, awful, my dear! But there's no evil without some compensation; your husband was no doubt a noble, wonderful, holy man, and such are more needed in Heaven than on earth."

Every line and feature in Marya Konstantinovna's face began quivering as though little needles were jumping up and down under her skin; she gave an almond-oily smile and said, breathlessly, enthusiastically:

"And so you are free, my dear. You can hold your head high now, and look people boldly in the face. Henceforth God and man will bless your union with Ivan Andreitch. It's enchanting. I am trembling with joy, I can find no words. My dear, I will give you away. . . . Nikodim Alexandritch and I have been so fond of you, you will allow us to give our blessing to your pure, lawful union. When, when do you think of being married?"

"I haven't thought of it," said Nadyezhda Fyodorovna, freeing her hands.

"That's impossible, my dear. You have thought of it, you have."

"Upon my word, I haven't," said Nadyezhda Fyodorovna, laughing. "What should we be married for? I see no necessity for it. We'll go on living as we have lived."

"What are you saying!" cried Marya Konstantinovna in horror. "For God's sake, what are you saying!"

"Our getting married won't make things any better. On the contrary, it will make them even worse. We shall lose our freedom."

"My dear, my dear, what are you saying!" exclaimed Marya Konstantinovna, stepping back and flinging up her hands. "You are talking wildly! Think what you are saying. You must settle down!"

"'Settle down.' How do you mean? I have not lived yet, and you tell me to settle down."

Nadyezhda Fyodorovna reflected that she really had not lived. She had finished her studies in a boarding-school and had been married to a man she did not love; then she had thrown in her lot with Laevsky, and had spent all her time with him on this empty, desolate coast, always expecting something better. Was that life?

"I ought to be married though," she thought, but remembering Kirilin and Atchmianov she flushed and said:

"No, it's impossible. Even if Ivan Andreitch begged me to on his knees—even then I would refuse."

Marya Konstantinovna sat on the sofa for a minute in silence, grave and mournful, gazing fixedly into space; then she got up and said coldly:

"Good-bye, my dear! Forgive me for having troubled you. Though it's not easy for me, it's my duty to tell you that from this day all is over between us, and, in spite of my profound respect for Ivan Andreitch, the door of my house is closed to you henceforth."

She uttered these words with great solemnity and was herself overwhelmed by her solemn tone. Her face began quivering again; it assumed a soft almond-oily expression. She held out both hands to

Nadyezhda Fyodorovna, who was overcome with alarm and confusion, and said in an imploring voice:

"My dear, allow me if only for a moment to be a mother or an elder sister to you! I will be as frank with you as a mother."

Nadyezhda Fyodorovna felt in her bosom warmth, gladness, and pity for herself, as though her own mother had really risen up and were standing before her. She impulsively embraced Marya Konstantinovna and pressed her face to her shoulder. Both of them shed tears. They sat down on the sofa and for a few minutes sobbed without looking at one another or being able to utter a word.

"My dear child," began Marya Konstantinovna, "I will tell you some harsh truths, without sparing you."

"For God's sake, for God's sake, do!"

"Trust me, my dear. You remember of all the ladies here, I was the only one to receive you. You horrified me from the very first day, but I had not the heart to treat you with disdain like all the rest. I grieved over dear, good Ivan Andreitch as though he were my son—a young man in a strange place, inexperienced, weak, with no mother; and I was worried, dreadfully worried. . . . My husband was opposed to our making his acquaintance, but I talked him over . . . persuaded him. . . . We began receiving Ivan Andreitch, and with him, of course, you. If we had not, he would have been insulted. I have a daughter, a son. . . . You understand the tender mind, the pure heart of childhood . . . 'whoso offendeth one of these little ones.' . . . I received you into my house and trembled for my children. Oh, when you become a mother, you will understand my fears. And every one was surprised at my receiving you, excuse my saying so, as a respectable woman, and hinted to me . . . well, of course, slanders, suppositions. . . . At the bottom of my heart I blamed you, but you were unhappy, flighty, to be pitied, and my heart was wrung with pity for you."

"But why, why?" asked Nadyezhda Fyodorovna, trembling all over. "What harm have I done any one?"

"You are a terrible sinner. You broke the vow you made your husband at the altar. You seduced a fine young man, who perhaps had he not met you might have taken a lawful partner for life from a good family in his own circle, and would have been like every one else now. You have ruined his youth. Don't speak, don't speak, my dear! I never believe that man is to blame for our sins. It is always the woman's fault. Men are frivolous in domestic life; they are guided by their minds, and not by their hearts. There's a great deal they don't understand; woman understands it all. Everything depends on her. To her much is given and from her much will be required. Oh, my dear, if she had been more foolish or weaker than man on that side, God would not have entrusted her with the education of boys and girls. And then, my dear, you entered on the path of vice, forgetting all modesty; any other woman in your place would have hidden herself from people, would have sat shut up at home, and would only have been seen in the temple of God, pale, dressed all in black and weeping, and every one would have said in genuine compassion: 'O Lord, this erring angel is coming back again to Thee. . . .' But you, my dear, have forgotten all discretion; have lived openly, extravagantly; have seemed to be proud of your sin; you have been gay and laughing, and I, looking at you, shuddered with horror, and have been afraid that thunder from Heaven would strike our house while you were sitting with us. My dear, don't speak, don't speak," cried Marya Konstantinovna, observing that Nadyezhda Fyodorovna wanted to speak. "Trust me, I will not deceive you, I will not hide one truth from the eyes of your soul. Listen to me, my dear. . . . God marks great sinners, and you have been marked out: only think—your costumes have always been appalling."

Nadyezhda Fyodorovna, who had always had the highest opinion of her costumes, left off crying and looked at her with surprise.

"Yes, appalling," Marya Konstantinovna went on. "Any one could judge of your behaviour from the elaboration and gaudiness of your attire. People laughed and shrugged their shoulders as they looked at you, and I grieved, I grieved. . . . And forgive me, my dear; you are not nice in your person! When we met in the bathing-place, you made me tremble. Your outer clothing was decent enough, but your petticoat, your chemise. . . . My dear, I blushed! Poor Ivan Andreitch! No one ever ties his cravat properly, and from his linen and his boots, poor fellow! one can see he has no one at home to look after him. And he is always hungry, my darling, and of course, if there is no one at home to think of the samovar and the coffee, one is forced to spend half one's salary at the pavilion. And it's simply awful, awful in your home! No one else in the town has flies, but there's no getting rid of them in your rooms: all the plates and dishes are black with them. If you look at the windows and the chairs, there's nothing but dust, dead flies, and glasses. . . . What do you want glasses standing about for? And, my dear, the table's not cleared till this time in the day. And one's ashamed to go into your bedroom: underclothes flung about everywhere, india-rubber tubes hanging on the walls, pails and basins standing about. . . . My dear! A husband ought to know nothing, and his wife ought to be as neat as a little angel in his presence. I wake up every morning before it is light, and wash my face with cold water that my Nikodim Alexandritch may not see me looking drowsy."

"That's all nonsense," Nadyezhda Fyodorovna sobbed. "If only I were happy, but I am so unhappy!"

"Yes, yes; you are very unhappy!" Marya Konstantinovna sighed, hardly able to restrain herself from weeping. "And there's terrible grief in store for you in the future! A solitary old age, ill-health; and then you will have to answer at the dread judgment seat. . . . It's awful, awful. Now fate itself holds out to you a helping hand, and you madly thrust it from you. Be married, make haste and be married!"

"Yes, we must, we must," said Nadyezhda Fyodorovna; "but it's impossible!"

"Why?"

"It's impossible. Oh, if only you knew!"

Nadyezhda Fyodorovna had an impulse to tell her about Kirilin, and how the evening before she had met handsome young Atchmianov at the harbour, and how the mad, ridiculous idea had occurred to her of cancelling her debt for three hundred; it had amused her very much, and she returned home late in the evening feeling that she had sold herself and was irrevocably lost. She did not know herself how it had happened. And she longed to swear to Marya Konstantinovna that she would certainly pay that debt, but sobs and shame prevented her from speaking.

"I am going away," she said. "Ivan Andreitch may stay, but I am going."

"Where?"

"To Russia."

"But how will you live there? Why, you have nothing."

"I will do translation, or . . . or I will open a library. . . ."

"Don't let your fancy run away with you, my dear. You must have money for a library. Well, I will leave you now, and you calm yourself and think things over, and to-morrow come and see me, bright and happy. That will be enchanting! Well, good-bye, my angel. Let me kiss you."

Marya Konstantinovna kissed Nadyezhda Fyodorovna on the forehead, made the sign of the cross over her, and softly withdrew. It was getting dark, and Olga lighted up in the kitchen. Still crying, Nadyezhda Fyodorovna went into the bedroom and lay down on the bed. She began to be very feverish. She undressed without getting up, crumpled up her clothes at her feet, and curled herself up under the bedclothes. She was thirsty, and there was no one to give her something to drink.

"I'll pay it back!" she said to herself, and it seemed to her in delirium that she was sitting beside some sick woman, and recognised her as herself. "I'll pay it back. It would be stupid to imagine that it was for money. I . . . I will go away and send him the money from Petersburg. At first a hundred . . . then another hundred . . . and then the third hundred. . . ."

It was late at night when Laevsky came in.

"At first a hundred . . ." Nadyezhda Fyodorovna said to him, "then another hundred . . ."

"You ought to take some quinine," he said, and thought, "To-morrow is Wednesday; the steamer goes and I am not going in it. So I shall have to go on living here till Saturday."

Nadyezhda Fyodorovna knelt up in bed.

"I didn't say anything just now, did I?" she asked, smiling and screwing up her eyes at the light.

"No, nothing. We shall have to send for the doctor to-morrow morning. Go to sleep."

He took his pillow and went to the door. Ever since he had finally made up his mind to go away and leave Nadyezhda Fyodorovna, she had begun to raise in him pity and a sense of guilt; he felt a little ashamed in her presence, as though in the presence of a sick or old horse whom one has decided to kill. He stopped in the doorway and looked round at her.

"I was out of humour at the picnic and said something rude to you. Forgive me, for God's sake!"

Saying this, he went off to his study, lay down, and for a long while could not get to sleep.

Next morning when Samoylenko, attired, as it was a holiday, in full-dress uniform with epaulettes on his shoulders and decorations on his breast, came out of the bedroom after feeling Nadyezhda Fyodorovna's pulse and looking at her tongue, Laevsky, who was standing in the doorway, asked him anxiously: "Well? Well?"

There was an expression of terror, of extreme uneasiness, and of hope on his face.

"Don't worry yourself; there's nothing dangerous," said Samoylenko; "it's the usual fever."

"I don't mean that." Laevsky frowned impatiently. "Have you got the money?"

"My dear soul, forgive me," he whispered, looking round at the door and overcome with confusion.

"For God's sake, forgive me! No one has anything to spare, and I've only been able to collect by five- and by ten-rouble notes. . . . Only a hundred and ten in all. To-day I'll speak to some one else. Have patience."

"But Saturday is the latest date," whispered Laevsky, trembling with impatience. "By all that's sacred, get it by Saturday! If I don't get away by Saturday, nothing's any use, nothing! I can't understand how a doctor can be without money!"

"Lord have mercy on us!" Samoylenko whispered rapidly and

intensely, and there was positively a breaking note in his throat. "I've been stripped of everything; I am owed seven thousand, and I'm in debt all round. Is it my fault?"

"Then you'll get it by Saturday? Yes?"

"I'll try."

"I implore you, my dear fellow! So that the money may be in my hands by Friday morning!"

Samoylenko sat down and prescribed solution of quinine and kalii bromati and tincture of rhubarb, tincturæ gentianæ, aquæ fœniculi— all in one mixture, added some pink syrup to sweeten it, and went away.

XI

"You look as though you were coming to arrest me," said Von Koren, seeing Samoylenko coming in, in his full-dress uniform.

"I was passing by and thought: 'Suppose I go in and pay my respects to zoology,'" said Samoylenko, sitting down at the big table, knocked together by the zoologist himself out of plain boards. "Good-morning, holy father," he said to the deacon, who was sitting in the window, copying something. "I'll stay a minute and then run home to see about dinner. It's time. . . . I'm not hindering you?"

"Not in the least," answered the zoologist, laying out over the table slips of paper covered with small writing. "We are busy copying."

"Ah! . . . Oh, my goodness, my goodness! . . ." sighed Samoylenko. He cautiously took up from the table a dusty book on which there was lying a dead dried spider, and said: "Only fancy, though; some little green beetle is going about its business, when suddenly a monster like this swoops down upon it. I can fancy its terror."

"Yes, I suppose so."

"Is poison given it to protect it from its enemies?"

"Yes, to protect it and enable it to attack."

"To be sure, to be sure. . . . And everything in nature, my dear fellows, is consistent and can be explained," sighed Samoylenko; "only I tell you what I don't understand. You're a man of very great intellect, so explain it to me, please. There are, you know, little beasts no bigger than rats, rather handsome to look at, but nasty and immoral in the extreme, let me tell you. Suppose such a little beast is running in the woods. He sees a bird; he catches it and devours it. He goes on and sees in the grass a nest of eggs; he does not want to eat them—he is not hungry, but yet he tastes one egg and scatters the others out of the nest with his paw. Then he meets a frog and begins to play with it; when he has tormented the frog he goes on licking himself and meets a beetle; he crushes the beetle with his paw . . . and so he spoils and destroys everything on his way. . . . He creeps into other beasts' holes, tears up the anthills, cracks the snail's shell. If he meets a rat, he fights with it; if he meets a snake or a mouse, he must strangle it; and so the whole day long. Come, tell me: what is the use of a beast like that? Why was he created?"

"I don't know what animal you are talking of," said Von Koren; "most likely one of the insectivora. Well, he got hold of the bird because it was incautious; he broke the nest of eggs because the bird was not skilful, had made the nest badly and did not know how to conceal it. The frog probably had some defect in its colouring or he would not have seen it, and so on. Your little beast only destroys the weak, the unskilful, the careless—in fact, those who have defects which nature does not think fit to hand on to posterity. Only the cleverer, the stronger, the more careful and developed survive; and so your little beast, without suspecting it, is serving the great ends of perfecting creation."

"Yes, yes, yes. . . . By the way, brother," said Samoylenko carelessly, "lend me a hundred roubles."

"Very good. There are some very interesting types among the insectivorous mammals. For instance, the mole is said to be useful because he devours noxious insects. There is a story that some German sent William I. a fur coat made of mole-skins, and the Emperor ordered him to be reproved for having destroyed so great a number of useful animals. And yet the mole is not a bit less cruel than your little beast, and is very mischievous besides, as he spoils meadows terribly."

Von Koren opened a box and took out a hundred-rouble note.

"The mole has a powerful thorax, just like the bat," he went on, shutting the box; "the bones and muscles are tremendously developed, the mouth is extraordinarily powerfully furnished. If it had the proportions of an elephant, it would be an all-destructive, invincible animal. It is interesting when two moles meet underground; they begin at once as though by agreement digging a little platform; they need the platform in order to have a battle more conveniently. When they have made it they enter upon a ferocious struggle and fight till the weaker one falls. Take the hundred roubles," said Von Koren, dropping his voice, "but only on condition that you're not borrowing it for Laevsky."

"And if it were for Laevsky," cried Samoylenko, flaring up, "what is that to you?"

"I can't give it to you for Laevsky. I know you like lending people money. You would give it to Kerim, the brigand, if he were to ask you; but, excuse me, I can't assist you in that direction."

"Yes, it is for Laevsky I am asking it," said Samoylenko, standing up and waving his right arm. "Yes! For Laevsky! And no one, fiend or devil, has a right to dictate to me how to dispose of my own money. It doesn't suit you to lend it me? No?"

The deacon began laughing.

"Don't get excited, but be reasonable," said the zoologist. "To shower benefits on Mr. Laevsky is, to my thinking, as senseless as to water weeds or to feed locusts."

"To my thinking, it is our duty to help our neighbours!" cried Samoylenko.

"In that case, help that hungry Turk who is lying under the fence! He is a workman and more useful and indispensable than your Laevsky. Give him that hundred-rouble note! Or subscribe a hundred roubles to my expedition!"

"Will you give me the money or not? I ask you!"

"Tell me openly: what does he want money for?"

"It's not a secret; he wants to go to Petersburg on Saturday."

"So that is it!" Von Koren drawled out. "Aha! . . . We understand. And is she going with him, or how is it to be?"

"She's staying here for the time. He'll arrange his affairs in Petersburg and send her the money, and then she'll go."

"That's smart!" said the zoologist, and he gave a short tenor laugh. "Smart, well planned."

He went rapidly up to Samoylenko, and standing face to face with him, and looking him in the eyes, asked: "Tell me now honestly: is he tired of her? Yes? tell me: is he tired of her? Yes?"

"Yes," Samoylenko articulated, beginning to perspire.

"How repulsive it is!" said Von Koren, and from his face it could be seen that he felt repulsion. "One of two things, Alexandr Daviditch: either you are in the plot with him, or, excuse my saying so, you are a simpleton. Surely you must see that he is taking you in like a child in the most shameless way? Why, it's as clear as day that he wants to get rid of her and abandon her here. She'll be left a burden on you. It is as clear as day that you will have to send her to Petersburg at your expense. Surely your fine friend can't have so blinded you by his dazzling qualities that you can't see the simplest thing?"

"That's all supposition," said Samoylenko, sitting down.

"Supposition? But why is he going alone instead of taking her with him? And ask him why he doesn't send her off first. The sly beast!"

Overcome with sudden doubts and suspicions about his friend, Samoylenko weakened and took a humbler tone.

"But it's impossible," he said, recalling the night Laevsky had spent at his house. "He is so unhappy!"

"What of that? Thieves and incendiaries are unhappy too!"

"Even supposing you are right . . ." said Samoylenko, hesitating. "Let us admit it. . . . Still, he's a young man in a strange place . . . a student. We have been students, too, and there is no one but us to come to his assistance."

"To help him to do abominable things, because he and you at

different times have been at universities, and neither of you did anything there! What nonsense!"

"Stop; let us talk it over coolly. I imagine it will be possible to make
some arrangement. . . ." Samoylenko reflected, twiddling his fingers.
"I'll give him the money, you see, but make him promise on his honour that within a week he'll send Nadyezhda Fyodorovna the money
for the journey."

"And he'll give you his word of honour—in fact, he'll shed tears and
believe in it himself; but what's his word of honour worth? He won't
keep it, and when in a year or two you meet him on the Nevsky
Prospect with a new mistress on his arm, he'll excuse himself on the
ground that he has been crippled by civilisation, and that he is made
after the pattern of Rudin. Drop him, for God's sake! Keep away from
the filth; don't stir it up with both hands!"

Samoylenko thought for a minute and said resolutely:

"But I shall give him the money all the same. As you please. I can't
bring myself to refuse a man simply on an assumption."

"Very fine, too. You can kiss him if you like."

"Give me the hundred roubles, then," Samoylenko asked timidly.

"I won't."

A silence followed. Samoylenko was quite crushed; his face wore a
guilty, abashed, and ingratiating expression, and it was strange to see
this pitiful, childish, shamefaced countenance on a huge man wearing
epaulettes and orders of merit.

"The bishop here goes the round of his diocese on horseback instead
of in a carriage," said the deacon, laying down his pen. "It's extremely
touching to see him sit on his horse. His simplicity and humility are
full of Biblical grandeur."

"Is he a good man?" asked Von Koren, who was glad to change the
conversation.

"Of course! If he hadn't been a good man, do you suppose he would
have been consecrated a bishop?"

"Among the bishops are to be found good and gifted men," said Von
Koren. "The only drawback is that some of them have the weakness to
imagine themselves statesmen. One busies himself with Russification,
another criticises the sciences. That's not their business. They had
much better look into their consistory a little."

"A layman cannot judge of bishops."

"Why so, deacon? A bishop is a man just the same as you or I."

"The same, but not the same." The deacon was offended and took
up his pen. "If you had been the same, the Divine Grace would have
rested upon you, and you would have been bishop yourself; and since
you are not bishop, it follows you are not the same."

"Don't talk nonsense, deacon," said Samoylenko dejectedly. "Listen to what I suggest," he said, turning to Von Koren. "Don't give me that hundred roubles. You'll be having your dinners with me for three months before the winter, so let me have the money beforehand for three months."

"I won't."

Samoylenko blinked and turned crimson; he mechanically drew towards him the book with the spider on it and looked at it, then he got up and took his hat.

Von Koren felt sorry for him.

"What it is to have to live and do with people like this," said the zoologist, and he kicked a paper into the corner with indignation. "You must understand that this is not kindness, it is not love, but cowardice, slackness, poison! What's gained by reason is lost by your flabby good-for-nothing hearts! When I was ill with typhoid as a schoolboy, my aunt in her sympathy gave me pickled mushrooms to eat, and I very nearly died. You, and my aunt too, must understand that love for man is not to be found in the heart or the stomach or the bowels, but here!"

Von Koren slapped himself on the forehead.

"Take it," he said, and thrust a hundred-rouble note into his hand.

"You've no need to be angry, Kolya," said Samoylenko mildly, folding up the note. "I quite understand you, but . . . you must put yourself in my place."

"You are an old woman, that's what you are."

The deacon burst out laughing.

"Hear my last request, Alexandr Daviditch," said Von Koren hotly. "When you give that scoundrel the money, make it a condition that he takes his lady with him, or sends her on ahead, and don't give it him without. There's no need to stand on ceremony with him. Tell him so, or, if you don't, I give you my word I'll go to his office and kick him downstairs, and I'll break off all acquaintance with you. So you'd better know it."

"Well! To go with her or send her on beforehand will be more convenient for him," said Samoylenko. "He'll be delighted indeed. Well, good-bye."

He said good-bye affectionately and went out, but before shutting the door after him, he looked round at Von Koren and, with a ferocious face, said:

"It's the Germans who have ruined you, brother! Yes! The Germans!"

XII

Next day, Thursday, Marya Konstantinovna was celebrating the birthday of her Kostya. All were invited to come at midday and eat pies, and in the evening to drink chocolate. When Laevsky and Nadyezhda

Fyodorovna arrived in the evening, the zoologist, who was already sitting in the drawing-room, drinking chocolate, asked Samoylenko:

"Have you talked to him?"

"Not yet."

"Mind now, don't stand on ceremony. I can't understand the insolence of these people! Why, they know perfectly well the view taken by this family of their cohabitation, and yet they force themselves in here."

"If one is to pay attention to every prejudice," said Samoylenko, "one could go nowhere."

"Do you mean to say that the repugnance felt by the masses for illicit love and moral laxity is a prejudice?"

"Of course it is. It's prejudice and hate. When the soldiers see a girl of light behaviour, they laugh and whistle; but just ask them what they are themselves."

"It's not for nothing they whistle. The fact that girls strangle their illegitimate children and go to prison for it, and that Anna Karenin flung herself under the train, and that in the villages they smear the gates with tar, and that you and I, without knowing why, are pleased by Katya's purity, and that every one of us feels a vague craving for pure love, though he knows there is no such love—is all that prejudice? That is the one thing, brother, which has survived intact from natural selection, and, if it were not for that obscure force regulating the relations of the sexes, the Laevskys would have it all their own way, and mankind would degenerate in two years."

Laevsky came into the drawing-room, greeted every one, and shaking hands with Von Koren, smiled ingratiatingly. He waited for a favourable moment and said to Samoylenko:

"Excuse me, Alexandr Daviditch, I must say two words to you."

Samoylenko got up, put his arm round Laevsky's waist, and both of them went into Nikodim Alexandritch's study.

"To-morrow's Friday," said Laevsky, biting his nails. "Have you got what you promised?"

"I've only got two hundred. I'll get the rest to-day or to-morrow. Don't worry yourself."

"Thank God . . ." sighed Laevsky, and his hands began trembling with joy. "You are saving me, Alexandr Daviditch, and I swear to you by God, by my happiness and anything you like, I'll send you the money as soon as I arrive. And I'll send you my old debt too."

"Look here, Vanya . . ." said Samoylenko, turning crimson and taking him by the button. "You must forgive my meddling in your private affairs, but . . . why shouldn't you take Nadyezhda Fyodorovna with you?"

"You queer fellow. How is that possible? One of us must stay, or our creditors will raise an outcry. You see, I owe seven hundred or more to the shops. Only wait, and I will send them the money. I'll stop their mouths, and then she can come away."

"I see. . . . But why shouldn't you send her on first?"

"My goodness, as though that were possible!" Laevsky was horrified. "Why, she's a woman; what would she do there alone? What does she know about it? That would only be a loss of time and a useless waste of money."

"That's reasonable . . ." thought Samoylenko, but remembering his conversation with Von Koren, he looked down and said sullenly: "I can't agree with you. Either go with her or send her first; otherwise. . . otherwise I won't give you the money. Those are my last words. . . ."

He staggered back, lurched backwards against the door, and went into the drawing-room, crimson, and overcome with confusion.

"Friday . . . Friday," thought Laevsky, going back into the drawing-room. "Friday. . . ."

He was handed a cup of chocolate; he burnt his lips and tongue with the scalding chocolate and thought: "Friday . . . Friday. . . ."

For some reason he could not get the word "Friday" out of his head; he could think of nothing but Friday, and the only thing that was clear to him, not in his brain but somewhere in his heart, was that he would not get off on Saturday. Before him stood Nikodim Alexandritch, very neat, with his hair combed over his temples, saying:

"Please take something to eat. . . ."

Marya Konstantinovna showed the visitors Katya's school report and said, drawling:

"It's very, very difficult to do well at school nowadays! So much is expected . . ."

"Mamma!" groaned Katya, not knowing where to hide her confusion at the praises of the company.

Laevsky, too, looked at the report and praised it. Scripture, Russian language, conduct, fives and fours, danced before his eyes, and all this, mixed with the haunting refrain of "Friday," with the carefully combed locks of Nikodim Alexandritch and the red cheeks of Katya, produced on him a sensation of such immense overwhelming boredom that he almost shrieked with despair and asked himself: "Is it possible, is it possible I shall not get away?"

They put two card tables side by side and sat down to play post. Laevsky sat down too.

"Friday . . . Friday . . ." he kept thinking, as he smiled and took a pencil out of his pocket. "Friday. . . ."

He wanted to think over his position, and was afraid to think. It was terrible to him to realise that the doctor had detected him in the deception which he had so long and carefully concealed from himself. Every time he thought of his future he would not let his thoughts have full rein. He would get into the train and set off, and thereby the problem of his life would be solved, and he did not let his thoughts go farther. Like a far-away dim light in the fields, the thought sometimes flickered in his mind that in one of the side-streets of Petersburg, in the remote future, he would have to have recourse to a tiny lie in order to get rid of Nadyezhda Fyodorovna and pay his debts; he would tell a lie only once, and then a completely new life would begin. And that was right: at the price of a small lie he would win so much truth.

Now when by his blunt refusal the doctor had crudely hinted at his deception, he began to understand that he would need deception not only in the remote future, but to-day, and to-morrow, and in a month's time, and perhaps up to the very end of his life. In fact, in order to get away he would have to lie to Nadyezhda Fyodorovna, to his creditors, and to his superiors in the Service; then, in order to get money in Petersburg, he would have to lie to his mother, to tell her that he had already broken with Nadyezhda Fyodorovna; and his mother would not give him more than five hundred roubles, so he had already deceived the doctor, as he would not be in a position to pay him back the money within a short time. Afterwards, when Nadyezhda Fyodorovna came to Petersburg, he would have to resort to a regular series of deceptions, little and big, in order to get free of her; and again there would be tears, boredom, a disgusting existence, remorse, and so there would be no new life. Deception and nothing more. A whole mountain of lies rose before Laevsky's imagination. To leap over it at one bound and not to do his lying piecemeal, he would have to bring himself to stern, uncompromising action; for instance, to getting up without saying a word, putting on his hat, and at once setting off without money and without explanation. But Laevsky felt that was impossible for him.

"Friday, Friday . . ." he thought. "Friday. . . ."

They wrote little notes, folded them in two, and put them in Nikodim Alexandritch's old top-hat. When there were a sufficient heap of notes, Kostya, who acted the part of postman, walked round the table and delivered them. The deacon, Katya, and Kostya, who received amusing notes and tried to write as funnily as they could, were highly delighted.

"We must have a little talk," Nadyezhda Fyodorovna read in a little note; she glanced at Marya Konstantinovna, who gave her an almond-oily smile and nodded.

"Talk of what?" thought Nadyezhda Fyodorovna. "If one can't tell the whole, it's no use talking."

Before going out for the evening she had tied Laevsky's cravat for him, and that simple action filled her soul with tenderness and sorrow. The anxiety in his face, his absent-minded looks, his pallor, and the incomprehensible change that had taken place in him of late, and the fact that she had a terrible revolting secret from him, and the fact that her hands trembled when she tied his cravat—all this seemed to tell her that they had not long left to be together. She looked at him as though he were an ikon, with terror and penitence, and thought: "Forgive, forgive."

Opposite her was sitting Atchmianov, and he never took his black, love-sick eyes off her. She was stirred by passion; she was ashamed of herself, and afraid that even her misery and sorrow would not prevent her from yielding to impure desire to-morrow, if not to-day—and that, like a drunkard, she would not have the strength to stop herself.

She made up her mind to go away that she might not continue this life, shameful for herself, and humiliating for Laevsky. She would beseech him with tears to let her go; and if he opposed her, she would go away secretly. She would not tell him what had happened; let him keep a pure memory of her.

"I love you, I love you, I love you," she read. It was from Atchmianov.

She would live in some far remote place, would work and send Laevsky, "anonymously," money, embroidered shirts, and tobacco, and would return to him only in old age or if he were dangerously ill and needed a nurse. When in his old age he learned what were her reasons for leaving him and refusing to be his wife, he would appreciate her sacrifice and forgive.

"You've got a long nose." That must be from the deacon or Kostya.

Nadyezhda Fyodorovna imagined how, parting from Laevsky, she would embrace him warmly, would kiss his hand, and would swear to love him all her life, all her life, and then, living in obscurity among strangers, she would every day think that somewhere she had a friend, some one she loved—a pure, noble, lofty man who kept a pure memory of her.

"If you don't give me an interview to-day, I shall take measures, I assure you on my word of honour. You can't treat decent people like this; you must understand that." That was from Kirilin.

XIII

Laevsky received two notes; he opened one and read: "Don't go away, my darling."

"Who could have written that?" he thought. "Not Samoylenko, of course. And not the deacon, for he doesn't know I want to go away. Von Koren, perhaps?"

The zoologist bent over the table and drew a pyramid. Laevsky fancied that his eyes were smiling.

"Most likely Samoylenko . . . has been gossiping," thought Laevsky.

In the other note, in the same disguised angular handwriting with long tails to the letters, was written: "Somebody won't go away on Saturday."

"A stupid gibe," thought Laevsky. "Friday, Friday. . . ."

Something rose in his throat. He touched his collar and coughed, but instead of a cough a laugh broke from his throat.

"Ha-ha-ha!" he laughed. "Ha-ha-ha! What am I laughing at? Ha-ha-ha!"

He tried to restrain himself, covered his mouth with his hand, but the laugh choked his chest and throat, and his hand could not cover his mouth.

"How stupid it is!" he thought, rolling with laughter. "Have I gone out of my mind?"

The laugh grew shriller and shriller, and became something like the bark of a lap-dog. Laevsky tried to get up from the table, but his legs would not obey him and his right hand was strangely, without his volition, dancing on the table, convulsively clutching and crumpling up the bits of paper. He saw looks of wonder, Samoylenko's grave, frightened face, and the eyes of the zoologist full of cold irony and disgust, and realised that he was in hysterics.

"How hideous, how shameful!" he thought, feeling the warmth of tears on his face. ". . . Oh, oh, what a disgrace! It has never happened to me. . . ."

They took him under his arms, and supporting his head from behind, led him away; a glass gleamed before his eyes and knocked against his teeth, and the water was spilt on his breast; he was in a little room, with two beds in the middle, side by side, covered by two snow-white quilts. He dropped on one of the beds and sobbed.

"It's nothing, it's nothing," Samoylenko kept saying; "it does happen . . . it does happen. . . ."

Chill with horror, trembling all over and dreading something awful, Nadyezhda Fyodorovna stood by the bedside and kept asking:

"What is it? What is it? For God's sake, tell me."

"Can Kirilin have written him something?" she thought.

"It's nothing," said Laevsky, laughing and crying; "go away, darling."

His face expressed neither hatred nor repulsion: so he knew nothing; Nadyezhda Fyodorovna was somewhat reassured, and she went into the drawing-room.

"Don't agitate yourself, my dear!" said Marya Konstantinovna, sitting down beside her and taking her hand. "It will pass. Men are just as weak as we poor sinners. You are both going through a crisis. . . . One can so well understand it! Well, my dear, I am waiting for an answer. Let us have a little talk."

"No, we are not going to talk," said Nadyezhda Fyodorovna, listening to Laevsky's sobs. "I feel depressed. . . . You must allow me to go home."

"What do you mean, what do you mean, my dear?" cried Marya Konstantinovna in alarm. "Do you think I could let you go without supper? We will have something to eat, and then you may go with my blessing."

"I feel miserable . . ." whispered Nadyezhda Fyodorovna, and she caught at the arm of the chair with both hands to avoid falling.

"He's got a touch of hysterics," said Von Koren gaily, coming into the drawing-room, but seeing Nadyezhda Fyodorovna, he was taken aback and retreated.

When the attack was over, Laevsky sat on the strange bed and thought.

"Disgraceful! I've been howling like some wretched girl! I must have been absurd and disgusting. I will go away by the back stairs. . . . But that would seem as though I took my hysterics too seriously. I ought to take it as a joke. . . ."

He looked in the looking-glass, sat there for some time, and went back into the drawing-room.

"Here I am," he said, smiling; he felt agonisingly ashamed, and he felt others were ashamed in his presence. "Fancy such a thing happening," he said, sitting down. "I was sitting here, and all of a sudden, do you know, I felt a terrible piercing pain in my side . . . unendurable, my nerves could not stand it, and . . . and it led to this silly performance. This is the age of nerves; there is no help for it."

At supper he drank some wine, and, from time to time, with an abrupt sigh rubbed his side as though to suggest that he still felt the pain. And no one, except Nadyezhda Fyodorovna, believed him, and he saw that.

After nine o'clock they went for a walk on the boulevard. Nadyezhda Fyodorovna, afraid that Kirilin would speak to her, did her best to keep all the time beside Marya Konstantinovna and the children. She felt weak with fear and misery, and felt she was going to be feverish; she was exhausted and her legs would hardly move, but she did not go home, because she felt sure that she would be followed by Kirilin or Atchmianov or both at once. Kirilin walked behind her with Nikodim Alexandritch, and kept humming in an undertone:

"I don't al-low people to play with me! I don't al-low it."

From the boulevard they went back to the pavilion and walked along the beach, and looked for a long time at the phosphorescence on the water. Von Koren began telling them why it looked phosphorescent.

XIV

"It's time I went to my *vint*. . . . They will be waiting for me," said Laevsky. "Good-bye, my friends."

"I'll come with you; wait a minute," said Nadyezhda Fyodorovna, and she took his arm.

They said good-bye to the company and went away. Kirilin took leave too, and saying that he was going the same way, went along beside them.

"What will be, will be," thought Nadyezhda Fyodorovna. "So be it. . . ."

And it seemed to her that all the evil memories in her head had taken shape and were walking beside her in the darkness, breathing heavily, while she, like a fly that had fallen into the inkpot, was crawling painfully along the pavement and smirching Laevsky's side and arm with blackness.

If Kirilin should do anything horrid, she thought, not he but she would be to blame for it. There was a time when no man would have talked to her as Kirilin had done, and she had torn up her security like a thread and destroyed it irrevocably—who was to blame for it? Intoxicated by her passions she had smiled at a complete stranger, probably just because he was tall and a fine figure. After two meetings she was weary of him, had thrown him over, and did not that, she thought now, give him the right to treat her as he chose?

"Here I'll say good-bye to you, darling," said Laevsky. "Ilya Mihalitch will see you home."

He nodded to Kirilin, and, quickly crossing the boulevard, walked along the street to Sheshkovsky's, where there were lights in the windows, and then they heard the gate bang as he went in.

"Allow me to have an explanation with you," said Kirilin. "I'm not a boy, not some Atchkasov or Latchkasov, Zatchkasov. . . . I demand serious attention."

Nadyezhda Fyodorovna's heart began beating violently. She made no reply.

"The abrupt change in your behaviour to me I put down at first to coquetry," Kirilin went on; "now I see that you don't know how to behave with gentlemanly people. You simply wanted to play with me, as you are playing with that wretched Armenian boy; but I'm a gentleman and I insist on being treated like a gentleman. And so I am at your service. . . ."

"I'm miserable," said Nadyezhda Fyodorovna beginning to cry, and to hide her tears she turned away.

"I'm miserable too," said Kirilin, "but what of that?"

Kirilin was silent for a space, then he said distinctly and emphatically:

"I repeat, madam, that if you do not give me an interview this evening, I'll make a scandal this very evening."

"Let me off this evening," said Nadyezhda Fyodorovna, and she did not recognise her own voice, it was so weak and pitiful.

"I must give you a lesson. . . . Excuse me for the roughness of my tone, but it's necessary to give you a lesson. Yes, I regret to say I must give you a lesson. I insist on two interviews—to-day and to-morrow. After to-morrow you are perfectly free and can go wherever you like with any one you choose. To-day and to-morrow."

Nadyezhda Fyodorovna went up to her gate and stopped.

"Let me go," she murmured, trembling all over and seeing nothing before her in the darkness but his white tunic. "You're right: I'm a horrible woman. . . . I'm to blame, but let me go . . . I beg you." She touched his cold hand and shuddered. "I beseech you. . . ."

"Alas!" sighed Kirilin, "alas! it's not part of my plan to let you go; I only mean to give you a lesson and make you realise. And what's more, madam, I've too little faith in women."

"I'm miserable. . . ."

Nadyezhda Fyodorovna listened to the even splash of the sea, looked at the sky studded with stars, and longed to make haste and end it all, and get away·from the cursed sensation of life, with its sea, stars, men, fever.

"Only not in my home," she said coldly. "Take me somewhere else."

"Come to Muridov's. That's better."

"Where's that?"

"Near the old·wall."

She walked quickly along the street and then turned into the side-street that led towards the mountains. It was dark. There were pale streaks of light here and there on the pavement, from the lighted windows, and it seemed to her that, like a fly, she kept falling into the ink and crawling out into the light again. At one point he stumbled, almost fell down and burst out laughing.

"He's drunk," thought Nadyezhda Fyodorovna. "Never mind. . . . Never mind. . . . So be it."

Atchmianov, too, soon took leave of the party and followed Nadyezhda Fyodorovna to ask her to go for a row. He went to her house and looked over the fence: the windows were wide open, there were no lights.

"Nadyezhda Fyodorovna!" he called.

A moment passed, he called again.

"Who's there?" he heard Olga's voice.

"Is Nadyezhda Fyodorovna at home?"

"No, she has not come in yet."

"Strange . . . very strange," thought Atchmianov, feeling very uneasy. "She went home. . . ."

He walked along the boulevard, then along the street, and glanced in at the windows of Sheshkovsky's. Laevsky was sitting at the table without his coat on, looking attentively at his cards.

"Strange, strange," muttered Atchmianov, and remembering Laevsky's hysterics, he felt ashamed. "If she is not at home, where is she?"

He went to Nadyezhda Fyodorovna's lodgings again, and looked at the dark windows.

"It's a cheat, a cheat . . ." he thought, remembering that, meeting him at midday at Marya Konstantinovna's, she had promised to go in a boat with him that evening.

The windows of the house where Kirilin lived were dark, and there was a policeman sitting asleep on a little bench at the gate. Everything was clear to Atchmianov when he looked at the windows and the policeman. He made up his mind to go home, and set off in that direction, but somehow found himself near Nadyezhda Fyodorovna's lodgings again. He sat down on the bench near the gate and took off his hat, feeling that his head was burning with jealousy and resentment.

The clock in the town church only struck twice in the twenty-four hours—at midday and midnight. Soon after it struck midnight he heard hurried footsteps.

"To-morrow evening, then, again at Muridov's," Atchmianov heard, and he recognised Kirilin' s voice. "At eight o'clock; good-bye!"

Nadyezhda Fyodorovna made her appearance near the garden. Without noticing that Atchmianov was sitting on the bench, she passed beside him like a shadow, opened the gate, and leaving it open, went into the house. In her own room she lighted the candle and quickly undressed, but instead of getting into bed, she sank on her knees before a chair, flung her arms round it, and rested her head on it.

It was past two when Laevsky came home.

XV

Having made up his mind to lie, not all at once but piecemeal, Laevsky went soon after one o'clock next day to Samoylenko to ask for the money that he might be sure to get off on Saturday. After his hysterical attack, which had added an acute feeling of shame to his depressed state of mind, it was unthinkable to remain in the town. If Samoylenko should insist on his conditions, he thought it would be possible to agree to them and take the money, and next day, just as he was starting, to say that Nadyezhda Fyodorovna refused to go. He would be able to persuade her that evening that the whole arrangement would be for her benefit. If Samoylenko, who was obviously under the influence of Von Koren, should refuse the money altogether or make fresh conditions, then he, Laevsky, would go off that very evening in a cargo vessel, or even in a sailing-boat, to Novy Athon or Novorossiisk, would send from there an humiliating telegram, and would stay there till his mother sent him the money for the journey.

When he went into Samoylenko's, he found Von Koren in the drawing-room. The zoologist had just arrived for dinner, and, as usual, was turning over the album and scrutinising the gentlemen in top-hats and the ladies in caps.

"How very unlucky!" thought Laevsky, seeing him. "He may be in the way. Good-morning."

"Good-morning," answered Von Koren, without looking at him.

"Is Alexandr Daviditch at home?"

"Yes, in the kitchen."

Laevsky went into the kitchen, but seeing from the door that Samoylenko was busy over the salad, he went back into the drawing-room and sat down. He always had a feeling of awkwardness in the zoologist's presence, and now he was afraid there would be talk about his attack of hysterics. There was more than a minute of silence. Von Koren suddenly raised his eyes to Laevsky and asked:

"How do you feel after yesterday?"

"Very well indeed," said Laevsky, flushing. "It really was nothing much. . . ."

"Until yesterday I thought it was only ladies who had hysterics, and so at first I thought you had St. Vitus's dance."

Laevsky smiled ingratiatingly, and thought:

"How indelicate on his part! He knows quite well how unpleasant it is for me. . . ."

"Yes, it was a ridiculous performance," he said, still smiling. "I've been laughing over it the whole morning. What's so curious in an attack of hysterics is that you know it is absurd, and are laughing at it in your heart, and at the same time you sob. In our neurotic age we are the slaves of our nerves; they are our masters and do as they like with us. Civilisation has done us a bad turn in that way. . . ."

As Laevsky talked, he felt it disagreeable that Von Koren listened to him gravely, and looked at him steadily and attentively as though studying him; and he was vexed with himself that in spite of his dislike of Von Koren, he could not banish the ingratiating smile from his face.

"I must admit, though," he added, "that there were immediate causes for the attack, and quite sufficient ones too. My health has been terribly shaky of late. To which one must add boredom, constantly being hard up . . . the absence of people and general interests. . . . My position is worse than a governor's."

"Yes, your position is a hopeless one," answered Von Koren.

These calm, cold words, implying something between a jeer and an uninvited prediction, offended Laevsky. He recalled the zoologist's eyes the evening before, full of mockery and disgust. He was silent for a space and then asked, no longer smiling:

"How do you know anything of my position?"

"You were only just speaking of it yourself. Besides, your friends take such a warm interest in you, that I am hearing about you all day long."

"What friends? Samoylenko, I suppose?"

"Yes, he too."

"I would ask Alexandr Daviditch and my friends in general not to trouble so much about me."

"Here is Samoylenko; you had better ask him not to trouble so much about you."

"I don't understand your tone," Laevsky muttered, suddenly feeling as though he had only just realised that the zoologist hated and despised him, and was jeering at him, and was his bitterest and most inveterate enemy.

"Keep that tone for some one else," he said softly, unable to speak aloud for the hatred with which his chest and throat were choking, as they had been the night before with laughter.

Samoylenko came in in his shirt-sleeves, crimson and perspiring from the stifling kitchen.

"Ah, you here?" he said. "Good-morning, my dear boy. Have you had dinner? Don't stand on ceremony. Have you had dinner?"

"Alexandr Daviditch," said Laevsky, standing up, "though I did appeal to you to help me in a private matter, it did not follow that I released you from the obligation of discretion and respect for other people's private affairs."

"What's this?" asked Samoylenko, in astonishment.

"If you have no money," Laevsky went on, raising his voice and shifting from one foot to the other in his excitement, "don't give it; refuse it. But why spread abroad in every back street that my position is hopeless, and all the rest of it? I can't endure such benevolence and friend's assistance where there's a shilling-worth of talk for a ha'p'orth of help! You can boast of your benevolence as much as you please, but no one has given you the right to gossip about my private affairs!"

"What private affairs?" asked Samoylenko, puzzled and beginning to be angry. "If you've come here to be abusive, you had better clear out. You can come again afterwards!"

He remembered the rule that when one is angry with one's neighbour, one must begin to count a hundred, and one will grow calm again; and he began rapidly counting.

"I beg you not to trouble yourself about me," Laevsky went on. "Don't pay any attention to me, and whose business is it what I do and how I live? Yes, I want to go away. Yes, I get into debt, I drink, I am living with another man's wife, I'm hysterical, I'm ordinary. I am not so profound as some people, but whose business is that? Respect other people's privacy."

"Excuse me, brother," said Samoylenko, who had counted up to thirty-five, "but . . ."

"Respect other people's individuality!" interrupted Laevsky. "This continual gossip about other people's affairs, this sighing and groaning and everlasting prying, this eavesdropping, this friendly sympathy . . . damn it all! They lend me money and make conditions as though I were a schoolboy! I am treated as the devil knows what! I don't want anything," shouted Laevsky, staggering with excitement and afraid that it might end in another attack of hysterics. "I shan't get away on Saturday, then," flashed through his mind. "I want nothing. All I ask of you is to spare me your protecting care. I'm not a boy, and I'm not mad, and I beg you to leave off looking after me."

The deacon came in, and seeing Laevsky pale and gesticulating, addressing his strange speech to the portrait of Prince Vorontsov, stood still by the door as though petrified.

"This continual prying into my soul," Laevsky went on, "is insulting to my human dignity, and I beg these volunteer detectives to give up their spying! Enough!"

"What's that . . . what did you say?" said Samoylenko, who had counted up to a hundred. He turned crimson and went up to Laevsky.

"It's enough," said Laevsky, breathing hard and snatching up his cap.

"I'm a Russian doctor, a nobleman by birth, and a civil councillor," said Samoylenko emphatically. "I've never been a spy, and I allow no one to insult me!" he shouted in a breaking voice, emphasising the last word. "Hold your tongue!"

The deacon, who had never seen the doctor so majestic, so swelling with dignity, so crimson and so ferocious, shut his mouth, ran out into the entry and there exploded with laughter.

As though through a fog, Laevsky saw Von Koren get up and, putting his hands in his trouser-pockets, stand still in an attitude of expectancy, as though waiting to see what would happen. This calm attitude struck Laevsky as insolent and insulting to the last degree.

"Kindly take back your words," shouted Samoylenko.

Laevsky, who did not by now remember what his words were, answered:

"Leave me alone! I ask for nothing. All I ask is that you and German upstarts of Jewish origin should let me alone! Or I shall take steps to make you! I will fight you!"

"Now we understand," said Von Koren, coming from behind the table.

"Mr. Laevsky wants to amuse himself with a duel before he goes away. I can give him that pleasure. Mr. Laevsky, I accept your challenge."

"A challenge," said Laevsky, in a low voice, going up to the zoologist and looking with hatred at his swarthy brow and curly hair. "A challenge? By all means! I hate you! I hate you!"

"Delighted. To-morrow morning early near Kerbalay's. I leave all details to your taste. And now, clear out!"

"I hate you," Laevsky said softly, breathing hard. "I have hated you a long while! A duel! Yes!"

"Get rid of him, Alexandr Daviditch, or else I'm going," said Von Koren. "He'll bite me."

Von Koren's cool tone calmed the doctor; he seemed suddenly to come to himself, to recover his reason; he put both arms round Laevsky's waist, and, leading him away from the zoologist, muttered in a friendly voice that shook with emotion:

"My friends . . . dear, good . . . you've lost your tempers and that's enough . . . and that's enough, my friends."

Hearing his soft, friendly voice, Laevsky felt that something unheard of, monstrous, had just happened to him, as though he had been nearly run over by a train; he almost burst into tears, waved his hand, and ran out of the room.

"To feel that one is hated, to expose oneself before the man who hates one, in the most pitiful, contemptible, helpless state. My God, how hard it is!" he thought a little while afterwards as he sat in the pavilion, feeling as though his body were scarred by the hatred of which he had just been the object.

"How coarse it is, my God!"

Cold water with brandy in it revived him. He vividly pictured Von Koren's calm, haughty face; his eyes the day before, his shirt like a rug, his voice, his white hand; and heavy, passionate, hungry hatred rankled in his breast and clamoured for satisfaction. In his thoughts he felled Von Koren to the ground, and trampled him underfoot. He remembered to the minutest detail all that had happened, and wondered how he could have smiled ingratiatingly to that insignificant man, and how he could care for the opinion of wretched petty people whom nobody knew, living in a miserable little town which was not, it seemed, even on the map, and of which not one decent person in Petersburg had heard. If this wretched little town suddenly fell into ruins or caught fire, the telegram with the news would be read in Russia with no more interest than an advertisement of the sale of second-hand furniture. Whether he killed Von Koren next day or left him alive, it would be just the same, equally useless and uninteresting. Better to shoot him in the leg or hand, wound him, then laugh at him, and let him, like an insect with a broken leg lost in the grass—let him be lost with his obscure sufferings in the crowd of insignificant people like himself.

Laevsky went to Sheshkovsky, told him all about it, and asked him to be his second; then they both went to the superintendent of the postal telegraph department, and asked him, too, to be a second, and stayed to dinner with him. At dinner there was a great deal of joking and laughing. Laevsky made jests at his own expense, saying he hardly knew how to fire off a pistol, calling himself a royal archer and William Tell.

"We must give this gentleman a lesson . . ." he said.

After dinner they sat down to cards. Laevsky played, drank wine, and thought that duelling was stupid and senseless, as it did not decide the question but only complicated it, but that it was sometimes impossible to get on without it. In the given case, for instance, one could not, of course, bring an action against Von Koren. And this duel was so far good in that it made it impossible for Laevsky to remain in the town afterwards. He got a little drunk and interested in the game, and felt at ease.

But when the sun had set and it grew dark, he was possessed by a feeling of uneasiness. It was not fear at the thought of death, because while he was dining and playing cards, he had for some reason a confident belief that the duel would end in nothing; it was dread at the thought of something unknown which was to happen next morning for the first time in his life, and dread of the coming night. . . . He knew that the night would be long and sleepless, and that he would have to think not only of Von Koren and his hatred, but also of the mountain of lies which he had to get through, and which he had not strength or ability to dispense with. It was as though he had been taken suddenly ill; all at once he lost all interest in the cards and in people, grew restless, and began asking them to let him go home. He was eager to get into bed, to lie without moving, and to prepare his thoughts for the night. Sheshkovsky and the postal superintendent saw him home and went on to Von Koren's to arrange about the duel.

Near his lodgings Laevsky met Atchmianov. The young man was breathless and excited.

"I am looking for you, Ivan Andreitch," he said. "I beg you to come quickly. . . ."

"Where?"

"Some one wants to see you, some one you don't know, about very important business; he earnestly begs you to come for a minute. He wants to speak to you of something. . . . For him it's a question of life and death. . . ." In his excitement Atchmianov spoke in a strong Armenian accent.

"Who is it?" asked Laevsky.

"He asked me not to tell you his name."

"Tell him I'm busy; to-morrow, if he likes. . . ."

"How can you!" Atchmianov was aghast. "He wants to tell you something very important for you . . . very important! If you don't come, something dreadful will happen."

"Strange . . ." muttered Laevsky, unable to understand why Atchmianov was so excited and what mysteries there could be in this dull, useless little town.

"Strange," he repeated in hesitation. "Come along, though; I don't care."

Atchmianov walked rapidly on ahead and Laevsky followed him. They walked down a street, then turned into an alley.

"What a bore this is!" said Laevsky.

"One minute, one minute . . . it's near."

Near the old rampart they went down a narrow alley between two empty enclosures, then they came into a sort of large yard and went towards a small house.

"That's Muridov's, isn't it?" asked Laevsky.

"Yes."

"But why we've come by the back yards I don't understand. We might have come by the street; it's nearer. . . ."

"Never mind, never mind. . . ."

It struck Laevsky as strange, too, that Atchmianov led him to a back entrance, and motioned to him as though bidding him go quietly and hold his tongue.

"This way, this way . . ." said Atchmianov, cautiously opening the door and going into the passage on tiptoe. "Quietly, quietly, I beg you . . . they may hear."

He listened, drew a deep breath and said in a whisper:

"Open that door, and go in . . . don't be afraid."

Laevsky, puzzled, opened the door and went into a room with a low ceiling and curtained windows.

There was a candle on the table.

"What do you want?" asked some one in the next room. "Is it you, Muridov?"

Laevsky turned into that room and saw Kirilin, and beside him Nadyezhda Fyodorovna.

He didn't hear what was said to him; he staggered back, and did not know how he found himself in the street. His hatred for Von Koren and his uneasiness—all had vanished from his soul. As he went home he waved his right arm awkwardly and looked carefully at the ground under his feet, trying to step where it was smooth. At home in his study he walked backwards and forwards, rubbing his hands, and awkwardly shrugging his shoulders and neck, as though his jacket and shirt were too tight; then he lighted a candle and sat down to the table. . . .

XVI

"The 'humane studies' of which you speak will only satisfy human thought when, as they advance, they meet the exact sciences and progress side by side with them. Whether they will meet under a new microscope, or in the monologues of a new Hamlet, or in a new religion, I do not know, but I expect the earth will be covered with a crust of ice before it comes to pass. Of all humane learning the most durable and living is, of course, the teaching of Christ; but look how differently even that is interpreted! Some teach that we must love all our neighbours but make an exception of soldiers, criminals, and lunatics. They allow the first to be killed in war, the second to be isolated or executed, and the third they forbid to marry. Other interpreters teach that we must love all our neighbours without exception, with no distinction of *plus* or *minus*. According to their teaching, if a consumptive or a murderer or an epileptic asks your daughter in marriage, you must let him have her. If *crêtins* go to war against the physically and mentally healthy, don't defend yourselves. This advocacy of love for love's sake, like art for art's sake, if it could have power, would bring mankind in the long run to complete extinction, and so would become the vastest crime that has ever been committed upon earth. There are very many interpretations, and since there are many of them, serious thought is not satisfied by any one of them, and hastens to add its own individual interpretation to the mass. For that reason you should never put a question on a philosophical or so-called Christian basis; by so doing you only remove the question further from solution."

The deacon listened to the zoologist attentively, thought a little, and asked:

"Have the philosophers invented the moral law which is innate in every man, or did God create it together with the body?"

"I don't know. But that law is so universal among all peoples and all ages that I fancy we ought to recognise it as organically connected with man. It is not invented, but exists and will exist. I don't tell you that one day it will be seen under the microscope, but its organic connection is shown, indeed, by evidence: serious affections of the brain and all so-called mental diseases, to the best of my belief, show themselves first of all in the perversion of the moral law."

"Good. So then, just as our stomach bids us eat, our moral sense bids us love our neighbours. Is that it? But our natural man through self-love opposes the voice of conscience and reason, and this gives rise to many brain-racking questions. To whom ought we to turn for the solution of those questions if you forbid us to put them on the philosophic basis?"

"Turn to what little exact science we have. Trust to evidence and the logic of facts. It is true it is but little, but, on the other hand, it is less fluid and shifting than philosophy. The moral law, let us suppose, demands that you love your neighbour. Well? Love ought to show itself in the removal of everything which in one way or another is injurious to men and threatens them with danger in the present or in the future. Our knowledge and the evidence tells us that the morally and physically abnormal are a menace to humanity. If so you must struggle against the abnormal; if you are not able to raise them to the normal standard you must have strength and ability to render them harmless— that is, to destroy them."

"So love consists in the strong overcoming the weak."

"Undoubtedly."

"But you know the strong crucified our Lord Jesus Christ," said the deacon hotly.

"The fact is that those who crucified Him were not the strong but the weak. Human culture weakens and strives to nullify the struggle for existence and natural selection; hence the rapid advancement of the weak and their predominance over the strong. Imagine that you succeeded in instilling into bees humanitarian ideas in their crude and elementary form. What would come of it? The drones who ought to be killed would remain alive, would devour the honey, would corrupt and stifle the bees, resulting in the predominance of the weak over the strong and the degeneration of the latter. The same process is taking place now with humanity; the weak are oppressing the strong. Among savages untouched by civilisation the strongest, cleverest, and most moral takes the lead; he is the chief and the master. But we civilised men have crucified Christ, and we go on crucifying Him, so there is something lacking in us. . . . And that something one ought to raise up in ourselves, or there will be no end to these errors."

"But what criterion have you to distinguish the strong from the weak?"

"Knowledge and evidence. The tuberculous and the scrofulous are recognised by their diseases, and the insane and the immoral by their actions."

"But mistakes may be made!"

"Yes, but it's no use to be afraid of getting your feet wet when you are threatened with the deluge!"

"That's philosophy," laughed the deacon.

"Not a bit of it. You are so corrupted by your seminary philosophy that you want to see nothing but fog in everything. The abstract studies

with which your youthful head is stuffed are called abstract just
because they abstract your minds from what is obvious. Look the devil
straight in the eye, and if he's the devil, tell him he's the devil, and
don't go calling to Kant or Hegel for explanations."

The zoologist paused and went on:

"Twice two's four, and a stone's a stone. Here to-morrow we have a
duel. You and I will say it's stupid and absurd, that the duel is out of
date, that there is no real difference between the aristocratic duel and
the drunken brawl in the pot-house, and yet we shall not stop, we shall
go there and fight. So there is some force stronger than our reasoning.
We shout that war is plunder, robbery, atrocity, fratricide; we cannot
look upon blood without fainting; but the French or the Germans have
only to insult us for us to feel at once an exaltation of spirit; in the most
genuine way we shout 'Hurrah!' and rush to attack the foe. You will
invoke the blessing of God on our weapons, and our valour will arouse
universal and general enthusiasm. Again it follows that there is a force,
if not higher, at any rate stronger, than us and our philosophy. We can
no more stop it than that cloud which is moving upwards over the sea.
Don't be hypocritical, don't make a long nose at it on the sly; and don't
say, 'Ah, old-fashioned, stupid! Ah, it's inconsistent with Scripture!' but
look it straight in the face, recognise its rational lawfulness, and when,
for instance, it wants to destroy a rotten, scrofulous, corrupt race, don't
hinder it with your pilules and misunderstood quotations from the
Gospel. Leskov has a story of a conscientious Danila who found a leper
outside the town, and fed and warmed him in the name of love and of
Christ. If that Danila had really loved humanity, he would have
dragged the leper as far as possible from the town, and would have
flung him in a pit, and would have gone to save the healthy. Christ, I
hope, taught us a rational, intelligent, practical love."

"What a fellow you are!" laughed the deacon. "You don't believe in
Christ. Why do you mention His name so often?"

"Yes, I do believe in Him. Only, of course, in my own way, not in
yours. Oh, deacon, deacon!" laughed the zoologist; he put his arm
round the deacon's waist, and said gaily: "Well? Are you coming with
us to the duel to-morrow?"

"My orders don't allow it, or else I should come."

"What do you mean by 'orders'?"

"I have been consecrated. I am in a state of grace."

"Oh, deacon, deacon," repeated Von Koren, laughing, "I love talking to you."

"You say you have faith," said the deacon. "What sort of faith is it?
Why, I have an uncle, a priest, and he believes so that when in time of
drought he goes out into the fields to pray for rain, he takes his

umbrella and leather overcoat for fear of getting wet through on his
way home. That's faith! When he speaks of Christ, his face is full of
radiance, and all the peasants, men and women, weep floods of tears.
He would stop that cloud and put all those forces you talk about to
flight. Yes . . . faith moves mountains."

The deacon laughed and slapped the zoologist on the shoulder.

"Yes . . ." he went on; "here you are teaching all the time, fathoming
the depths of the ocean, dividing the weak and the strong, writing books
and challenging to duels—and everything remains as it is; but, behold!
some feeble old man will mutter just one word with a holy spirit, or a
new Mahomet, with a sword, will gallop from Arabia, and everything
will be topsy-turvy, and in Europe not one stone will be left standing
upon another."

"Well, deacon, that's on the knees of the gods."

"Faith without works is dead, but works without faith are worse
still—mere waste of time and nothing more."

The doctor came into sight on the sea-front. He saw the deacon and
the zoologist, and went up to them.

"I believe everything is ready," he said, breathing hard. "Govorovsky
and Boyko will be the seconds. They will start at five o'clock in the
morning. How it has clouded over," he said, looking at the sky. "One
can see nothing; there will be rain directly."

"I hope you are coming with us?" said the zoologist.

"No, God preserve me; I'm worried enough as it is. Ustimovitch is
going instead of me. I've spoken to him already."

Far over the sea was a flash of lightning, followed by a hollow roll of
thunder.

"How stifling it is before a storm!" said Von Koren. "I bet you've been
to Laevsky already and have been weeping on his bosom."

"Why should I go to him?" answered the doctor in confusion. "What
next?"

Before sunset he had walked several times along the boulevard and
the street in the hope of meeting Laevsky. He was ashamed of his hasti-
ness and the sudden outburst of friendliness which had followed it. He
wanted to apologise to Laevsky in a joking tone, to give him a good talking to, to soothe him and to tell him that the duel was a survival of
mediæval barbarism, but that Providence itself had brought them to
the duel as a means of reconciliation; that the next day, both being
splendid and highly intelligent people, they would, after exchanging
shots, appreciate each other's noble qualities and would become
friends. But he could not come across Laevsky.

"What should I go and see him for?" repeated Samoylenko. "I did
not insult him; he insulted me. Tell me, please, why he attacked me.

What harm had I done him? I go into the drawing-room, and, all of a sudden, without the least provocation: 'Spy!' There's a nice thing! Tell me, how did it begin? What did you say to him?"

"I told him his position was hopeless. And I was right. It is only honest men or scoundrels who can find an escape from any position, but one who wants to be at the same time an honest man and a scoundrel—it is a hopeless position. But it's eleven o'clock, gentlemen, and we have to be up early to-morrow."

There was a sudden gust of wind; it blew up the dust on the sea-front, whirled it round in eddies, with a howl that drowned the roar of the sea.

"A squall," said the deacon. "We must go in, our eyes are getting full of dust."

As they went, Samoylenko sighed and, holding his hat, said:

"I suppose I shan't sleep to-night."

"Don't you agitate yourself," laughed the zoologist. "You can set your mind at rest; the duel will end in nothing. Laevsky will magnanimously fire into the air—he can do nothing else; and I daresay I shall not fire at all. To be arrested and lose my time on Laevsky's account—the game's not worth the candle. By the way, what is the punishment for duelling?"

"Arrest, and in the case of the death of your opponent a maximum of three years' imprisonment in the fortress."

"The fortress of St. Peter and St. Paul?"

"No, in a military fortress, I believe."

"Though this fine gentleman ought to have a lesson!"

Behind them on the sea, there was a flash of lightning, which for an instant lighted up the roofs of the houses and the mountains. The friends parted near the boulevard. When the doctor disappeared in the darkness and his steps had died away, Von Koren shouted to him:

"I only hope the weather won't interfere with us to-morrow!"

"Very likely it will! Please God it may!"

"Good-night!"

"What about the night? What do you say?"

In the roar of the wind and the sea and the crashes of thunder, it was difficult to hear.

"It's nothing," shouted the zoologist, and hurried home.

XVII

> "Upon my mind, weighed down with woe,
>   Crowd thoughts, a heavy multitude:
>   In silence memory unfolds
>   Her long, long scroll before my eyes.

Loathing and shuddering I curse
And bitterly lament in vain,
And bitter though the tears I weep
I do not wash those lines away."

PUSHKIN.

Whether they killed him next morning, or mocked at him—that is, left him his life—he was ruined, anyway. Whether this disgraced woman killed herself in her shame and despair, or dragged on her pitiful existence, she was ruined anyway.

So thought Laevsky as he sat at the table late in the evening, still rubbing his hands. The windows suddenly blew open with a bang; a violent gust of wind burst into the room, and the papers fluttered from the table. Laevsky closed the windows and bent down to pick up the papers. He was aware of something new in his body, a sort of awkwardness he had not felt before, and his movements were strange to him. He moved timidly, jerking with his elbows and shrugging his shoulders; and when he sat down to the table again, he again began rubbing his hands. His body had lost its suppleness.

On the eve of death one ought to write to one's nearest relation. Laevsky thought of this. He took a pen and wrote with a tremulous hand: "Mother!"

He wanted to write to beg his mother, for the sake of the merciful God in whom she believed, that she would give shelter and bring a little warmth and kindness into the life of the unhappy woman who, by his doing, had been disgraced and was in solitude, poverty, and weakness, that she would forgive and forget everything, everything, everything, and by her sacrifice atone to some extent for her son's terrible sin. But he remembered how his mother, a stout, heavily-built old woman in a lace cap, used to go out into the garden in the morning, followed by her companion with the lap-dog; how she used to shout in a peremptory way to the gardener and the servants, and how proud and haughty her face was—he remembered all this and scratched out the word he had written.

There was a vivid flash of lightning at all three windows, and it was followed by a prolonged, deafening roll of thunder, beginning with a hollow rumble and ending with a crash so violent that all the window-panes rattled. Laevsky got up, went to the window, and pressed his forehead against the pane. There was a fierce, magnificent storm. On the horizon lightning-flashes were flung in white streams from the storm-clouds into the sea, lighting up the high, dark waves over the far-away expanse. And to right and to left, and, no doubt, over the house too, the lightning flashed.

"The storm!" whispered Laevsky; he had a longing to pray to some one or to something, if only to the lightning or the storm-clouds. "Dear storm!"

He remembered how as a boy he used to run out into the garden without a hat on when there was a storm, and how two fair-haired girls with blue eyes used to run after him, and how they got wet through with the rain; they laughed with delight, but when there was a loud peal of thunder, the girls used to nestle up to the boy confidingly, while he crossed himself and made haste to repeat: "Holy, holy, holy. . . ." Oh, where had they vanished to! In what sea were they drowned, those dawning days of pure, fair life? He had no fear of the storm, no love of nature now; he had no God. All the confiding girls he had ever known had by now been ruined by him and those like him. All his life he had not planted one tree in his own garden, nor grown one blade of grass; and living among the living, he had not saved one fly; he had done nothing but destroy and ruin, and lie, lie. . . .

"What in my past was not vice?" he asked himself, trying to clutch at some bright memory as a man falling down a precipice clutches at the bushes.

School? The university? But that was a sham. He had neglected his work and forgotten what he had learnt. The service of his country? That, too, was a sham, for he did nothing in the Service, took a salary for doing nothing, and it was an abominable swindling of the State for which one was not punished.

He had no craving for truth, and had not sought it; spellbound by vice and lying, his conscience had slept or been silent. Like a stranger, like an alien from another planet, he had taken no part in the common life of men, had been indifferent to their sufferings, their ideas, their religion, their sciences, their strivings, and their struggles. He had not said one good word, not written one line that was not useless and vulgar; he had not done his fellows one ha'p'orth of service, but had eaten their bread, drunk their wine, seduced their wives, lived on their thoughts, and to justify his contemptible, parasitic life in their eyes and in his own, he had always tried to assume an air of being higher and better than they. Lies, lies, lies. . . .

He vividly remembered what he had seen that evening at Muridov's, and he was in an insufferable anguish of loathing and misery. Kirilin and Atchmianov were loathsome, but they were only continuing what he had begun; they were his accomplices and his disciples. This young weak woman had trusted him more than a brother, and he had deprived her of her husband, of her friends and of her country, and had brought her here—to the heat, to fever, and to boredom; and from day to day she was bound to reflect, like a mirror, his idleness, his viciousness and falsity—

and that was all she had had to fill her weak, listless, pitiable life. Then he had grown sick of her, had begun to hate her, but had not had the pluck to abandon her, and he had tried to entangle her more and more closely in a web of lies. . . . These men had done the rest.

Laevsky sat at the table, then got up and went to the window; at one minute he put out the candle and then he lighted it again. He cursed himself aloud, wept and wailed, and asked forgiveness; several times he ran to the table in despair, and wrote:

"Mother!"

Except his mother, he had no relations or near friends; but how could his mother help him? And where was she? He had an impulse to run to Nadyezhda Fyodorovna, to fall at her feet, to kiss her hands and feet, to beg her forgiveness; but she was his victim, and he was afraid of her as though she were dead.

"My life is ruined," he repeated, rubbing his hands. "Why am I still alive, my God! . . ."

He had cast out of heaven his dim star; it had fallen, and its track was lost in the darkness of night. It would never return to the sky again, because life was given only once and never came a second time. If he could have turned back the days and years of the past, he would have replaced the falsity with truth, the idleness with work, the boredom with happiness; he would have given back purity to those whom he had robbed of it. He would have found God and goodness, but that was as impossible as to put back the fallen star into the sky, and because it was impossible he was in despair.

When the storm was over he sat by the open window and thought calmly of what was before him. Von Koren would most likely kill him. The man's clear, cold theory of life justified the destruction of the rotten and the useless; if it changed at the crucial moment, it would be the hatred and the repugnance that Laevsky inspired in him that would save him. If he missed his aim or, in mockery of his hated opponent, only wounded him, or fired in the air, what could he do then? Where could he go?

"Go to Petersburg?" Laevsky asked himself. But that would mean beginning over again the old life which he cursed. And the man who seeks salvation in change of place like a migrating bird would find nothing anywhere, for all the world is alike to him. Seek salvation in men? In whom and how? Samoylenko's kindness and generosity could no more save him than the deacon's laughter or Von Koren's hatred. He must look for salvation in himself alone, and if there were no finding it, why waste time? He must kill himself, that was all. . . .

He heard the sound of a carriage. It was getting light. The carriage passed by, turned, and crunching on the wet sand, stopped near the house. There were two men in the carriage.

"Wait a minute; I'm coming directly," Laevsky said to them out of the window. "I'm not asleep. Surely it's not time yet?"

"Yes, it's four o'clock. By the time we get there . . ."

Laevsky put on his overcoat and cap, put some cigarettes in his pocket, and stood still hesitating. He felt as though there was something else he must do. In the street the seconds talked in low voices and the horses snorted, and this sound in the damp, early morning, when everybody was asleep and light was hardly dawning in the sky, filled Laevsky's soul with a disconsolate feeling which was like a presentiment of evil. He stood for a little, hesitating, and went into the bedroom.

Nadyezhda Fyodorovna was lying stretched out on the bed, wrapped from head to foot in a rug. She did not stir, and her whole appearance, especially her head, suggested an Egyptian mummy. Looking at her in silence, Laevsky mentally asked her forgiveness, and thought that if the heavens were not empty and there really were a God, then He would save her; if there were no God, then she had better perish—there was nothing for her to live for.

All at once she jumped up, and sat up in bed. Lifting her pale face and looking with horror at Laevsky, she asked:

"Is it you? Is the storm over?"

"Yes."

She remembered; put both hands to her head and shuddered all over.

"How miserable I am!" she said. "If only you knew how miserable I am! I expected," she went on, half closing her eyes, "that you would kill me or turn me out of the house into the rain and storm, but you delay . . . delay . . ."

Warmly and impulsively he put his arms round her and covered her knees and hands with kisses. Then when she muttered something and shuddered with the thought of the past, he stroked her hair, and looking into her face, realised that this unhappy, sinful woman was the one creature near and dear to him, whom no one could replace.

When he went out of the house and got into the carriage he wanted to return home alive.

XVIII

The deacon got up, dressed, took his thick, gnarled stick and slipped quietly out of the house. It was dark, and for the first minute when he went into the street, he could not even see his white stick. There was not a single star in the sky, and it looked as though there would be rain again. There was a smell of wet sand and sea.

"It's to be hoped that the mountaineers won't attack us," thought the deacon, hearing the tap of the stick on the pavement, and noticing how loud and lonely the taps sounded in the stillness of the night.

When he got out of town, he began to see both the road and his stick. Here and there in the black sky there were dark cloudy patches, and soon a star peeped out and timidly blinked its one eye. The deacon walked along the high rocky coast and did not see the sea; it was slumbering below, and its unseen waves broke languidly and heavily on the shore, as though sighing "Ouf!" and how slowly! One wave broke—the deacon had time to count eight steps; then another broke, and six steps; later a third. As before, nothing could be seen, and in the darkness one could hear the languid, drowsy drone of the sea. One could hear the infinitely far-away, inconceivable time when God moved above chaos.

The deacon felt uncanny. He hoped God would not punish him for keeping company with infidels, and even going to look at their duels. The duel would be nonsensical, bloodless, absurd, but however that might be, it was a heathen spectacle, and it was altogether unseemly for an ecclesiastical person to be present at it. He stopped and wondered—should he go back? But an intense, restless curiosity triumphed over his doubts, and he went on.

"Though they are infidels they are good people, and will be saved," he assured himself. "They are sure to be saved," he said aloud, lighting a cigarette.

By what standard must one measure men's qualities, to judge rightly of them? The deacon remembered his enemy, the inspector of the clerical school, who believed in God, lived in chastity, and did not fight duels; but he used to feed the deacon on bread with sand in it, and on one occasion almost pulled off the deacon's ear. If human life was so artlessly constructed that every one respected this cruel and dishonest inspector who stole the Government flour, and his health and salvation were prayed for in the schools, was it just to shun such men as Von Koren and Laevsky, simply because they were unbelievers? The deacon was weighing this question, but he recalled how absurd Samoylenko had looked yesterday, and that broke the thread of his ideas. What fun they would have next day! The deacon imagined how he would sit under a bush and look on, and when Von Koren began boasting next day at dinner, he, the deacon, would begin laughing and telling him all the details of the duel.

"How do you know all about it?" the zoologist would ask.

"Well, there you are! I stayed at home, but I know all about it."

It would be nice to write a comic description of the duel. His father-in-law would read it and laugh. A good story, told or written, was more than meat and drink to his father-in-law.

The valley of the Yellow River opened before him. The stream was broader and fiercer for the rain, and instead of murmuring as before, it was raging. It began to get light. The grey, dingy morning, and the clouds racing towards the west to overtake the storm-clouds, the mountains girt with mist, and the wet trees, all struck the deacon as ugly and sinister. He washed at the brook, repeated his morning prayer, and felt a longing for tea and hot rolls, with sour cream, which were served every morning at his father-in-law's. He remembered his wife and the "Days past Recall," which she played on the piano. What sort of woman was she? His wife had been introduced, betrothed, and married to him all in one week: he had lived with her less than a month when he was ordered here, so that he had not had time to find out what she was like. All the same, he rather missed her.

"I must write her a nice letter . . ." he thought. The flag on the *duhan* hung limp, soaked by the rain, and the *duhan* itself with its wet roof seemed darker and lower than it had been before. Near the door was standing a cart; Kerbalay, with two mountaineers and a young Tatar woman in trousers—no doubt Kerbalay's wife or daughter—were bringing sacks of something out of the *duhan*, and putting them on maize straw in the cart.

Near the cart stood a pair of asses hanging their heads. When they had put in all the sacks, the mountaineers and the Tatar woman began covering them over with straw, while Kerbalay began hurriedly harnessing the asses.

"Smuggling, perhaps," thought the deacon.

Here was the fallen tree with the dried pine-needles, here was the blackened patch from the fire. He remembered the picnic and all its incidents, the fire, the singing of the mountaineers, his sweet dreams of becoming a bishop, and of the Church procession. . . . The Black River had grown blacker and broader with the rain. The deacon walked cautiously over the narrow bridge, which by now was reached by the topmost crests of the dirty water, and went up through the little copse to the drying-shed.

"A splendid head," he thought, stretching himself on the straw, and thinking of Von Koren. "A fine head—God grant him health; only there is cruelty in him. . . ."

Why did he hate Laevsky and Laevsky hate him? Why were they going to fight a duel? If from their childhood they had known poverty as the deacon had; if they had been brought up among ignorant, hardhearted, grasping, coarse and ill-mannered people who grudged you a crust of bread, who spat on the floor and hiccoughed at dinner and at prayers; if they had not been spoilt from childhood by the pleasant surroundings and the select circle of friends they lived in—how they would have rushed at each other, how readily they would have over-looked each other's shortcomings and would have prized each other's strong points! Why, how few even outwardly decent people there were in the world! It was true that Laevsky was flighty, dissipated, queer, but he did not steal, did not spit loudly on the floor; he did not abuse his wife and say, "You'll eat till you burst, but you don't want to work"; he would not beat a child with reins, or give his servants stinking meat to eat—surely this was reason enough to be indulgent to him? Besides, he was the chief sufferer from his failings, like a sick man from his sores. Instead of being led by boredom and some sort of misunderstanding to look for degeneracy, extinction, heredity, and other such incompre-hensible things in each other, would they not do better to stoop a little lower and turn their hatred and anger where whole streets resounded with moanings from coarse ignorance, greed, scolding, impurity, swear-ing, the shrieks of women. . . .

The sound of a carriage interrupted the deacon's thoughts. He glanced out of the door and saw a carriage and in it three persons: Laevsky, Sheshkovsky, and the superintendent of the post-office.

"Stop!" said Sheshkovsky.

All three got out of the carriage and looked at one another.

"They are not here yet," said Sheshkovsky, shaking the mud off. "Well? Till the show begins, let us go and find a suitable spot; there's not room to turn round here."

They went further up the river and soon vanished from sight. The Tatar driver sat in the carriage with his head resting on his shoulder and fell asleep. After waiting ten minutes the deacon came out of the drying-shed, and taking off his black hat that he might not be noticed, he began threading his way among the bushes and strips of maize along the bank, crouching and looking about him. The grass and maize were wet, and big drops fell on his head from the trees and bushes. "Disgraceful!" he muttered, picking up his wet and muddy skirt. "Had I realised it, I would not have come."

Soon he heard voices and caught sight of them. Laevsky was walking rapidly to and fro in the small glade with bowed back and hands thrust in his sleeves; his seconds were standing at the water's edge, rolling cigarettes.

"Strange," thought the deacon, not recognising Laevsky's walk; "he looks like an old man. . . ."

"How rude it is of them!" said the superintendent of the post-office, looking at his watch. "It may be learned manners to be late, but to my thinking it's hoggish."

Sheshkovsky, a stout man with a black beard, listened and said:

"They're coming!"

XIX

"It's the first time in my life I've seen it! How glorious!" said Von Koren, pointing to the glade and stretching out his hands to the east. "Look: green rays!"

In the east behind the mountains rose two green streaks of light, and it really was beautiful. The sun was rising.

"Good-morning!" the zoologist went on, nodding to Laevsky's seconds. "I'm not late, am I?"

He was followed by his seconds, Boyko and Govorovsky, two very young officers of the same height, wearing white tunics, and Ustimovitch, the thin, unsociable doctor; in one hand he had a bag of some sort, and in the other hand, as usual, a cane which he held behind him. Laying the bag on the ground and greeting no one, he put the other hand, too, behind his back and began pacing up and down the glade.

Laevsky felt the exhaustion and awkwardness of a man who is soon perhaps to die, and is for that reason an object of general attention. He wanted to be killed as soon as possible or taken home. He saw the sunrise now for the first time in his life; the early morning, the green rays of light, the dampness, and the men in wet boots, seemed to him to have nothing to do with his life, to be superfluous and embarrassing. All this had no connection with the night he had been through, with his thoughts and his feeling of guilt, and so he would have gladly gone away without waiting for the duel.

Von Koren was noticeably excited and tried to conceal it, pretending that he was more interested in the green light than anything. The seconds were confused, and looked at one another as though wondering why they were here and what they were to do.

"I imagine, gentlemen, there is no need for us to go further," said Sheshkovsky. "This place will do."

"Yes, of course," Von Koren agreed.

A silence followed. Ustimovitch, pacing to and fro, suddenly turned sharply to Laevsky and said in a low voice, breathing into his face:

"They have very likely not told you my terms yet. Each side is to pay me fifteen roubles, and in the case of the death of one party, the survivor is to pay thirty."

Laevsky was already acquainted with the man, but now for the first time he had a distinct view of his lustreless eyes, his stiff moustaches, and wasted, consumptive neck; he was a money-grubber, not a doctor; his breath had an unpleasant smell of beef.

"What people there are in the world!" thought Laevsky, and answered: "Very good."

The doctor nodded and began pacing to and fro again, and it was evident he did not need the money at all, but simply asked for it from hatred. Every one felt it was time to begin, or to end what had been begun, but instead of beginning or ending, they stood about, moved to and fro and smoked. The young officers, who were present at a duel for the first time in their lives, and even now hardly believed in this civilian and, to their thinking, unnecessary duel, looked critically at their tunics and stroked their sleeves. Sheshkovsky went up to them and said softly: "Gentlemen, we must use every effort to prevent this duel; they ought to be reconciled."

He flushed crimson and added:

"Kirilin was at my rooms last night complaining that Laevsky had found him with Nadyezhda Fyodorovna, and all that sort of thing."

"Yes, we know that too," said Boyko.

"Well, you see, then . . . Laevsky's hands are trembling and all that sort of thing . . . he can scarcely hold a pistol now. To fight with him is as inhuman as to fight a man who is drunk or who has typhoid. If a reconciliation cannot be arranged, we ought to put off the duel, gentlemen, or something. . . . It's such a sickening business, I can't bear to see it."

"Talk to Von Koren."

"I don't know the rules of duelling, damnation take them, and I don't want to either; perhaps he'll imagine Laevsky funks it and has sent me to him, but he can think what he likes—I'll speak to him."

Sheshkovsky hesitatingly walked up to Von Koren with a slight limp, as though his leg had gone to sleep; and as he went towards him, clearing his throat, his whole figure was a picture of indolence.

"There's something I must say to you, sir," he began, carefully scrutinising the flowers on the zoologist's shirt. "It's confidential. I don't know the rules of duelling, damnation take them, and I don't want to, and I look on the matter not as a second and that sort of thing, but as a man, and that's all about it."

"Yes. Well?"

"When seconds suggest reconciliation they are usually not listened to; it is looked upon as a formality. *Amour propre* and all that. But I humbly beg you to look carefully at Ivan Andreitch. He's not in a normal state, so to speak, to-day—not in his right mind, and a pitiable object. He has had a misfortune. I can't endure gossip. . . ."

Sheshkovsky flushed crimson and looked round.

"But in view of the duel, I think it necessary to inform you, Laevsky found his madam last night at Muridov's with . . . another gentleman."

"How disgusting!" muttered the zoologist; he turned pale, frowned, and spat loudly. "Tfoo!"

His lower lip quivered, he walked away from Sheshkovsky, unwilling to hear more, and as though he had accidentally tasted something bitter, spat loudly again, and for the first time that morning looked with hatred at Laevsky. His excitement and awkwardness passed off; he tossed his head and said aloud:

"Gentlemen, what are we waiting for, I should like to know? Why don't we begin?"

Sheshkovsky glanced at the officers and shrugged his shoulders.

"Gentlemen," he said aloud, addressing no one in particular. "Gentlemen, we propose that you should be reconciled."

"Let us make haste and get the formalities over," said Von Koren. "Reconciliation has been discussed already. What is the next formality? Make haste, gentlemen, time won't wait for us."

"But we insist on reconciliation all the same," said Sheshkovsky in a guilty voice, as a man compelled to interfere in another man's business; he flushed, laid his hand on his heart, and went on: "Gentlemen, we see no grounds for associating the offence with the duel. There's nothing in common between duelling and offences against one another of which we are sometimes guilty through human weakness. You are university men and men of culture, and no doubt you see in the duel nothing but a foolish and out-of-date formality, and all that sort of thing. That's how we look at it ourselves, or we shouldn't have come, for we cannot allow that in our presence men should fire at one another, and all that." Sheshkovsky wiped the perspiration off his face and went on: "Make an end to your misunderstanding, gentlemen; shake hands, and let us go home and drink to peace. Upon my honour, gentlemen!"

Von Koren did not speak. Laevsky, seeing that they were looking at him, said:

"I have nothing against Nikolay Vassilitch; if he considers I'm to blame, I'm ready to apologise to him."

Von Koren was offended.

"It is evident, gentlemen," he said, "you want Mr. Laevsky to return home a magnanimous and chivalrous figure, but I cannot give you and him that satisfaction. And there was no need to get up early and drive eight miles out of town simply to drink to peace, to have breakfast, and to explain to me that the duel is an out-of-date formality. A duel is a duel, and there is no need to make it more false and stupid than it is in reality. I want to fight!"

A silence followed. Boyko took a pair of pistols out of a box; one was given to Von Koren and one to Laevsky, and then there followed a difficulty which afforded a brief amusement to the zoologist and the seconds. It appeared that of all the people present not one had ever in his life been at a duel, and no one knew precisely how they ought to stand,

and what the seconds ought to say and do. But then Boyko remembered and began, with a smile, to explain.

"Gentlemen, who remembers the description in Lermontov?" asked Von Koren, laughing. "In Turgenev, too, Bazarov had a duel with some one. . . ."

"There's no need to remember," said Ustimovitch impatiently. "Measure the distance, that's all."

And he took three steps as though to show how to measure it. Boyko counted out the steps while his companion drew his sabre and scratched the earth at the extreme points to mark the barrier. In complete silence the opponents took their places.

"Moles," the deacon thought, sitting in the bushes.

Sheshkovsky said something, Boyko explained something again, but Laevsky did not hear—or rather heard, but did not understand. He cocked his pistol when the time came to do so, and raised the cold, heavy weapon with the barrel upwards. He forgot to unbutton his overcoat, and it felt very tight over his shoulder and under his arm, and his arm rose as awkwardly as though the sleeve had been cut out of tin. He remembered the hatred he had felt the night before for the swarthy brow and curly hair, and felt that even yesterday at the moment of intense hatred and anger he could not have shot a man. Fearing that the bullet might somehow hit Von Koren by accident, he raised the pistol higher and higher, and felt that this too obvious magnanimity was indelicate and anything but magnanimous, but he did not know how else to do and could do nothing else. Looking at the pale, ironically smiling face of Von Koren, who evidently had been convinced from the beginning that his opponent would fire in the air, Laevsky thought that, thank God, everything would be over directly, and all that he had to do was to press the trigger rather hard. . . .

He felt a violent shock on the shoulder; there was the sound of a shot and an answering echo in the mountains: ping-ting!

Von Koren cocked his pistol and looked at Ustimovitch, who was pacing as before with his hands behind his back, taking no notice of any one.

"Doctor," said the zoologist, "be so good as not to move to and fro like a pendulum. You make me dizzy."

The doctor stood still. Von Koren began to take aim at Laevsky.

"It's all over!" thought Laevsky.

The barrel of the pistol aimed straight at his face, the expression of hatred and contempt in Von Koren's attitude and whole figure, and the murder just about to be committed by a decent man in broad daylight, in the presence of decent men, and the stillness and the unknown force that compelled Laevsky to stand still and not to run—how mysterious it all was, how incomprehensible and terrible!

The moment while Von Koren was taking aim seemed to Laevsky longer than a night: he glanced imploringly at the seconds; they were pale and did not stir.

"Make haste and fire," thought Laevsky, and felt that his pale, quivering, and pitiful face must arouse even greater hatred in Von Koren.

"I'll kill him directly," thought Von Koren, aiming at his forehead, with his finger already on the catch. "Yes, of course I'll kill him. . . ."

"He'll kill him!" A despairing shout was suddenly heard somewhere very close at hand.

A shot rang out at once. Seeing that Laevsky remained standing where he was and did not fall, they all looked in the direction from which the shout had come, and saw the deacon. With pale face and wet hair sticking to his forehead and his cheeks, wet through and muddy, he was standing in the maize on the further bank, smiling rather queerly and waving his wet hat. Sheshkovsky laughed with joy, burst into tears, and moved away. . . .

XX

A little while afterwards, Von Koren and the deacon met near the little bridge. The deacon was excited; he breathed hard, and avoided looking in people's faces. He felt ashamed both of his terror and his muddy, wet garments.

"I thought you meant to kill him . . ." he muttered. "How contrary to human nature it is! How utterly unnatural it is!"

"But how did you come here?" asked the zoologist.

"Don't ask," said the deacon, waving his hand. "The evil one tempted me, saying: 'Go, go. . . .' So I went and almost died of fright in the maize. But now, thank God, thank God. . . . I am awfully pleased with you," muttered the deacon. "Old Grandad Tarantula will be glad. . . . It's funny, it's too funny! Only I beg of you most earnestly don't tell anybody I was there, or I may get into hot water with the authorities. They will say: 'The deacon was a second.'"

"Gentlemen," said Von Koren, "the deacon asks you not to tell any one you've seen him here. He might get into trouble."

"How contrary to human nature it is!" sighed the deacon. "Excuse my saying so, but your face was so dreadful that I thought you were going to kill him."

"I was very much tempted to put an end to that scoundrel," said Von Koren, "but you shouted close by, and I missed my aim. The whole procedure is revolting to any one who is not used to it, and it has exhausted me, deacon. I feel awfully tired. Come along. . . ."

"No, you must let me walk back. I must get dry, for I am wet and cold."

"Well, as you like," said the zoologist, in a weary tone, feeling dispirited, and, getting into the carriage, he closed his eyes. "As you like. . . ."

While they were moving about the carriages and taking their seats, Kerbalay stood in the road, and, laying his hands on his stomach, he bowed low, showing his teeth; he imagined that the gentry had come to enjoy the beauties of nature and drink tea, and could not understand why they were getting into the carriages. The party set off in complete silence and only the deacon was left by the *duhan*.

"Come to the *duhan*, drink tea," he said to Kerbalay. "Me wants to eat."

Kerbalay spoke good Russian, but the deacon imagined that the Tatar would understand him better if he talked to him in broken Russian. "Cook omelette, give cheese. . . ."

"Come, come, father," said Kerbalay, bowing. "I'll give you everything. . . . I've cheese and wine. . . . Eat what you like."

"What is 'God' in Tatar?" asked the deacon, going into the *duhan*.

"Your God and my God are the same," said Kerbalay, not understanding him. "God is the same for all men, only men are different. Some are Russian, some are Turks, some are English—there are many sorts of men, but God is one."

"Very good. If all men worship the same God, why do you Mohammedans look upon Christians as your everlasting enemies?"

"Why are you angry?" said Kerbalay, laying both hands on his stomach. "You are a priest; I am a Mussulman: you say, 'I want to eat'—I give it you. . . . Only the rich man distinguishes your God from my God; for the poor man it is all the same. If you please, it is ready."

While this theological conversation was taking place at the *duhan*, Laevsky was driving home thinking how dreadful it had been driving there at daybreak, when the roads, the rocks, and the mountains were wet and dark, and the uncertain future seemed like a terrible abyss, of which one could not see the bottom; while now the raindrops hanging on the grass and on the stones were sparkling in the sun like diamonds, nature was smiling joyfully, and the terrible future was left behind. He looked at Sheshkovsky's sullen, tear-stained face, and at the two carriages ahead of them in which Von Koren, his seconds, and the doctor were sitting, and it seemed to him as though they were all coming back from a graveyard in which a wearisome, insufferable man who was a burden to others had just been buried.

"Everything is over," he thought of his past, cautiously touching his neck with his fingers.

On the right side of his neck was a small swelling, of the length and breadth of his little finger, and he felt a pain, as though some one had passed a hot iron over his neck. The bullet had bruised it.

Afterwards, when he got home, a strange, long, sweet day began for him, misty as forgetfulness. Like a man released from prison or from hospital, he stared at the long-familiar objects and wondered that the tables, the windows, the chairs, the light, and the sea stirred in him a keen, childish delight such as he had not known for long, long years. Nadyezhda Fyodorovna, pale and haggard, could not understand his gentle voice and strange movements; she made haste to tell him every-thing that had happened to her. . . . It seemed to her that very likely he scarcely heard and did not understand her, and that if he did know everything he would curse her and kill her, but he listened to her, stroked her face and hair, looked into her eyes and said:

"I have nobody but you. . . ."

Then they sat a long while in the garden, huddled close together, saying nothing, or dreaming aloud of their happy life in the future, in brief, broken sentences, while it seemed to him that he had never spo-ken at such length or so eloquently.

XXI

More than three months had passed.

The day came that Von Koren had fixed on for his departure. A cold, heavy rain had been falling from early morning, a north-east wind was blowing, and the waves were high on the sea. It was said that the steamer would hardly be able to come into the harbour in such weather. By the time-table it should have arrived at ten o'clock in the morning, but Von Koren, who had gone on to the sea-front at midday and again after dinner, could see nothing through the field-glass but grey waves and rain covering the horizon.

Towards the end of the day the rain ceased and the wind began to drop perceptibly. Von Koren had already made up his mind that he would not be able to get off that day, and had settled down to play chess with Samoylenko; but after dark the orderly announced that there were lights on the sea and that a rocket had been seen.

Von Koren made haste. He put his satchel over his shoulder, and kissed Samoylenko and the deacon. Though there was not the slightest necessity, he went through the rooms again, said good-bye to the orderly and the cook, and went out into the street, feeling that he had left something behind, either at the doctor's or his lodging. In the street he walked beside Samoylenko, behind them came the deacon with a box, and last of all the orderly with two portmanteaus. Only Samoylenko and the orderly could distinguish the dim lights on the sea. The others gazed into the darkness and saw nothing. The steamer had stopped a long way from the coast.

"Make haste, make haste," Von Koren hurried them. "I am afraid it will set off."

As they passed the little house with three windows, into which Laevsky had moved soon after the duel, Von Koren could not resist peeping in at the window. Laevsky was sitting, writing, bent over the table, with his back to the window.

"I wonder at him!" said the zoologist softly. "What a screw he has put on himself!"

"Yes, one may well wonder," said Samoylenko. "He sits from morning till night, he's always at work. He works to pay off his debts. And he lives, brother, worse than a beggar!"

Half a minute of silence followed. The zoologist, the doctor, and the deacon stood at the window and went on looking at Laevsky.

"So he didn't get away from here, poor fellow," said Samoylenko. "Do you remember how hard he tried?"

"Yes, he has put a screw on himself," Von Koren repeated. "His marriage, the way he works all day long for his daily bread, a new expression in his face, and even in his walk—it's all so extraordinary that I don't know what to call it."

The zoologist took Samoylenko's sleeve and went on with emotion in his voice:

"You tell him and his wife that when I went away I was full of admiration for them and wished them all happiness . . . and I beg him, if he can, not to remember evil against me. He knows me. He knows that if I could have foreseen this change, then I might have become his best friend."

"Go in and say good-bye to him."

"No, that wouldn't do."

"Why? God knows, perhaps you'll never see him again."

The zoologist reflected, and said:

"That's true."

Samoylenko tapped softly at the window. Laevsky started and looked round.

"Vanya, Nikolay Vassilitch wants to say goodbye to you," said Samoylenko. "He is just going away."

Laevsky got up from the table, and went into the passage to open the door. Samoylenko, the zoologist, and the deacon went into the house.

"I can only come for one minute," began the zoologist, taking off his goloshes in the passage, and already wishing he had not given way to his feelings and come in, uninvited. "It is as though I were forcing myself on him," he thought, "and that's stupid."

"Forgive me for disturbing you," he said as he went into the room with Laevsky, "but I'm just going away, and I had an impulse to see you. God knows whether we shall ever meet again."

"I am very glad to see you. ... Please come in," said Laevsky, and he awkwardly set chairs for his visitors as though he wanted to bar their way, and stood in the middle of the room, rubbing his hands.

"I should have done better to have left my audience in the street," thought Von Koren, and he said firmly: "Don't remember evil against me, Ivan Andreitch. To forget the past is, of course, impossible—it is too painful, and I've not come here to apologise or to declare that I was not to blame. I acted sincerely, and I have not changed my convictions since then. . . . It is true that I see, to my great delight, that I was mistaken in regard to you, but it's easy to make a false step even on a smooth road, and, in fact, it's the natural human lot: if one is not mistaken in the main, one is mistaken in the details. Nobody knows the real truth."

"No, no one knows the truth," said Laevsky.

"Well, good-bye. . . . God give you all happiness."

Von Koren gave Laevsky his hand; the latter took it and bowed.

"Don't remember evil against me," said Von Koren. "Give my greetings to your wife, and say I am very sorry not to say good-bye to her."

"She is at home."

Laevsky went to the door of the next room, and said:

"Nadya, Nikolay Vassilitch wants to say goodbye to you."

Nadyezhda Fyodorovna came in; she stopped near the doorway and looked shyly at the visitors. There was a look of guilt and dismay on her face, and she held her hands like a schoolgirl receiving a scolding.

"I'm just going away, Nadyezhda Fyodorovna," said Von Koren, "and have come to say good-bye."

She held out her hand uncertainly, while Laevsky bowed.

"What pitiful figures they are, though!" thought Von Koren. "The life they are living does not come easy to them. I shall be in Moscow and Petersburg; can I send you anything?" he asked.

"Oh!" said Nadyezhda Fyodorovna, and she looked anxiously at her husband. "I don't think there's anything. . . ."

"No, nothing . . ." said Laevsky, rubbing his hands. "Our greetings."

Von Koren did not know what he could or ought to say, though as he went in he thought he would say a very great deal that would be warm and good and important. He shook hands with Laevsky and his wife in silence, and left them with a depressed feeling.

"What people!" said the deacon in a low voice, as he walked behind them. "My God, what people! Of a truth, the right hand of God has planted this vine! Lord! Lord! One man vanquishes thousands and another tens of thousands. Nikolay Vassilitch," he said ecstatically, "let me tell you that to-day you have conquered the greatest of man's enemies—pride."

"Hush, deacon! Fine conquerors we are! Conquerors ought to look like eagles, while he's a pitiful figure, timid, crushed; he bows like a Chinese idol and I, I am sad. . . ."

They heard steps behind them. It was Laevsky, hurrying after them to see him off. The orderly was standing on the quay with the two portmanteaus, and at a little distance stood four boatmen.

"There is a wind, though. . . . Brrr!" said Samoylenko. "There must be a pretty stiff storm on the sea now! You are not going off at a nice time, Koyla."

"I'm not afraid of sea-sickness."

"That's not the point. . . . I only hope these rascals won't upset you. You ought to have crossed in the agent's sloop. Where's the agent's sloop?" he shouted to the boatmen.

"It has gone, Your Excellency."

"And the Customs-house boat?"

"That's gone, too."

"Why didn't you let us know," said Samoylenko angrily. "You dolts!"

"It's all the same, don't worry yourself . . ." said Von Koren. "Well, good-bye. God keep you."

Samoylenko embraced Von Koren and made the sign of the cross over him three times.

"Don't forget us, Kolya. . . . Write. . . . We shall look out for you next spring."

"Good-bye, deacon," said Von Koren, shaking hands with the deacon. "Thank you for your company and for your pleasant conversation. Think about the expedition."

"Oh Lord, yes! to the ends of the earth," laughed the deacon. "I've nothing against it."

Von Koren recognised Laevsky in the darkness, and held out his hand without speaking. The boatmen were by now below, holding the boat, which was beating against the piles, though the breakwater screened it from the breakers. Von Koren went down the ladder, jumped into the boat, and sat at the helm.

"Write!" Samoylenko shouted to him. "Take care of yourself."

"No one knows the real truth," thought Laevsky, turning up the collar of his coat and thrusting his hands into his sleeves.

The boat turned briskly out of the harbour into the open sea. It vanished in the waves, but at once from a deep hollow glided up onto a high breaker, so that they could distinguish the men and even the oars. The boat moved three yards forward and was sucked two yards back.

"Write!" shouted Samoylenko; "it's devilish weather for you to go in."

"Yes, no one knows the real truth . . ." thought Laevsky, looking wearily at the dark, restless sea.

"It flings the boat back," he thought; "she makes two steps forward and one step back; but the boatmen are stubborn, they work the oars unceasingly, and are not afraid of the high waves. The boat goes on and on. Now she is out of sight, but in half an hour the boatmen will see the steamer lights distinctly, and within an hour they will be by the steamer ladder. So it is in life. . . . In the search for truth man makes two steps forward and one step back. Suffering, mistakes, and weariness of life thrust them back, but the thirst for truth and stubborn will drive them on and on. And who knows? Perhaps they will reach the real truth at last."

"Go—o—od-by—e," shouted Samoylenko.

"There's no sight or sound of them," said the deacon. "Good luck on the journey!"

It began to spot with rain.

"ANNA ON THE NECK"

I

AFTER THE wedding they had not even light refreshments; the happy pair simply drank a glass of champagne, changed into their travelling things, and drove to the station. Instead of a gay wedding ball and supper, instead of music and dancing, they went on a journey to pray at a shrine a hundred and fifty miles away. Many people commended this, saying that Modest Alexeitch was a man high up in the service and no longer young, and that a noisy wedding might not have seemed quite suitable; and music is apt to sound dreary when a government official of fifty-two marries a girl who is only just eighteen. People said, too, that Modest Alexeitch, being a man of principle, had arranged this visit to the monastery expressly in order to make his young bride realize that even in marriage he put religion and morality above everything.

The happy pair were seen off at the station. The crowd of relations and colleagues in the service stood, with glasses in their hands, waiting for the train to start to shout "Hurrah!" and the bride's father, Pyotr Leontyitch, wearing a top-hat and the uniform of a teacher, already drunk and very pale, kept craning towards the window, glass in hand and saying in an imploring voice:

"Anyuta! Anya, Anya! one word!"

Anna bent out of the window to him, and he whispered something to her, enveloping her in a stale smell of alcohol, blew into her ear— she could make out nothing—and made the sign of the cross over her face, her bosom, and her hands; meanwhile he was breathing in gasps and tears were shining in his eyes. And the schoolboys, Anna's brothers, Petya and Andrusha, pulled at his coat from behind, whispering in confusion:

"Father, hush! . . . Father, that's enough. . . ."

When the train started, Anna saw her father run a little way after the train, staggering and spilling his wine, and what a kind, guilty, pitiful face he had:

"Hurra—ah!" he shouted.

The happy pair were left alone. Modest Alexeitch looked about the compartment, arranged their things on the shelves, and sat down, smiling, opposite his young wife. He was an official of medium height, rather stout and puffy, who looked exceedingly well nourished, with long whiskers and no moustache. His clean-shaven, round, sharply defined chin looked like the heel of a foot. The most characteristic point in his face was the absence of moustache, the bare, freshly shaven place, which gradually passed into the fat cheeks, quivering like jelly. His deportment was dignified, his movements were deliberate, his manner was soft.

"I cannot help remembering now one circumstance," he said, smiling. "When, five years ago, Kosorotov received the order of St. Anna of the second grade, and went to thank His Excellency, His Excellency expressed himself as follows: 'So now you have three Annas: one in your buttonhole and two on your neck.' And it must be explained that at that time Kosorotov's wife, a quarrelsome and frivolous person, had just returned to him, and that her name was Anna. I trust that when I receive the Anna of the second grade His Excellency will not have occasion to say the same thing to me."

He smiled with his little eyes. And she, too, smiled, troubled at the thought that at any moment this man might kiss her with his thick damp lips, and that she had no right to prevent his doing so. The soft movements of his fat person frightened her; she felt both fear and disgust. He got up, without haste took off the order from his neck, took off his coat and waistcoat, and put on his dressing-gown.

"That's better," he said, sitting down beside Anna.

Anna remembered what agony the wedding had been, when it had seemed to her that the priest, and the guests, and every one in church had been looking at her sorrowfully and asking why, why was she, such a sweet, nice girl, marrying such an elderly, uninteresting gentleman. Only that morning she was delighted that everything had been satisfactorily arranged, but at the time of the wedding, and now in the railway carriage, she felt cheated, guilty, and ridiculous. Here she had married a rich man and yet she had no money, her wedding-dress had been bought on credit, and when her father and brothers had been saying good-bye, she could see from their faces that they had not a farthing. Would they have any supper that day? And tomorrow? And for some reason it seemed to her that her father and the boys were sitting tonight hungry without her, and feeling the same misery as they had the day after their mother's funeral.

"Oh, how unhappy I am!" she thought. "Why am I so unhappy?"

With the awkwardness of a man with settled habits, unaccustomed to deal with women, Modest Alexeitch touched her on the waist and patted her on the shoulder, while she went on thinking about money, about her mother and her mother's death. When her mother died, her father, Pyotr Leontyitch, a teacher of drawing and writing in the high school, had taken to drink, impoverishment had followed, the boys had not had boots or goloshes, their father had been hauled up before the magistrate, the warrant officer had come and made an inventory of the furniture. . . . What a disgrace! Anna had had to look after her drunken father, darn her brothers' stockings, go to market, and when she was complimented on her youth, her beauty, and her elegant manners, it seemed to her that every one was looking at her cheap hat and the holes in her boots that were inked over. And at night there had been tears and a haunting dread that her father would soon, very soon, be dismissed from the school for his weakness, and that he would not survive it, but would die, too, like their mother. But ladies of their acquaintance had taken the matter in hand and looked about for a good match for Anna. This Modest Alexeitch, who was neither young nor good-looking but had money, was soon found. He had a hundred thousand in the bank and the family estate, which he had let on lease. He was a man of principle and stood well with His Excellency; it would be nothing to him, so they told Anna, to get a note from His Excellency to the directors of the high school, or even to the Education Commissioner, to prevent Pyotr Leontyitch from being dismissed.

While she was recalling these details, she suddenly heard strains of music which floated in at the window, together with the sound of voices. The train was stopping at a station. In the crowd beyond the platform an accordion and a cheap squeaky fiddle were being briskly played, and the sound of a military band came from beyond the villas and the tall birches and poplars that lay bathed in the moonlight; there must have been a dance in the place. Summer visitors and townspeople, who used to come out here by train in fine weather for a breath of fresh air, were parading up and down on the platform. Among them was the wealthy owner of all the summer villas—a tall, stout, dark man called Artynov. He had prominent eyes and looked like an Armenian. He wore a strange costume; his shirt was unbuttoned, showing his chest; he wore high boots with spurs, and a black cloak hung from his shoulders and dragged on the ground like a train. Two boar-hounds followed him with their sharp noses to the ground.

Tears were still shining in Anna's eyes, but she was not thinking now of her mother, nor of money, nor of her marriage; but shaking hands with school-boys and officers she knew, she laughed gaily and said quickly:

"How do you do? How are you?"

She went out on to the platform between the carriages into the moonlight, and stood so that they could all see her in her new splendid dress and hat.

"Why are we stopping here?" she asked.

"This is a junction. They are waiting for the mail train to pass."

Seeing that Artynov was looking at her, she screwed up her eyes coquettishly and began talking aloud in French; and because her voice sounded so pleasant, and because she heard music and the moon was reflected in the pond, and because Artynov, the notorious Don Juan and spoiled child of fortune, was looking at her eagerly and with curiosity, and because every one was in good spirits—she suddenly felt joyful, and when the train started and the officers of her acquaintance saluted her, she was humming the polka the strains of which reached her from the military band playing beyond the trees; and she returned to her compartment feeling as though it had been proved to her at the station that she would certainly be happy in spite of everything.

The happy pair spent two days at the monastery, then went back to town. They lived in a rent-free flat. When Modest Alexeitch had gone to the office, Anna played the piano, or shed tears of depression, or lay down on a couch and read novels or looked through fashion papers. At dinner Modest Alexeitch ate a great deal and talked about politics, about appointments, transfers, and promotions in the service, about the necessity of hard work, and said that, family life not being a pleasure but a duty, if you took care of the kopecks the roubles would take care of themselves, and that he put religion and morality before everything else in the world. And holding his knife in his fist as though it were a sword, he would say:

"Every one ought to have his duties!"

And Anna listened to him, was frightened, and could not eat, and she usually got up from the table hungry. After dinner her husband lay down for a nap and snored loudly, while Anna went to see her own people. Her father and the boys looked at her in a peculiar way, as though just before she came in they had been blaming her for having married for money a tedious, wearisome man she did not love; her rustling skirts, her bracelets, and her general air of a married lady, offended them and made them uncomfortable. In her presence they felt a little embarrassed and did not know what to talk to her about; but yet they still loved her as before, and were not used to having dinner without her. She sat down with them to cabbage soup, porridge, and fried potatoes, smelling of mutton dripping. Pyotr Leontyitch filled his glass from the decanter with a trembling hand and drank it off hurriedly, greedily, with repulsion, then poured out a second glass and then a third. Petya and Andrusha, thin, pale boys with big eyes, would take the decanter and say desperately:

"You mustn't, father. . . . Enough, father. . . ."

And Anna, too, was troubled and entreated him to drink no more; and he would suddenly fly into a rage and beat the table with his fists:

"I won't allow any one to dictate to me!" he would shout. "Wretched boys! wretched girl! I'll turn you all out!"

But there was a note of weakness, of good-nature in his voice, and no one was afraid of him. After dinner he usually dressed in his best. Pale, with a cut on his chin from shaving, craning his thin neck, he would stand for half an hour before the glass, prinking, combing his hair, twisting his black moustache, sprinkling himself with scent, tying his cravat in a bow; then he would put on his gloves and his top-hat, and go off to give his private lessons. Or if it was a holiday he would stay at home and paint, or play the harmonium, which wheezed and growled; he would try to wrest from it pure harmonious sounds and would sing to it; or would storm at the boys:

"Wretches! Good-for-nothing boys! You have spoiled the instrument!"

In the evening Anna's husband played cards with his colleagues, who lived under the same roof in the government quarters. The wives of these gentlemen would come in—ugly, tastelessly dressed women, as coarse as cooks—and gossip would begin in the flat as tasteless and unattractive as the ladies themselves. Sometimes Modest Alexeitch would take Anna to the theatre. In the intervals he would never let her stir a step from his side, but walked about arm in arm with her through the corridors and the foyer. When he bowed to some one, he immediately whispered to Anna: "A civil councillor . . . visits at His Excellency's"; or, "A man of means . . . has a house of his own." When they passed the buffet Anna had a great longing for something sweet; she was fond of chocolate and apple cakes, but she had no money, and she did not like to ask her husband. He would take a pear, pinch it with his fingers, and ask uncertainly:

"How much?"

"Twenty-five kopecks!"

"I say!" he would reply, and put it down; but as it was awkward to leave the buffet without buying anything, he would order some seltzer-water and drink the whole bottle himself, and tears would come into his eyes. And Anna hated him at such times.

And suddenly flushing crimson, he would say to her rapidly:

"Bow to that old lady!"

"But I don't know her."

"No matter. That's the wife of the director of the local treasury! Bow, I tell you," he would grumble insistently. "Your head won't drop off."

Anna bowed and her head certainly did not drop off, but it was agonizing. She did everything her husband wanted her to, and was furious with herself for having let him deceive her like the veriest idiot. She had only married him for his money, and yet she had less money now than before her marriage. In old days her father would sometimes give her twenty kopecks, but now she had not a farthing. To take money by stealth or ask for it, she could not; she was afraid of her husband, she trembled before him. She felt as though she had been afraid of him for years. In her childhood the director of the high school had always seemed the most impressive and terrifying force in the world, sweeping down like a thunderstorm or a steam-engine ready to crush her; another similar force of which the whole family talked, and of which they were for some reason afraid, was His Excellency; then there were a dozen others, less formidable, and among them the teachers at the high school, with shaven upper lips, stern, implacable; and now finally, there was Modest Alexeitch, a man of principle, who even resembled the director in the face. And in Anna's imagination all these forces blended together into one, and, in the form of a terrible, huge white bear, menaced the weak and erring such as her father. And she was afraid to say anything in opposition to her husband, and gave a forced smile, and tried to make a show of pleasure when she was coarsely caressed and defiled by embraces that excited her terror.

Only once Pyotr Leontyitch had the temerity to ask for a loan of fifty roubles in order to pay some very irksome debt, but what an agony it had been!

"Very good; I'll give it to you," said Modest Alexeitch after a moment's thought; "but I warn you I won't help you again till you give up drinking. Such a failing is disgraceful in a man in the government service! I must remind you of the well-known fact that many capable people have been ruined by that passion, though they might possibly, with temperance, have risen in time to a very high position."

And long-winded phrases followed: "inasmuch as . . . ," "following upon which proposition . . . ," in view of the aforesaid contention . . ."; and Pyotr Leontyitch was in agonies of humiliation and felt an intense craving for alcohol.

And when the boys came to visit Anna, generally in broken boots and threadbare trousers, they, too, had to listen to sermons.

"Every man ought to have his duties!" Modest Alexeitch would say to them.

And he did not give them money. But he did give Anna bracelets, rings, and brooches, saying that these things would come in useful for a rainy day. And he often unlocked her drawer and made an inspection to see whether they were all safe.

II

Meanwhile winter came on. Long before Christmas there was an announcement in the local papers that the usual winter ball would take place on the twenty-ninth of December in the Hall of Nobility. Every evening after cards Modest Alexeitch was excitedly whispering with his colleagues' wives and glancing at Anna, and then paced up and down the room for a long while, thinking. At last, late one evening, he stood still, facing Anna, and said:

"You ought to get yourself a ball dress. Do you understand? Only please consult Marya Grigoryevna and Natalya Kuzminishna."

And he gave her a hundred roubles. She took the money, but she did not consult any one when she ordered the ball dress; she spoke to no one but her father, and tried to imagine how her mother would have dressed for a ball. Her mother had always dressed in the latest fashion and had always taken trouble over Anna, dressing her elegantly like a doll, and had taught her to speak French and dance the mazurka superbly (she had been a governess for five years before her marriage). Like her mother, Anna could make a new dress out of an old one, clean gloves with benzine, hire jewels; and, like her mother, she knew how to screw up her eyes, lisp, assume graceful attitudes, fly into raptures when necessary, and throw a mournful and enigmatic look into her eyes. And from her father she had inherited the dark colour of her hair and eyes, her highly-strung nerves, and the habit of always making herself look her best.

When, half an hour before setting off for the ball, Modest Alexeitch went into her room without his coat on, to put his order round his neck before her pier-glass, dazzled by her beauty and the splendour of her fresh, ethereal dress, he combed his whiskers complacently and said:

"So that's what my wife can look like . . . so that's what you can look like! Anyuta!" he went on, dropping into a tone of solemnity, "I have made your fortune, and now I beg you to do something for mine. I beg you to get introduced to the wife of His Excellency! For God's sake, do! Through her I may get the post of senior reporting clerk!"

They went to the ball. They reached the Hall of Nobility, the entrance with the hall porter. They came to the vestibule with the hat-stands, the fur coats; footmen scurrying about, and ladies with low necks putting up their fans to screen themselves from the draughts. There was a smell of gas and of soldiers. When Anna, walking upstairs

on her husband's arm, heard the music and saw herself full length in
the looking-glass in the full glow of the lights, there was a rush of joy in
her heart, and she felt the same presentiment of happiness as in the
moonlight at the station. She walked in proudly, confidently, for the
first time feeling herself not a girl but a lady, and unconsciously imi-
tating her mother in her walk and in her manner. And for the first time
in her life she felt rich and free. Even her husband's presence did not
oppress her, for as she crossed the threshold of the hall she had guessed
instinctively that the proximity of an old husband did not detract from
her in the least, but, on the contrary, gave her that shade of piquant
mystery that is so attractive to men. The orchestra was already playing
and the dances had begun. After their flat Anna was overwhelmed by
the lights, the bright colours, the music, the noise, and looking round
the room, thought, "Oh, how lovely!" She at once distinguished in the
crowd all her acquaintances, every one she had met before at parties or
on picnics—all the officers, the teachers, the lawyers, the officials, the
landowners, His Excellency, Artynov, and the ladies of the highest
standing, dressed up and very *décolletées*, handsome and ugly, who had
already taken up their positions in the stalls and pavilions of the charity bazaar, to begin selling things for the benefit of the poor. A huge
officer in epaulettes—she had been introduced to him in Staro-Kievsky
Street when she was a schoolgirl, but now she could not remember his
name—seemed to spring from out of the ground, begging her for a
waltz, and she flew away from her husband, feeling as though she were
floating away in a sailing-boat in a violent storm, while her husband
was left far away on the shore. She danced passionately, with fervour, a
waltz, then a polka and a quadrille, being snatched by one partner as
soon as she was left by another, dizzy with music and the noise, mixing
Russian with French, lisping, laughing, and with no thought of her
husband or anything else. She excited great admiration among the
men—that was evident, and indeed it could not have been otherwise;
she was breathless with excitement, felt thirsty, and convulsively
clutched her fan. Pyotr Leontyitch, her father, in a crumpled dress-coat
that smelt of benzine, came up to her, offering her a plate of pink ice.

"You are enchanting this evening," he said, looking at her rapturously,
"and I have never so much regretted that you were in such a hurry to get
married. . . . What was it for? I know you did it for our sake, but . . ." With
a shaking hand he drew out a roll of notes and said: "I got the money for
my lessons today, and can pay your husband what I owe him."

She put the plate back into his hand, and was pounced upon by
some one and borne off to a distance. She caught a glimpse over her
partner's shoulder of her father gliding over the floor, putting his arm
round a lady and whirling down the ball-room with her.

"How sweet he is when he is sober!" she thought.

She danced the mazurka with the same huge officer; he moved gravely, as heavily as a dead carcase in a uniform, twitched his shoulders and his chest, stamped his feet very languidly—he felt fearfully disinclined to dance. She fluttered round him, provoking him by her beauty, her bare neck; her eyes glowed defiantly, her movements were passionate, while he became more and more indifferent, and held out his hands to her as graciously as a king.

"Bravo, bravo!" said people watching them.

But little by little the huge officer, too, broke out; he grew lively, excited, and, overcome by her fascination, was carried away and danced lightly, youthfully, while she merely moved her shoulders and looked slyly at him as though she were now the queen and he were her slave; and at that moment it seemed to her that the whole room was looking at them, and that everybody was thrilled and envied them. The huge officer had hardly had time to thank her for the dance, when the crowd suddenly parted and the men drew themselves up in a strange way, with their hands at their sides. His Excellency, with two stars on his dress-coat, was walking up to her. Yes, His Excellency was walking straight towards her, for he was staring directly at her with a sugary smile, while he licked his lips as he always did when he saw a pretty woman.

"Delighted, delighted . . ." he began. "I shall order your husband to be clapped in a lock-up for keeping such a treasure hidden from us till now. I've come to you with a message from my wife," he went on, offering her his arm. "You must help us. . . . M-m-yes. . . . We ought to give you the prize for beauty as they do in America. . . . M-m-yes. . . . The Americans. . . . My wife is expecting you impatiently."

He led her to a stall and presented her to a middle-aged lady, the lower part of whose face was disproportionately large, so that she looked as though she were holding a big stone in her mouth.

"You must help us," she said through her nose in a sing-song voice. "All the pretty women are working for our charity bazaar, and you are the only one enjoying yourself. Why won't you help us?"

She went away, and Anna took her place by the cups and the silver samovar. She was soon doing a lively trade. Anna asked no less than a rouble for a cup of tea, and made the huge officer drink three cups. Artynov, the rich man with prominent eyes, who suffered from asthma, came up, too; he was not dressed in the strange costume in which Anna had seen him in the summer at the station, but wore a dress-coat like every one else. Keeping his eyes fixed on Anna, he drank a glass of champagne and paid a hundred roubles for it, then drank some tea and gave another hundred—all this without saying a word, as he was short of breath through asthma. . . . Anna invited purchasers and got money out of them, firmly convinced by now that her smiles and glances could not fail to afford these people great pleasure. She realized now that she was created exclusively for this noisy, brilliant, laughing life, with its music, its dancers, its adorers, and her old terror of a force that was sweeping down upon her and menacing to crush her seemed to her ridiculous: she was afraid of no one now, and only regretted that her mother could not be there to rejoice at her success.

Pyotr Leontyitch, pale by now but still steady on his legs, came up to the stall and asked for a glass of brandy. Anna turned crimson, expecting him to say something inappropriate (she was already ashamed of having such a poor and ordinary father); but he emptied his glass, took ten roubles out of his roll of notes, flung it down, and walked away with dignity without uttering a word. A little later she saw him dancing in the grand chain, and by now he was staggering and kept shouting something, to the great confusion of his partner; and Anna remembered how at the ball three years before he had staggered and shouted in the same way, and it had ended in the police-sergeant's taking him home to bed, and next day the director had threatened to dismiss him from his post. How inappropriate that memory was!

When the samovars were put out in the stalls and the exhausted ladies handed over their takings to the middle-aged lady with the stone in her mouth, Artynov took Anna on his arm to the hall where supper was served to all who had assisted at the bazaar. There were some twenty people at supper, not more, but it was very noisy. His Excellency proposed a toast: "In this magnificent dining-room it will be appropriate to drink to the success of the cheap dining-rooms, which are the object of today's bazaar."

The brigadier-general proposed the toast: "To the power by which even the artillery is vanquished," and all the company clinked glasses with the ladies. It was very, very gay.

When Anna was escorted home it was daylight and the cooks were going to market. Joyful, intoxicated, full of new sensations, exhausted, she undressed, dropped into bed, and at once fell asleep. . . .

It was past one in the afternoon when the servant waked her and announced that M. Artynov had called. She dressed quickly and went down into the drawing-room. Soon after Artynov, His Excellency called to thank her for her assistance in the bazaar. With a sugary smile, chewing his lips, he kissed her hand, and asking her permission to come again, took his leave, while she remained standing in the middle of the drawing-room, amazed, enchanted, unable to believe that this change in her life, this marvellous change, had taken place so quickly; and at that moment Modest Alexeitch walked in . . . and he, too, stood before her now with the same ingratiating, sugary, cringingly respectful expression which she was accustomed to see on his face in the presence of the great and powerful; and with rapture, with indignation, with contempt, convinced that no harm would come to her from it, she said, articulating distinctly each word:

"Be off, you blockhead!"

From this time forward Anna never had one day free, as she was always taking part in picnics, expeditions, performances. She returned home every day after midnight, and went to bed on the floor in the drawing-room, and afterwards used to tell every one, touchingly, how she slept under flowers. She needed a very great deal of money, but she was no longer afraid of Modest Alexeitch, and spent his money as though it were her own; and she did not ask, did not demand it, simply sent him in the bills. "Give bearer two hundred roubles," or "Pay one hundred roubles at once."

At Easter Modest Alexeitch received the Anna of the second grade. When he went to offer his thanks, His Excellency put aside the paper he was reading and settled himself more comfortably in his chair.

"So now you have three Annas," he said, scrutinizing his white hands and pink nails—"one on your buttonhole and two on your neck."

Modest Alexeitch put two fingers to his lips as a precaution against laughing too loud and said:

"Now I have only to look forward to the arrival of a little Vladimir. I make bold to beg your Excellency to stand godfather."

He was alluding to Vladimir of the fourth grade, and was already imagining how he would tell everywhere the story of this pun, so happy in its readiness and audacity, and he wanted to say something equally happy, but His Excellency was buried again in his newspaper, and merely gave him a nod.

And Anna went on driving about with three horses, going out hunting with Artynov, playing in one-act dramas, going out to supper, and was more and more rarely with her own family; they dined now alone. Pyotr Leontyitch was drinking more heavily than ever; there was no money, and the harmonium had been sold long ago for debt. The boys did not let him go out alone in the street now, but looked after him for fear he might fall down; and whenever they met Anna driving in Staro-Kievsky Street with a pair of horses and Artynov on the box instead of a coachman, Pyotr Leontyitch took off his top-hat, and was about to shout to her, but Petya and Andrusha took him by the arm, and said imploringly:

"You mustn't, father. Hush, father!"

THE MAN IN A CASE

At the furthest end of the village of Mironositskoe some belated sportsmen lodged for the night in the elder Prokofy's barn. There were two of them, the veterinary surgeon Ivan Ivanovitch and the schoolmaster Burkin. Ivan Ivanovitch had a rather strange double-barrelled surname—Tchimsha-Himalaisky—which did not suit him at all, and he was called simply Ivan Ivanovitch all over the province. He lived at a stud-farm near the town, and had come out shooting now to get a breath of fresh air. Burkin, the high-school teacher, stayed every summer at Count P——'s, and had been thoroughly at home in this district for years.

They did not sleep. Ivan Ivanovitch, a tall, lean old fellow with long moustaches, was sitting outside the door, smoking a pipe in the moonlight. Burkin was lying within on the hay, and could not be seen in the darkness.

They were telling each other all sorts of stories. Among other things, they spoke of the fact that the elder's wife, Mavra, a healthy and by no means stupid woman, had never been beyond her native village, had never seen a town nor a railway in her life, and had spent the last ten years sitting behind the stove, and only at night going out into the street.

"What is there wonderful in that!" said Burkin. "There are plenty of people in the world, solitary by temperament, who try to retreat into their shell like a hermit crab or a snail. Perhaps it is an instance of atavism, a return to the period when the ancestor of man was not yet a social animal and lived alone in his den, or perhaps it is only one of the diversities of human character—who knows? I am not a natural science man, and it is not my business to settle such questions; I only mean to say that people like Mavra are not uncommon. There is no need to look far; two months ago a man called Byelikov, a colleague of mine, the Greek master, died in our town. You have heard of him, no doubt. He was remarkable for always wearing goloshes and a warm wadded coat, and carrying an umbrella even in the very finest weather. And his umbrella was in a case, and his watch was in a case made of grey chamois leather, and when he took out his penknife to sharpen his pencil, his penknife, too, was in a little case; and his face seemed to be in a case too, because he always hid it in his turned-up collar. He wore dark spectacles and flannel vests, stuffed up his ears with cotton-wool, and when he got into a cab always told the driver to put up the hood. In short, the man displayed a constant and insurmountable impulse to wrap himself in a covering, to make himself, so to speak, a case which would isolate him and protect him from external influences. Reality irritated him, frightened him, kept him in continual agitation, and, perhaps to justify his timidity, his aversion for the actual, he always praised the past and what had never existed; and even the classical languages which he taught were in reality for him goloshes and umbrellas in which he sheltered himself from real life.

"'Oh, how sonorous, how beautiful is the Greek language!' he would say, with a sugary expression; and as though to prove his words he would screw up his eyes and, raising his finger, would pronounce 'Anthropos!'

"And Byelikov tried to hide his thoughts also in a case. The only things that were clear to his mind were government circulars and newspaper articles in which something was forbidden. When some proclamation prohibited the boys from going out in the streets after nine o'clock in the evening, or some article declared carnal love unlawful, it was to his mind clear and definite; it was forbidden, and that was enough. For him there was always a doubtful element, something vague and not fully expressed, in any sanction or permission. When a dramatic club or a reading-room or a tea-shop was licensed in the town, he would shake his head and say softly:

"It is all right, of course; it is all very nice, but I hope it won't lead to anything!"

"Every sort of breach of order, deviation or departure from rule, depressed him, though one would have thought it was no business of his. If one of his colleagues was late for church or if rumours reached him of some prank of the high-school boys, or one of the mistresses was seen late in the evening in the company of an officer, he was much disturbed, and said he hoped that nothing would come of it. At the teachers' meetings he simply oppressed us with his caution, his circumspection, and his characteristic reflection on the ill-behaviour of the young people in both male and female high-schools, the uproar in the classes. . . .

"Oh, he hoped it would not reach the ears of the authorities; oh, he hoped nothing would come of it; and he thought it would be a very good thing if Petrov were expelled from the second class and Yegorov from the fourth. And, do you know, by his sighs, his despondency, his black spectacles on his pale little face, a little face like a pole-cat's, you know, he crushed us all, and we gave way, reduced Petrov's and Yegorov's marks for conduct, kept them in, and in the end expelled them both. He had a strange habit of visiting our lodgings. He would come to a teacher's, would sit down, and remain silent, as though he were carefully inspecting something. He would sit like this in silence for an hour or two and then go away. This he called 'maintaining good relations with his colleagues'; and it was obvious that coming to see us and sitting there was tiresome to him, and that he came to see us simply because he considered it his duty as our colleague. We teachers were afraid of him. And even the headmaster was afraid of him. Would you believe it, our teachers were all intellectual, right-minded people, brought up on Turgenev and Shtchedrin, yet this little chap, who always went about with goloshes and an umbrella, had the whole high-school under his thumb for fifteen long years! High-school, indeed — he had the whole town under his thumb! Our ladies did not get up private theatricals on Saturdays for fear he should hear of it, and the clergy dared not eat meat or play cards in his presence. Under the influence of people like Byelikov we have got into the way of being afraid of everything in our town for the last ten or fifteen years. They are afraid to speak aloud, afraid to send letters, afraid to make acquaintances, afraid to read books, afraid to help the poor, to teach people to read and write. . . ."

Ivan Ivanovitch cleared his throat, meaning to say something, but first lighted his pipe, gazed at the moon, and then said, with pauses:

"Yes, intellectual, right-minded people read Shtchedrin and Turgenev, Buckle, and all the rest of them, yet they knocked under and put up with it . . . that's just how it is."

"Byelikov lived in the same house as I did," Burkin went on, "on the same storey, his door facing mine; we often saw each other, and I knew how he lived when he was at home. And at home it was the same story: dressing-gown, nightcap, blinds, bolts, a perfect succession of prohibitions and restrictions of all sorts, and — 'Oh, I hope nothing will come of it!' Lenten fare was bad for him, yet he could not eat meat, as people might perhaps say Byelikov did not keep the fasts, and he ate fresh-water fish with butter — not a Lenten dish, yet one could not say that it was meat. He did not keep a female servant for fear people might think evil of him, but had as cook an old man of sixty, called Afanasy, half-witted and given to tippling, who had once been an officer's servant and could cook after a fashion. This Afanasy was usually standing at the door with his arms folded; with a deep sigh, he would mutter always the same thing:

"'There are plenty of *them* about nowadays!'

"Byelikov had a little bedroom like a box; his bed had curtains. When he went to bed he covered his head over; it was hot and stuffy; the wind battered on the closed doors; there was a droning noise in the stove and a sound of sighs from the kitchen—ominous sighs. . . . And he felt frightened under the bed-clothes. He was afraid that something might happen, that Afanasy might murder him, that thieves might break in, and so he had troubled dreams all night, and in the morning, when we went together to the high-school, he was depressed and pale, and it was evident that the high-school full of people excited dread and aversion in his whole being, and that to walk beside me was irksome to a man of his solitary temperament.

"'They make a great noise in our classes,' he used to say, as though trying to find an explanation for his depression. 'It's beyond anything.'

"And the Greek master, this man in a case—would you believe it?—almost got married."

Ivan Ivanovitch glanced quickly into the barn, and said:

"You are joking!"

"Yes, strange as it seems, he almost got married. A new teacher of history and geography, Mihail Savvitch Kovalenko, a Little Russian, was appointed. He came, not alone, but with his sister Varinka. He was a tall, dark young man with huge hands, and one could see from his face that he had a bass voice, and, in fact, he had a voice that seemed to come out of a barrel—'boom, boom, boom!' And she was not so young, about thirty, but she, too, was tall, well-made, with black eyebrows and red cheeks—in fact, she was a regular sugar-plum, and so sprightly, so noisy; she was always singing Little Russian songs and laughing. For the least thing she would go off into a ringing laugh—'Ha-ha-ha!' We made our first thorough acquaintance with the Kovalenkos at the headmaster's name-day party. Among the glum and intensely bored teachers who came even to the name-day party as a duty we suddenly saw a new Aphrodite risen from the waves; she walked with her arms akimbo, laughed, sang, danced. . . . She sang with feeling 'The Winds do Blow,' then another song, and another, and she fascinated us all—all, even Byelikov. He sat down by her and said with a honeyed smile:

"'The Little Russian reminds one of the ancient Greek in its softness and agreeable resonance.'

"That flattered her, and she began telling him with feeling and earnestness that they had a farm in the Gadyatchsky district, and that her mamma lived at the farm, and that they had such pears, such melons, such *kabaks!* The Little Russians call pumpkins *kabaks* (*i.e.*, pothouses), while their pothouses they call *shinki*, and they make a beetroot soup with tomatoes and aubergines in it, 'which was so nice—awfully nice!'

"We listened and listened, and suddenly the same idea dawned upon us all:

"'It would be a good thing to make a match of it,' the headmaster's wife said to me softly.

"We all for some reason recalled the fact that our friend Byelikov was not married, and it now seemed to us strange that we had hitherto failed to observe, and had in fact completely lost sight of, a detail so important in his life. What was his attitude to woman? How had he settled this vital question for himself? This had not interested us in the least till then; perhaps we had not even admitted the idea that a man who went out in all weathers in goloshes and slept under curtains could be in love.

"'He is a good deal over forty and she is thirty,' the headmaster's wife went on, developing her idea. 'I believe she would marry him.'

"All sorts of things are done in the provinces through boredom, all sorts of unnecessary and nonsensical things! And that is because what is necessary is not done at all. What need was there, for instance, for us to make a match for this Byelikov, whom one could not even imagine married? The headmaster's wife, the inspector's wife, and all our high-school ladies, grew livelier and even better-looking, as though they had suddenly found a new object in life. The headmaster's wife would take a box at the theatre, and we beheld sitting in her box Varinka, with such a fan, beaming and happy, and beside her Byelikov, a little bent figure, looking as though he had been extracted from his house by pincers. I would give an evening party, and the ladies would insist on my inviting Byelikov and Varinka. In short, the machine was set in motion. It appeared that Varinka was not averse to matrimony. She had not a very cheerful life with her brother; they could do nothing but quarrel and scold one another from morning till night. Here is a scene, for instance. Kovalenko would be coming along the street, a tall, sturdy young ruffian, in an embroidered shirt, his love-locks falling on his forehead under his cap, in one hand a bundle of books, in the other a thick knotted stick, followed by his sister, also with books in her hand.

"'But you haven't read it, Mihalik!' she would be arguing loudly. 'I tell you, I swear you have not read it at all!'

"'And I tell you I have read it,' cries Kovalenko, thumping his stick on the pavement.

"'Oh, my goodness, Mihalik! why are you so cross? We are arguing about principles.'

"'I tell you that I have read it!' Kovalenko would shout, more loudly than ever.

"And at home, if there was an outsider present, there was sure to be a skirmish. Such a life must have been wearisome, and of course she must have longed for a home of her own. Besides, there was her age to be considered; there was no time left to pick and choose; it was a case of marrying anybody, even a Greek master. And, indeed, most of our young ladies don't mind whom they marry so long as they do get married. However that may be, Varinka began to show an unmistakable partiality for Byelikov.

"And Byelikov? He used to visit Kovalenko just as he did us. He would arrive, sit down, and remain silent. He would sit quiet, and Varinka would sing to him 'The Winds do Blow,' or would look pensively at him with her dark eyes, or would suddenly go off into a peal—'Ha-ha-ha!'

"Suggestion plays a great part in love affairs, and still more in getting married. Everybody—both his colleagues and the ladies—began assuring Byelikov that he ought to get married, that there was nothing left for him in life but to get married; we all congratulated him, with solemn countenances delivered ourselves of various platitudes, such as 'Marriage is a serious step.' Besides, Varinka was good-looking and interesting; she was the daughter of a civil councillor, and had a farm; and what was more, she was the first woman who had been warm and friendly in her manner to him. His head was turned, and he decided that he really ought to get married."

"Well, at that point you ought to have taken away his goloshes and umbrella," said Ivan Ivanovitch.

"Only fancy! that turned out to be impossible. He put Varinka's portrait on his table, kept coming to see me and talking about Varinka, and home life, saying marriage was a serious step. He was frequently at Kovalenko's, but he did not alter his manner of life in the least; on the contrary, indeed, his determination to get married seemed to have a depressing effect on him. He grew thinner and paler, and seemed to retreat further and further into his case.

"'I like Varvara Savvishna,' he used to say to me, with a faint and wry smile, 'and I know that every one ought to get married, but . . . you know all this has happened so suddenly. . . . One must think a little.'

"'What is there to think over?' I used to say to him. 'Get married—that is all.'

"'No; marriage is a serious step. One must first weigh the duties before one, the responsibilities . . . that nothing may go wrong afterwards. It worries me so much that I don't sleep at night. And I must confess I am afraid: her brother and she have a strange way of thinking; they look at things strangely, you know, and her disposition is very impetuous. One may get married, and then, there is no knowing, one may find oneself in an unpleasant position.'

"And he did not make an offer; he kept putting it off, to the great vexation of the headmaster's wife and all our ladies; he went on weighing his future duties and responsibilities, and meanwhile he went for a walk with Varinka almost every day—possibly he thought that this was necessary in his position—and came to see me to talk about family life. And in all probability in the end he would have proposed to her, and would have made one of those unnecessary, stupid marriages such as are made by thousands among us from being bored and having nothing to do, if it had not been for a *kolossalische scandal.* I must mention that Varinka's brother, Kovalenko, detested Byelikov from the first day of their acquaintance, and could not endure him.

"'I don't understand,' he used to say to us, shrugging his shoulders — 'I don't understand how you can put up with that sneak, that nasty phiz. Ugh! how can you live here! The atmosphere is stifling and unclean! Do you call yourselves schoolmasters, teachers? You are paltry government clerks. You keep, not a temple of science, but a department for red tape and loyal behaviour, and it smells as sour as a police-station. No, my friends; I will stay with you for a while, and then I will go to my farm and there catch crabs and teach the Little Russians. I shall go, and you can stay here with your Judas—damn his soul!'

"Or he would laugh till he cried, first in a loud bass, then in a shrill, thin laugh, and ask me, waving his hands:

"'What does he sit here for? What does he want? He sits and stares.'

"He even gave Byelikov a nickname, 'The Spider.' And it will readily be understood that we avoided talking to him of his sister's being about to marry 'The Spider.'

"And on one occasion, when the headmaster's wife hinted to him what a good thing it would be to secure his sister's future with such a reliable, universally respected man as Byelikov, he frowned and muttered:

"'It's not my business; let her marry a reptile if she likes. I don't like meddling in other people's affairs.'

"Now hear what happened next. Some mischievous person drew a caricature of Byelikov walking along in his goloshes with his trousers tucked up, under his umbrella, with Varinka on his arm; below, the inscription 'Anthropos in love.' The expression was caught to a marvel, you know. The artist must have worked for more than one night, for the teachers of both the boys' and girls' high-schools, the teachers of the seminary, the government officials, all received a copy. Byelikov received one, too. The caricature made a very painful impression on him.

"We went out together; it was the first of May, a Sunday, and all of us, the boys and the teachers, had agreed to meet at the high-school and then to go for a walk together to a wood beyond the town. We set off, and he was green in the face and gloomier than a storm-cloud.

"'What wicked, ill-natured people there are!' he said, and his lips quivered.

"I felt really sorry for him. We were walking along, and all of a sudden—would you believe it?—Kovalenko came bowling along on a bicycle, and after him, also on a bicycle, Varinka, flushed and exhausted, but good-humoured and gay.

"'We are going on ahead,' she called. 'What lovely weather! Awfully lovely!'

"And they both disappeared from our sight. Byelikov turned white instead of green, and seemed petrified. He stopped short and stared at me. . . .

"'What is the meaning of it? Tell me, please!' he asked. 'Can my eyes have deceived me? Is it the proper thing for high-school masters and ladies to ride bicycles?'

"'What is there improper about it?' I said. 'Let them ride and enjoy themselves.'

"'But how can that be?' he cried, amazed at my calm. 'What are you saying?'

"And he was so shocked that he was unwilling to go on, and returned home.

"Next day he was continually twitching and nervously rubbing his hands, and it was evident from his face that he was unwell. And he left before his work was over, for the first time in his life. And he ate no dinner. Towards evening he wrapped himself up warmly, though it was quite warm weather, and sallied out to the Kovalenkos'. Varinka was out; he found her brother, however.

"'Pray sit down,' Kovalenko said coldly, with a frown. His face looked sleepy; he had just had a nap after dinner, and was in a very bad humour.

"Byelikov sat in silence for ten minutes, and then began:

"'I have come to see you to relieve my mind. I am very, very much troubled. Some scurrilous fellow has drawn an absurd caricature of me and another person, in whom we are both deeply interested. I regard it as a duty to assure you that I have had no hand in it. . . . I have given no sort of ground for such ridicule—on the contrary, I have always behaved in every way like a gentleman.'

"Kovalenko sat sulky and silent. Byelikov waited a little, and went on slowly in a mournful voice:

"'And I have something else to say to you. I have been in the service for years, while you have only lately entered it, and I consider it my duty as an older colleague to give you a warning. You ride on a bicycle, and that pastime is utterly unsuitable for an educator of youth.'

"'Why so?' asked Kovalenko in his bass.

"'Surely that needs no explanation, Mihail Savvitch—surely you can understand that? If the teacher rides a bicycle, what can you expect the pupils to do? You will have them walking on their heads next! And so long as there is no formal permission to do so, it is out of the question. I was horrified yesterday! When I saw your sister everything seemed dancing before my eyes. A lady or a young girl on a bicycle—it's awful!'

"'What is it you want exactly?'

"'All I want is to warn you, Mihail Savvitch. You are a young man, you have a future before you, you must be very, very careful in your behaviour, and you are so careless—oh, so careless! You go about in an embroidered shirt, are constantly seen in the street carrying books, and now the bicycle, too. The headmaster will learn that you and your sister ride the bicycle, and then it will reach the higher authorities. . . . Will that be a good thing?'

"'It's no business of anybody else if my sister and I do bicycle!' said Kovalenko, and he turned crimson. 'And damnation take any one who meddles in my private affairs!'

"Byelikov turned pale and got up.

"'If you speak to me in that tone I cannot continue,' he said. 'And I beg you never to express yourself like that about our superiors in my presence; you ought to be respectful to the authorities.'

"'Why, have I said any harm of the authorities?' asked Kovalenko, looking at him wrathfully. 'Please leave me alone. I am an honest man, and do not care to talk to a gentleman like you. I don't like sneaks!'

"Byelikov flew into a nervous flutter, and began hurriedly putting on his coat, with an expression of horror on his face. It was the first time in his life he had been spoken to so rudely.

"'You can say what you please,' he said, as he went out from the entry to the landing on the staircase. 'I ought only to warn you: possibly some one may have overheard us, and that our conversation may not be misunderstood and harm come of it, I shall be compelled to inform our headmaster of our conversation . . . in its main features. I am bound to do so.'

"'Inform him? You can go and make your report!'

"Kovalenko seized him from behind by the collar and gave him a push, and Byelikov rolled downstairs, thudding with his goloshes. The staircase was high and steep, but he rolled to the bottom unhurt, got up, and touched his nose to see whether his spectacles were all right.

But just as he was falling down the stairs Varinka came in, and with her two ladies; they stood below staring, and to Byelikov this was more terrible than anything. I believe he would rather have broken his neck or both legs than have been an object of ridicule. Why, now the whole town would hear of it; it would come to the headmaster's ears, would reach the higher authorities—oh, it might lead to something! There would be another caricature, and it would all end in his being asked to resign his post. . . .

"When he got up, Varinka recognized him, and, looking at his ridiculous face, his crumpled overcoat, and his goloshes, not understanding what had happened and supposing that he had slipped down by accident, could not restrain herself, and laughed loud enough to be heard by all the flats:

"'Ha-ha-ha!'

"And this pealing, ringing 'Ha-ha-ha!' was the last straw that put an end to everything: to the proposed match and to Byelikov's earthly existence. He did not hear what Varinka said to him; he saw nothing. On reaching home, the first thing he did was to remove her portrait from the table; then he went to bed, and he never got up again.

"Three days later Afanasy came to me and asked whether we should not send for the doctor, as there was something wrong with his master. I went in to Byelikov. He lay silent behind the curtain, covered with a quilt; if one asked him a question, he said 'Yes' or 'No' and not another sound. He lay there while Afanasy, gloomy and scowling, hovered about him, sighing heavily, and smelling like a pothouse.

"A month later Byelikov died. We all went to his funeral—that is, both the high-schools and the seminary. Now when he was lying in his coffin his expression was mild, agreeable, even cheerful, as though he were glad that he had at last been put into a case which he would never leave again. Yes, he had attained his ideal! And, as though in his honour, it was dull, rainy weather on the day of his funeral, and we all wore goloshes and took our umbrellas. Varinka, too, was at the funeral, and when the coffin was lowered into the grave she burst into tears. I have noticed that Little Russian women are always laughing or crying—no intermediate mood.

"One must confess that to bury people like Byelikov is a great pleasure. As we were returning from the cemetery we wore discreet Lenten faces; no one wanted to display this feeling of pleasure—a feeling like that we had experienced long, long ago as children when our elders had gone out and we ran about the garden for an hour or two, enjoying complete freedom. Ah, freedom, freedom! The merest hint, the faintest hope of its possibility gives wings to the soul, does it not?

"We returned from the cemetery in a good humour. But not more than a week had passed before life went on as in the past, as gloomy, oppressive, and senseless—a life not forbidden by government prohibition, but not fully permitted, either: it was no better. And, indeed, though we had buried Byelikov, how many such men in cases were left, how many more of them there will be!"

"That's just how it is," said Ivan Ivanovitch and he lighted his pipe.

"How many more of them there will be!" repeated Burkin.

The schoolmaster came out of the barn. He was a short, stout man, completely bald, with a black beard down to his waist. The two dogs came out with him.

"What a moon!" he said, looking upwards.

It was midnight. On the right could be seen the whole village, a long street stretching far away for four miles. All was buried in deep silent slumber; not a movement, not a sound; one could hardly believe that nature could be so still. When on a moonlight night you see a broad village street, with its cottages, haystacks, and slumbering willows, a feeling of calm comes over the soul; in this peace, wrapped away from care, toil, and sorrow in the darkness of night, it is mild, melancholy, beautiful, and it seems as though the stars look down upon it kindly and with tenderness, and as though there were no evil on earth and all were well. On the left the open country began from the end of the village; it could be seen stretching far away to the horizon, and there was no movement, no sound in that whole expanse bathed in moonlight.

"Yes, that is just how it is," repeated Ivan Ivanovitch; "and isn't our living in town, airless and crowded, our writing useless papers, our playing *vint*—isn't that all a sort of case for us? And our spending our whole lives among trivial, fussy men and silly, idle women, our talking and our listening to all sorts of nonsense—isn't that a case for us, too? If you like, I will tell you a very edifying story."

"No; it's time we were asleep," said Burkin.

"Tell it tomorrow."

They went into the barn and lay down on the hay. And they were both covered up and beginning to doze when they suddenly heard light footsteps—patter, patter. . . . Some one was walking not far from the barn, walking a little and stopping, and a minute later, patter, patter again. . . . The dogs began growling.

"That's Mavra," said Burkin.

The footsteps died away.

"You see and hear that they lie," said Ivan Ivanovitch, turning over on the other side, "and they call you a fool for putting up with their lying. You endure insult and humiliation, and dare not openly say that you are on the side of the honest and the free, and you lie and smile yourself; and all that for the sake of a crust of bread, for the sake of a warm corner, for the sake of a wretched little worthless rank in the service. No, one can't go on living like this."

"Well, you are off on another tack now, Ivan Ivanovitch," said the schoolmaster. "Let us go to sleep!"

And ten minutes later Burkin was asleep. But Ivan Ivanovitch kept sighing and turning over from side to side; then he got up, went outside again, and, sitting in the doorway, lighted his pipe.

THE DARLING

OLENKA, THE daughter of the retired collegiate assessor, Plemyanniakov, was sitting in her back porch, lost in thought. It was hot, the flies were persistent and teasing, and it was pleasant to reflect that it would soon be evening. Dark rainclouds were gathering from the east, and bringing from time to time a breath of moisture in the air.

Kukin, who was the manager of an open-air theatre called the Tivoli, and who lived in the lodge, was standing in the middle of the garden looking at the sky.

"Again!" he observed despairingly. "It's going to rain again! Rain every day, as though to spite me. I might as well hang myself! It's ruin! Fearful losses every day."

He flung up his hands, and went on, addressing Olenka:

"There! that's the life we lead, Olga Semyonovna. It's enough to make one cry. One works and does one's utmost, one wears oneself out, getting no sleep at night, and racks one's brain what to do for the best. And then what happens? To begin with, one's public is ignorant, boorish. I give them the very best operetta, a dainty masque, first rate music-hall artists. But do you suppose that's what they want! They don't understand anything of that sort. They want a clown; what they ask for is vulgarity. And then look at the weather! Almost every evening it rains. It started on the tenth of May, and it's kept it up all May and June. It's simply awful! The public doesn't come, but I've to pay the rent just the same, and pay the artists."

The next evening the clouds would gather again, and Kukin would say with an hysterical laugh:

"Well, rain away, then! Flood the garden, drown me! Damn my luck in this world and the next! Let the artists have me up! Send me to prison!—to Siberia!—the scaffold! Ha, ha, ha!"

And next day the same thing.

Olenka listened to Kukin with silent gravity, and sometimes tears came into her eyes. In the end his misfortunes touched her; she grew to love him. He was a small thin man, with a yellow face, and curls combed forward on his forehead. He spoke in a thin tenor; as he talked his mouth worked on one side, and there was always an expression of despair on his face; yet he aroused a deep and genuine affection in her. She was always fond of some one, and could not exist without loving. In earlier days she had loved her papa, who now sat in a darkened room, breathing with difficulty; she had loved her aunt who used to come every other year from Bryansk; and before that, when she was at school, she had loved her French master. She was a gentle, soft-hearted, compassionate girl, with mild, tender eyes and very good health. At the sight of her full rosy cheeks, her soft white neck with a little dark mole on it, and the kind, naïve smile, which came into her face when she listened to anything pleasant, men thought, "Yes, not half bad," and smiled too, while lady visitors could not refrain from seizing her hand in the middle of a conversation, exclaiming in a gush of delight, "You darling!"

The house in which she had lived from her birth upwards, and which was left her in her father's will, was at the extreme end of the town, not far from the Tivoli. In the evenings and at night she could head the band playing, and the crackling and banging of fireworks, and it seemed to her that it was Kukin struggling with his destiny, storming the entrenchments of his chief foe, the indifferent public; there was a sweet thrill at her heart, she had no desire to sleep, and when he returned home at daybreak, she tapped softly at her bedroom window, and showing him only her face and one shoulder through the curtain, she gave him a friendly smile. . . .

He proposed to her, and they were married. And when he had a closer view of her neck and her plump, fine shoulders, he threw up his hands, and said:

"You darling!"

He was happy, but as it rained on the day and night of his wedding, his face still retained an expression of despair.

They got on very well together. She used to sit in his office, to look after things in the Tivoli, to put down the accounts and pay the wages. And her rosy cheeks, her sweet, naïve, radiant smile, were to be seen now at the office window, now in the refreshment bar or behind the scenes of the theatre. And already she used to say to her acquaintances that the theatre was the chief and most important thing in life, and that it was only through the drama that one could derive true enjoyment and become cultivated and humane.

"But do you suppose the public understands that?" she used to say.

"What they want is a clown. Yesterday we gave 'Faust Inside Out,' and almost all the boxes were empty; but if Vanitchka and I had been producing some vulgar thing, I assure you the theatre would have been packed. Tomorrow Vanitchka and I are doing 'Orpheus in Hell.' Do come."

And what Kukin said about the theatre and the actors she repeated. Like him she despised the public for their ignorance and their indifference to art; she took part in the rehearsals, she corrected the actors, she kept an eye on the behaviour of the musicians, and when there was an unfavourable notice in the local paper, she shed tears, and then went to the editor's office to set things right.

The actors were fond of her and used to call her "Vanitchka and I," and "the darling"; she was sorry for them and used to lend them small sums of money, and if they deceived her, she used to shed a few tears in private, but did not complain to her husband.

They got on well in the winter too. They took the theatre in the town for the whole winter, and let it for short terms to a Little Russian company, or to a conjurer, or to a local dramatic society. Olenka grew stouter, and was always beaming with satisfaction, while Kukin grew thinner and yellower, and continually complained of their terrible losses, although he had not done badly all the winter. He used to cough at night, and she used to give him hot raspberry tea or lime-flower water, to rub him with eau-de-Cologne and to wrap him in her warm shawls.

"You're such a sweet pet!" she used to say with perfect sincerity, stroking his hair. "You're such a pretty dear!"

Towards Lent he went to Moscow to collect a new troupe, and without him she could not sleep, but sat all night at her window, looking at the stars, and she compared herself with the hens, who are awake all night and uneasy when the cock is not in the hen-house. Kukin was detained in Moscow, and wrote that he would be back at Easter, adding some instructions about the Tivoli. But on the Sunday before Easter, late in the evening, came a sudden ominous knock at the gate; some one was hammering on the gate as though on a barrel—boom, boom, boom! The drowsy cook went flopping with her bare feet through the puddles, as she ran to open the gate.

"Please open," said some one outside in a thick bass. "There is a telegram for you."

Olenka had received telegrams from her husband before, but this time for some reason she felt numb with terror. With shaking hands she opened the telegram and read as follows:

"IVAN PETROVITCH DIED SUDDENLY TO-DAY. AWAITING IMMATE INSTRUCTIONS FUFUNERAL TUESDAY."

That was how it was written in the telegram—"fufuneral," and the utterly incomprehensible word "immate." It was signed by the stage manager of the operatic company.

"My darling!" sobbed Olenka. "Vanitchka, my precious, my darling! Why did I ever meet you! Why did I know you and love you! Your poor heart-broken Olenka is all alone without you!"

Kukin's funeral took place on Tuesday in Moscow, Olenka returned home on Wednesday, and as soon as she got indoors she threw herself on her bed and sobbed so loudly that it could be heard next door, and in the street.

"Poor darling!" the neighbours said, as they crossed themselves. "Olga Semyonovna, poor darling! How she does take on!"

Three months later Olenka was coming home from mass, melancholy and in deep mourning. It happened that one of her neighbours, Vassily Andreitch Pustovalov, returning home from church, walked back beside her. He was the manager at Babakayev's, the timber merchant's. He wore a straw hat, a white waistcoat, and a gold watch-chain, and looked more like a country gentleman than a man in trade.

"Everything happens as it is ordained, Olga Semyonovna," he said gravely, with a sympathetic note in his voice; "and if any of our dear ones die, it must be because it is the will of God, so we ought to have fortitude and bear it submissively."

After seeing Olenka to her gate, he said good-bye and went on. All day afterwards she heard his sedately dignified voice, and whenever she shut her eyes she saw his dark beard. She liked him very much. And apparently she had made an impression on him too, for not long afterwards an elderly lady, with whom she was only slightly acquainted, came to drink coffee with her, and as soon as she was seated at table began to talk about Pustovalov, saying that he was an excellent man whom one could thoroughly depend upon, and that any girl would be glad to marry him. Three days later Pustovalov came himself. He did not stay long, only about ten minutes, and he did not say much, but when he left, Olenka loved him—loved him so much that she lay awake all night in a perfect fever, and in the morning she sent for the elderly lady. The match was quickly arranged, and then came the wedding.

Pustovalov and Olenka got on very well together when they were married.

Usually he sat in the office till dinner-time, then he went out on business, while Olenka took his place, and sat in the office till evening, making up accounts and booking orders.

"Timber gets dearer every year; the price rises twenty per cent," she would say to her customers and friends. "Only fancy we used to sell

local timber, and now Vassitchka always has to go for wood to the
Mogilev district. And the freight!" she would add, covering her cheeks
with her hands in horror. "The freight!"

It seemed to her that she had been in the timber trade for ages and
ages, and that the most important and necessary thing in life was timber; and there was something intimate and touching to her in the very
sound of words such as "baulk," "post," "beam," "pole," "scantling,"
"batten," "lath," "plank," etc.

At night when she was asleep she dreamed of perfect mountains of
planks and boards, and long strings of wagons, carting timber somewhere far away. She dreamed that a whole regiment of six-inch beams
forty feet high, standing on end, was marching upon the timber-yard;
that logs, beams, and boards knocked together with the resounding
crash of dry wood, kept falling and getting up again, piling themselves
on each other. Olenka cried out in her sleep, and Pustovalov said to her
tenderly: "Olenka, what's the matter, darling? Cross yourself!"

Her husband's ideas were hers. If he thought the room was too hot,
or that business was slack, she thought the same. Her husband did not
care for entertainments, and on holidays he stayed at home. She did
likewise.

"You are always at home or in the office," her friends said to her.
"You should go to the theatre, darling, or to the circus."

"Vassitchka and I have no time to go to theatres," she would answer
sedately. "We have no time for nonsense. What's the use of these
theatres?"

On Saturdays Pustovalov and she used to go to the evening service;
on holidays to early mass, and they walked side by side with softened
faces as they came home from church. There was a pleasant fragrance
about them both, and her silk dress rustled agreeably. At home they
drank tea, with fancy bread and jams of various kinds, and afterwards
they ate pie. Every day at twelve o'clock there was a savoury smell of
beet-root soup and of mutton or duck in their yard, and on fast-days of
fish, and no one could pass the gate without feeling hungry. In the
office the samovar was always boiling, and customers were regaled with
tea and cracknels. Once a week the couple went to the baths and
returned side by side, both red in the face.

"Yes, we have nothing to complain of, thank God," Olenka used to
say to her acquaintances. "I wish every one were as well off as
Vassitchka and I."

When Pustovalov went away to buy wood in the Mogilev district, she
missed him dreadfully, lay awake and cried. A young veterinary surgeon
in the army, called Smirnin, to whom they had let their lodge, used
sometimes to come in in the evening. He used to talk to her and play

cards with her, and this entertained her in her husband's absence. She was particularly interested in what he told her of his home life. He was married and had a little boy, but was separated from his wife because she had been unfaithful to him, and now he hated her and used to send her forty roubles a month for the maintenance of their son. And hearing of all this, Olenka sighed and shook her head. She was sorry for him.

"Well, God keep you," she used to say to him at parting, as she lighted him down the stairs with a candle. "Thank you for coming to cheer me up, and may the Mother of God give you health."

And she always expressed herself with the same sedateness and dignity, the same reasonableness, in imitation of her husband. As the veterinary surgeon was disappearing behind the door below, she would say:

"You know, Vladimir Platonitch, you'd better make it up with your wife. You should forgive her for the sake of your son. You may be sure the little fellow understands."

And when Pustovalov came back, she told him in a low voice about the veterinary surgeon and his unhappy home life, and both sighed and shook their heads and talked about the boy, who, no doubt, missed his father, and by some strange connection of ideas, they went up to the holy ikons, bowed to the ground before them and prayed that God would give them children.

And so the Pustovalovs lived for six years quietly and peaceably in love and complete harmony.

But behold! one winter day after drinking hot tea in the office, Vassily Andreitch went out into the yard without his cap on to see about sending off some timber, caught cold and was taken ill. He had the best doctors, but he grew worse and died after four months' illness. And Olenka was a widow once more.

"I've nobody, now you've left me, my darling," she sobbed, after her husband's funeral. "How can I live without you, in wretchedness and misery! Pity me, good people, all alone in the world!"

She went about dressed in black with long "weepers," and gave up wearing hat and gloves for good. She hardly ever went out, except to church, or to her husband's grave, and led the life of a nun. It was not till six months later that she took off the weepers and opened the shutters of the windows. She was sometimes seen in the mornings, going with her cook to market for provisions, but what went on in her house and how she lived now could only be surmised. People guessed, from seeing her drinking tea in her garden with the veterinary surgeon, who read the newspaper aloud to her, and from the fact that, meeting a lady she knew at the post-office, she said to her:

"There is no proper veterinary inspection in our town, and that's the cause of all sorts of epidemics. One is always hearing of people's getting infection from the milk supply, or catching diseases from horses and cows. The health of domestic animals ought to be as well cared for as the health of human beings."

She repeated the veterinary surgeon's words, and was of the same opinion as he about everything. It was evident that she could not live a year without some attachment, and had found new happiness in the lodge. In any one else this would have been censured, but no one could think ill of Olenka; everything she did was so natural. Neither she nor the veterinary surgeon said anything to other people of the change in their relations, and tried, indeed, to conceal it, but without success, for Olenka could not keep a secret. When he had visitors, men serving in his regiment, and she poured out tea or served the supper, she would begin talking of the cattle plague, of the foot and mouth disease, and of the municipal slaughterhouses. He was dreadfully embarrassed, and when the guests had gone, he would seize her by the hand and hiss angrily:

"I've asked you before not to talk about what you don't understand. When we veterinary surgeons are talking among ourselves, please don't put your word in. It's really annoying."

And she would look at him with astonishment and dismay, and ask him in alarm: "But, Voloditchka, what *am* I to talk about?"

And with tears in her eyes she would embrace him, begging him not to be angry, and they were both happy.

But this happiness did not last long. The veterinary surgeon departed, departed for ever with his regiment, when it was transferred to a distant place—to Siberia, it may be. And Olenka was left alone.

Now she was absolutely alone. Her father had long been dead, and his armchair lay in the attic, covered with dust and lame of one leg. She got thinner and plainer, and when people met her in the street they did not look at her as they used to, and did not smile to her; evidently her best years were over and left behind, and now a new sort of life had begun for her, which did not bear thinking about. In the evening Olenka sat in the porch, and heard the band playing and the fireworks popping in the Tivoli, but now the sound stirred no response. She looked into her yard without interest, thought of nothing, wished for nothing, and afterwards, when night came on she went to bed and dreamed of her empty yard. She ate and drank as it were unwillingly.

And what was worst of all, she had no opinions of any sort. She saw the objects about her and understood what she saw, but could not form any opinion about them, and did not know what to talk about. And how awful it is not to have any opinions! One sees a bottle, for instance, or the rain, or a peasant driving in his cart, but what the bottle is for, or the rain, or the peasant, and what is the meaning of it, one can't say, and could not even for a thousand roubles. When she had Kukin, or Pustovalov, or the veterinary surgeon, Olenka could explain everything, and give her opinion about anything you like, but now there was the same emptiness in her brain and in her heart as there was in her yard outside. And it was as harsh and as bitter as wormwood in the mouth.

Little by little the town grew in all directions. The road became a street, and where the Tivoli and the timber-yard had been, there were new turnings and houses. How rapidly time passes! Olenka's house grew dingy, the roof got rusty, the shed sank on one side, and the whole yard was overgrown with docks and stinging-nettles. Olenka herself had grown plain and elderly; in summer she sat in the porch, and her soul, as before, was empty and dreary and full of bitterness. In winter she sat at her window and looked at the snow. When she caught the scent of spring, or heard the chime of the church bells, a sudden rush of memories from the past came over her, there was a tender ache in her heart, and her eyes brimmed over with tears; but this was only for a minute, and then came emptiness again and the sense of the futility of life. The black kitten, Briska, rubbed against her and purred softly, but Olenka was not touched by these feline caresses. That was not what she needed. She wanted a love that would absorb her whole being, her whole soul and reason—that would give her ideas and an object in life, and would warm her old blood. And she would shake the kitten off her skirt and say with vexation:

"Get along; I don't want you!"

And so it was, day after day and year after year, and no joy, and no opinions. Whatever Mavra, the cook, said she accepted.

One hot July day, towards evening, just as the cattle were being driven away, and the whole yard was full of dust, some one suddenly knocked at the gate. Olenka went to open it herself and was dumbfounded when she looked out: she saw Smirnin, the veterinary surgeon, grey-headed, and dressed as a civilian. She suddenly remembered everything. She could not help crying and letting her head fall on his breast without uttering a word, and in the violence of her feeling she did not notice how they both walked into the house and sat down to tea.

"My dear Vladimir Platonitch! What fate has brought you?" she muttered, trembling with joy.

"I want to settle here for good, Olga Semyonovna," he told her. "I have resigned my post, and have come to settle down and try my luck on my own account. Besides, it's time for my boy to go to school. He's a big boy. I am reconciled with my wife, you know."

"Where is she?" asked Olenka.

"She's at the hotel with the boy, and I'm looking for lodgings."

"Good gracious, my dear soul! Lodgings? Why not have my house? Why shouldn't that suit you? Why, my goodness, I wouldn't take any rent!" cried Olenka in a flutter, beginning to cry again. "You live here, and the lodge will do nicely for me. Oh dear! how glad I am!"

Next day the roof was painted and the walls were whitewashed, and Olenka, with her arms akimbo, walked about the yard giving directions. Her face was beaming with her old smile, and she was brisk and alert as though she had waked from a long sleep. The veterinary's wife arrived—a thin, plain lady, with short hair and a peevish expression. With her was her little Sasha, a boy of ten, small for his age, blue-eyed, chubby, with dimples in his cheeks. And scarcely had the boy walked into the yard when he ran after the cat, and at once there was the sound of his gay, joyous laugh.

"Is that your puss, auntie?" he asked Olenka. "When she has little ones, do give us a kitten. Mamma is awfully afraid of mice."

Olenka talked to him, and gave him tea. Her heart warmed and there was a sweet ache in her bosom, as though the boy had been her own child. And when he sat at the table in the evening, going over his lessons, she looked at him with deep tenderness and pity as she murmured to herself:

"You pretty pet! . . . my precious! . . . Such a fair little thing, and so clever."

"'An island is a piece of land which is entirely surrounded by water,'" he read aloud.

"An island is a piece of land," she repeated, and this was the first opinion to which she gave utterance with positive conviction after so many years of silence and dearth of ideas.

Now she had opinions of her own, and at supper she talked to Sasha's parents, saying how difficult the lessons were at the high schools, but that yet the high-school was better than a commercial one, since with a high-school education all careers were open to one, such as being a doctor or an engineer.

Sasha began going to the high-school. His mother departed to Harkov to her sister's and did not return; his father used to go off every day to inspect cattle, and would often be away from home for three days together, and it seemed to Olenka as though Sasha was entirely abandoned, that he was not wanted at home, that he was being starved, and she carried him off to her lodge and gave him a little room there.

And for six months Sasha had lived in the lodge with her. Every morning Olenka came into his bedroom and found him fast asleep, sleeping noiselessly with his hand under his cheek. She was sorry to wake him.

"Sashenka," she would say mournfully, "get up, darling. It's time for school."

He would get up, dress and say his prayers, and then sit down to breakfast, drink three glasses of tea, and eat two large cracknels and half a buttered roll. All this time he was hardly awake and a little ill-humoured in consequence.

"You don't quite know your fable, Sashenka," Olenka would say, looking at him as though he were about to set off on a long journey. "What a lot of trouble I have with you! You must work and do your best, darling, and obey your teachers."

"Oh, do leave me alone!" Sasha would say.

Then he would go down the street to school, a little figure, wearing a big cap and carrying a satchel on his shoulder. Olenka would follow him noiselessly.

"Sashenka!" she would call after him, and she would pop into his hand a date or a caramel. When he reached the street where the school was, he would feel ashamed of being followed by a tall, stout woman; he would turn round and say:

"You'd better go home, auntie. I can go the rest of the way alone."

She would stand still and look after him fixedly till he had disappeared at the school-gate.

Ah, how she loved him! Of her former attachments not one had been so deep; never had her soul surrendered to any feeling so spontaneously, so disinterestedly, and so joyously as now that her maternal instincts were aroused. For this little boy with the dimple in his cheek and the big school cap, she would have given her whole life, she would have given it with joy and tears of tenderness. Why? Who can tell why?

When she had seen the last of Sasha, she returned home, contented and serene, brimming over with love; her face, which had grown younger during the last six months, smiled and beamed; people meeting her looked at her with pleasure.

"Good-morning, Olga Semyonovna, darling. How are you, darling?"

"The lessons at the high-school are very difficult now," she would relate at the market. "It's too much; in the first class yesterday they gave him a fable to learn by heart, and a Latin translation and a problem. You know it's too much for a little chap."

And she would begin talking about the teachers, the lessons, and the school books, saying just what Sasha said.

At three o'clock they had dinner together: in the evening they learned their lessons together and cried. When she put him to bed, she would stay a long time making the Cross over him and murmuring a prayer; then she would go to bed and dream of that far-away misty future when Sasha would finish his studies and become a doctor or an engineer, would have a big house of his own with horses and a carriage, would get married and have children. . . . She would fall asleep still thinking of the same thing, and tears would run down her cheeks from her closed eyes, while the black cat lay purring beside her: "Mrr, mrr, mrr."

Suddenly there would come a loud knock at the gate.

Olenka would wake up breathless with alarm, her heart throbbing. Half a minute later would come another knock.

"It must be a telegram from Harkov," she would think, beginning to tremble from head to foot. "Sasha's mother is sending for him from Harkov. . . . Oh, mercy on us!"

She was in despair. Her head, her hands, and her feet would turn chill, and she would feel that she was the most unhappy woman in the world. But another minute would pass, voices would be heard: it would turn out to be the veterinary surgeon coming home from the club.

"Well, thank God!" she would think.

And gradually the load in her heart would pass off, and she would feel at ease. She would go back to bed thinking of Sasha, who lay sound asleep in the next room, sometimes crying out in his sleep:

"I'll give it you! Get away! Shut up!"

DOVER·THRIFT·EDITIONS

FICTION

FLATLAND: A ROMANCE OF MANY DIMENSIONS, Edwin A. Abbott. 96pp. 27263-X

SHORT STORIES, Louisa May Alcott. 64pp. 29063-8

WINESBURG, OHIO, Sherwood Anderson. 160pp. 28269-4

PERSUASION, Jane Austen. 224pp. 29555-9

PRIDE AND PREJUDICE, Jane Austen. 272pp. 28473-5

SENSE AND SENSIBILITY, Jane Austen. 272pp. 29049-2

LOOKING BACKWARD, Edward Bellamy. 160pp. 29038-7

BEOWULF, Beowulf (trans. by R. K. Gordon). 64pp. 27264-8

CIVIL WAR STORIES, Ambrose Bierce. 128pp. 28038-1

"THE MOONLIT ROAD" AND OTHER GHOST AND HORROR STORIES, Ambrose Bierce (John Grafton, ed.) 96pp. 40056-5

WUTHERING HEIGHTS, Emily Brontë. 256pp. 29256-8

THE THIRTY-NINE STEPS, John Buchan. 96pp. 28201-5

TARZAN OF THE APES, Edgar Rice Burroughs. 224pp. (Available in U.S. only.) 29570-2

ALICE'S ADVENTURES IN WONDERLAND, Lewis Carroll, 96pp. 27543-4

THROUGH THE LOOKING-GLASS, Lewis Carroll. 128pp. 40878-7

MY ÁNTONIA, Willa Cather. 176pp. 28240-6

O PIONEERS!, Willa Cather. 128pp. 27785-2

PAUL'S CASE AND OTHER STORIES, Willa Cather. 64pp. 29057-3

FIVE GREAT SHORT STORIES, Anton Chekhov. 96pp. 26463-7

TALES OF CONJURE AND THE COLOR LINE, Charles Waddell Chesnutt. 128pp. 40426-9

FAVORITE FATHER BROWN STORIES, G. K. Chesterton. 96pp. 27545-0

THE AWAKENING, Kate Chopin. 128pp. 27786-0

A PAIR OF SILK STOCKINGS AND OTHER STORIES, Kate Chopin. 64pp. 29264-9

HEART OF DARKNESS, Joseph Conrad. 80pp. 26464-5

LORD JIM, Joseph Conrad. 256pp. 40650-4

THE SECRET SHARER AND OTHER STORIES, Joseph Conrad. 128pp. 27546-9

THE "LITTLE REGIMENT" AND OTHER CIVIL WAR STORIES, Stephen Crane. 80pp. 29557-5

THE OPEN BOAT AND OTHER STORIES, Stephen Crane. 128pp. 27547-7

THE RED BADGE OF COURAGE, Stephen Crane. 112pp. 26465-3

MOLL FLANDERS, Daniel Defoe. 256pp. 29093-X

ROBINSON CRUSOE, Daniel Defoe. 288pp. 40427-7

A CHRISTMAS CAROL, Charles Dickens. 80pp. 26865-9

THE CRICKET ON THE HEARTH AND OTHER CHRISTMAS STORIES, Charles Dickens. 128pp. 28039-X

A TALE OF TWO CITIES, Charles Dickens. 304pp. 40651-2

THE DOUBLE, Fyodor Dostoyevsky. 128pp. 29572-9

THE GAMBLER, Fyodor Dostoyevsky. 112pp. 29081-6

NOTES FROM THE UNDERGROUND, Fyodor Dostoyevsky. 96pp. 27053-X

THE ADVENTURE OF THE DANCING MEN AND OTHER STORIES, Sir Arthur Conan Doyle. 80pp. 29558-3

THE HOUND OF THE BASKERVILLES, Arthur Conan Doyle. 128pp. 28214-7

THE LOST WORLD, Arthur Conan Doyle. 176pp. 40060-3

DOVER·THRIFT·EDITIONS

FICTION

SIX GREAT SHERLOCK HOLMES STORIES, Sir Arthur Conan Doyle. 112pp. 27055-6

SHORT STORIES, Theodore Dreiser. 112pp. 28215-5

SILAS MARNER, George Eliot. 160pp. 29246-0

THIS SIDE OF PARADISE, F. Scott Fitzgerald. 208pp. 28999-0

"THE DIAMOND AS BIG AS THE RITZ" AND OTHER STORIES, F. Scott Fitzgerald. 29991-0

MADAME BOVARY, Gustave Flaubert. 256pp. 29257-6

THE REVOLT OF "MOTHER" AND OTHER STORIES, Mary E. Wilkins Freeman. 128pp. 40428-5

A ROOM WITH A VIEW, E. M. Forster. 176pp. (Available in U.S. only.) 28467-0

WHERE ANGELS FEAR TO TREAD, E. M. Forster. 128pp. (Available in U.S. only.) 27791-7

THE IMMORALIST, André Gide. 112pp. (Available in U.S. only.) 29237-1

HERLAND, Charlotte Perkins Gilman. 128pp. 40429-3

"THE YELLOW WALLPAPER" AND OTHER STORIES, Charlotte Perkins Gilman. 80pp. 29857-4

THE OVERCOAT AND OTHER STORIES, Nikolai Gogol. 112pp. 27057-2

CHELKASH AND OTHER STORIES, Maxim Gorky. 64pp. 40652-0

GREAT GHOST STORIES, John Grafton (ed.). 112pp. 27270-2

DETECTION BY GASLIGHT, Douglas G. Greene (ed.). 272pp. 29928-7

THE MABINOGION, Lady Charlotte E. Guest. 192pp. 29541-9

"THE FIDDLER OF THE REELS" AND OTHER SHORT STORIES, Thomas Hardy. 80pp. 29960-0

THE LUCK OF ROARING CAMP AND OTHER STORIES, Bret Harte. 96pp. 27271-0

THE HOUSE OF THE SEVEN GABLES, Nathaniel Hawthorne. 272pp. 40882-5

THE SCARLET LETTER, Nathaniel Hawthorne. 192pp. 28048-9

YOUNG GOODMAN BROWN AND OTHER STORIES, Nathaniel Hawthorne. 128pp. 27060-2

THE GIFT OF THE MAGI AND OTHER SHORT STORIES, O. Henry. 96pp. 27061-0

THE NUTCRACKER AND THE GOLDEN POT, E. T. A. Hoffmann. 128pp. 27806-9

THE BEAST IN THE JUNGLE AND OTHER STORIES, Henry James. 128pp. 27552-3

DAISY MILLER, Henry James. 64pp. 28773-4

THE TURN OF THE SCREW, Henry James. 96pp. 26684-2

WASHINGTON SQUARE, Henry James. 176pp. 40431-5

THE COUNTRY OF THE POINTED FIRS, Sarah Orne Jewett. 96pp. 28196-5

THE AUTOBIOGRAPHY OF AN EX-COLORED MAN, James Weldon Johnson. 112pp. 28512-X

DUBLINERS, James Joyce. 160pp. 26870-5

A PORTRAIT OF THE ARTIST AS A YOUNG MAN, James Joyce. 192pp. 28050-0

THE METAMORPHOSIS AND OTHER STORIES, Franz Kafka. 96pp. 29030-1

THE MAN WHO WOULD BE KING AND OTHER STORIES, Rudyard Kipling. 128pp. 28051-9

YOU KNOW ME AL, Ring Lardner. 128pp. 28513-8

SELECTED SHORT STORIES, D. H. Lawrence. 128pp. 27794-1

GREEN TEA AND OTHER GHOST STORIES, J. Sheridan LeFanu. 96pp. 27795-X

THE CALL OF THE WILD, Jack London. 64pp. 26472-6

FIVE GREAT SHORT STORIES, Jack London. 96pp. 27063-7

THE SEA-WOLF, Jack London. iv+244pp. 41108-7

WHITE FANG, Jack London. 160pp. 26968-X

DEATH IN VENICE, Thomas Mann. 96pp. (Available in U.S. only.) 28714-9

IN A GERMAN PENSION: 13 Stories, Katherine Mansfield. 112pp. 28719-X

DOVER·THRIFT·EDITIONS

FICTION

THE NECKLACE AND OTHER SHORT STORIES, Guy de Maupassant. 128pp. 27064-5
BARTLEBY AND BENITO CERENO, Herman Melville. 112pp. 26473-4
THE OIL JAR AND OTHER STORIES, Luigi Pirandello. 96pp. 28459-X
THE GOLD-BUG AND OTHER TALES, Edgar Allan Poe. 128pp. 26875-6
TALES OF TERROR AND DETECTION, Edgar Allan Poe. 96pp. 28744-0
THE QUEEN OF SPADES AND OTHER STORIES, Alexander Pushkin. 128pp. 28054-3
THE STORY OF AN AFRICAN FARM, Olive Schreiner. 256pp. 40165-0
FRANKENSTEIN, Mary Shelley. 176pp. 28211-2
THREE LIVES, Gertrude Stein. 176pp. (Available in U.S. only.) 28059-4
THE STRANGE CASE OF DR. JEKYLL AND MR. HYDE, Robert Louis Stevenson. 64pp. 26688-5
TREASURE ISLAND, Robert Louis Stevenson. 160pp. 27559-0
GULLIVER'S TRAVELS, Jonathan Swift. 240pp. 29273-8
THE KREUTZER SONATA AND OTHER SHORT STORIES, Leo Tolstoy. 144pp. 27805-0
THE WARDEN, Anthony Trollope. 176pp. 40076-X
FIRST LOVE AND DIARY OF A SUPERFLUOUS MAN, Ivan Turgenev. 96pp. 28775-0
FATHERS AND SONS, Ivan Turgenev. 176pp. 40073-5
ADVENTURES OF HUCKLEBERRY FINN, Mark Twain. 224pp. 28061-6
THE ADVENTURES OF TOM SAWYER, Mark Twain. 192pp. 40077-8
THE MYSTERIOUS STRANGER AND OTHER STORIES, Mark Twain. 128pp. 27069-6
HUMOROUS STORIES AND SKETCHES, Mark Twain. 80pp. 29279-7
AROUND THE WORLD IN EIGHTY DAYS, Jules Verne. 160pp. 41111-7
CANDIDE, Voltaire (François-Marie Arouet). 112pp. 26689-3
GREAT SHORT STORIES BY AMERICAN WOMEN, Candace Ward (ed.). 192pp. 28776-9
"THE COUNTRY OF THE BLIND" AND OTHER SCIENCE-FICTION STORIES, H. G. Wells. 160pp. (Available in U.S. only.) 29569-9
THE ISLAND OF DR. MOREAU, H. G. Wells. 112pp. (Available in U.S. only.) 29027-1
THE INVISIBLE MAN, H. G. Wells. 112pp. (Available in U.S. only.) 27071-8
THE TIME MACHINE, H. G. Wells. 80pp. (Available in U.S. only.) 28472-7
THE WAR OF THE WORLDS, H. G. Wells. 160pp. (Available in U.S. only.) 29506-0
ETHAN FROME, Edith Wharton. 96pp. 26690-7
SHORT STORIES, Edith Wharton. 128pp. 28235-X
THE AGE OF INNOCENCE, Edith Wharton. 288pp. 29803-5
THE PICTURE OF DORIAN GRAY, Oscar Wilde. 192pp. 27807-7
JACOB'S ROOM, Virginia Woolf. 144pp. (Available in U.S. only.) 40109-X
MONDAY OR TUESDAY: Eight Stories, Virginia Woolf. 64pp. (Available in U.S. only.) 29453-6

NONFICTION

POETICS, Aristotle. 64pp. 29577-X
POLITICS, Aristotle. 368pp. 41424-8
NICOMACHEAN ETHICS, Aristotle. 256pp. 40096-4
MEDITATIONS, Marcus Aurelius. 128pp. 29823-X
THE LAND OF LITTLE RAIN, Mary Austin. 96pp. 29037-9
THE DEVIL'S DICTIONARY, Ambrose Bierce. 144pp. 27542-6
THE ANALECTS, Confucius. 128pp. 28484-0
CONFESSIONS OF AN ENGLISH OPIUM EATER, Thomas De Quincey. 80pp. 28742-4
NARRATIVE OF THE LIFE OF FREDERICK DOUGLASS, Frederick Douglass. 96pp. 28499-9

DOVER · THRIFT · EDITIONS

PLAYS

FAUST, PART ONE, Johann Wolfgang von Goethe. 192pp. 28046-2
THE INSPECTOR GENERAL, Nikolai Gogol. 80pp. 28500-6
SHE STOOPS TO CONQUER, Oliver Goldsmith. 80pp. 26867-5
A DOLL'S HOUSE, Henrik Ibsen. 80pp. 27062-9
GHOSTS, Henrik Ibsen. 64pp. 29852-3
HEDDA GABLER, Henrik Ibsen. 80pp. 26469-6
THE WILD DUCK, Henrik Ibsen. 96pp. 41116-8
VOLPONE, Ben Jonson. 112pp. 28049-7
DR. FAUSTUS, Christopher Marlowe. 64pp. 28208-2
THE MISANTHROPE, Molière. 64pp. 27065-3
ANNA CHRISTIE, Eugene O'Neill. 80pp. 29985-6
BEYOND THE HORIZON, Eugene O'Neill. 96pp. 29085-9
THE EMPEROR JONES, Eugene O'Neill. 64pp. 29268-1
THE LONG VOYAGE HOME AND OTHER PLAYS, Eugene O'Neill. 80pp. 28755-6
RIGHT YOU ARE, IF YOU THINK YOU ARE, Luigi Pirandello. 64pp. (Available in U.S. only.) 29576-1
SIX CHARACTERS IN SEARCH OF AN AUTHOR, Luigi Pirandello. 64pp. (Available in U.S. only.) 29992-9
HANDS AROUND, Arthur Schnitzler. 64pp. 28724-6
ANTONY AND CLEOPATRA, William Shakespeare. 128pp. 40062-X
AS YOU LIKE IT, William Shakespeare. 80pp. 40432-3
HAMLET, William Shakespeare. 128pp. 27278-8
HENRY IV, William Shakespeare. 96pp. 29584-2
JULIUS CAESAR, William Shakespeare. 80pp. 26876-4
KING LEAR, William Shakespeare. 112pp. 28058-6
MACBETH, William Shakespeare. 96pp. 27802-6
MEASURE FOR MEASURE, William Shakespeare. 96pp. 40889-2
THE MERCHANT OF VENICE, William Shakespeare. 96pp. 28492-1
A MIDSUMMER NIGHT'S DREAM, William Shakespeare. 80pp. 27067-X
MUCH ADO ABOUT NOTHING, William Shakespeare. 80pp. 28272-4
OTHELLO, William Shakespeare. 112pp. 29097-2
RICHARD III, William Shakespeare. 112pp. 28747-5
ROMEO AND JULIET, William Shakespeare. 96pp. 27557-4
THE TAMING OF THE SHREW, William Shakespeare. 96pp. 29765-9
THE TEMPEST, William Shakespeare. 96pp. 40658-X
TWELFTH NIGHT; OR, WHAT YOU WILL, William Shakespeare. 80pp. 29290-8
ARMS AND THE MAN, George Bernard Shaw. 80pp. (Available in U.S. only.) 26476-9
HEARTBREAK HOUSE, George Bernard Shaw. 128pp. (Available in U.S. only.) 29291-6
PYGMALION, George Bernard Shaw. 96pp. (Available in U.S. only.) 28222-8
THE RIVALS, Richard Brinsley Sheridan. 96pp. 40433-1
THE SCHOOL FOR SCANDAL, Richard Brinsley Sheridan. 96pp. 26687-7
ANTIGONE, Sophocles. 64pp. 27804-2
OEDIPUS AT COLONUS, Sophocles. 64pp. 40659-8
OEDIPUS REX, Sophocles. 64pp. 26877-2
ELECTRA, Sophocles. 64pp. 28482-4
MISS JULIE, August Strindberg. 64pp. 27281-8
THE PLAYBOY OF THE WESTERN WORLD AND RIDERS TO THE SEA, J. M. Synge. 80pp. 27562-0
THE DUCHESS OF MALFI, John Webster. 96pp. 40660-1
THE IMPORTANCE OF BEING EARNEST, Oscar Wilde. 64pp. 26478-5
LADY WINDERMERE'S FAN, Oscar Wilde. 64pp. 40078-6

DOVER·THRIFT·EDITIONS

BOXED SETS

FAVORITE JANE AUSTEN NOVELS: *Pride and Prejudice*, *Sense and Sensibility* and *Persuasion* (Complete and Unabridged), Jane Austen. 800pp. 29748-9

BEST WORKS OF MARK TWAIN: Four Books, Dover. 624pp. 40226-6

EIGHT GREAT GREEK TRAGEDIES: Six Books, Dover. 480pp. 40203-7

FIVE GREAT ENGLISH ROMANTIC POETS, Dover. 496pp. 27893-X

FIVE GREAT PLAYS, Dover. 368pp. 27179-X

FIVE GREAT PLAYS OF SHAKESPEARE, Dover. 496pp. 27892-1

FIVE GREAT POETS: Poems by Shakespeare, Keats, Poe, Dickinson, and Whitman, Dover. 416pp. 26942-6

47 GREAT SHORT STORIES: Stories by Poe, Chekhov, Maupassant, Gogol, O. Henry, and Twain, Dover. 688pp. 27178-1

GREAT AFRICAN-AMERICAN WRITERS: Seven Books, Dover. 704pp. 29995-3

GREAT AMERICAN NOVELS, Dover. 720pp. 28665-7

GREAT ENGLISH NOVELS, Dover. 704pp. 28666-5

GREAT IRISH WRITERS: Five Books, Dover. 672pp. 29996-1

GREAT MODERN WRITERS: Five Books, Dover. 720pp. (Available in U.S. only.) 29458-7

GREAT WOMEN POETS: 4 Complete Books, Dover. 256pp. (Available in U.S. only.) 28388-7

MASTERPIECES OF RUSSIAN LITERATURE: Seven Books, Dover. 880pp. 40665-2

NINE GREAT ENGLISH POETS: Poems by Shakespeare, Keats, Blake, Coleridge, Wordsworth, Mrs. Browning, FitzGerald, Tennyson, and Kipling, Dover. 704pp. 27633-3

SEVEN GREAT ENGLISH VICTORIAN POETS: Seven Volumes, Dover. 592pp. 40204-5

SIX GREAT AMERICAN POETS: Poems by Poe, Dickinson, Whitman, Longfellow, Frost, and Millay, Dover. 512pp. (Available in U.S. only.) 27425-X

38 SHORT STORIES BY AMERICAN WOMEN WRITERS: Five Books, Dover. 512pp. 29459-5

26 GREAT TALES OF TERROR AND THE SUPERNATURAL, Dover. 608pp. (Available in U.S. only.) 27891-3

For a complete descriptive list of all volumes in the Dover Thrift Editions series write for a free Dover Literature and Language Catalog (59047-X) to Dover Publications, Inc., Dept. DTE, 31 E. 2nd Street, Mineola, NY 11501